PRAISE FOR THE FIDDLER AND FIORA SERIES

The King of Nothing

"For relentless action with classy, inventive plotting, it's hard to beat the Fiddler series. . . . The highest recommendation." —*Orange County Register*

"A. E. Maxwell writes with cheerful vigor, the swiftly paced plot never falters and the quirky humor is superbly timed. A new Fiddler is always a welcome event."
—*St. Louis Post-Dispatch*

"Fiddler and Fiora are the '90s equivalents of Nick and Nora Charles—the perfect couple to deal with the complexities of murder and mayhem in an imperfect world."
—*The Drood Review of Mystery*

Money Burns

"Tightly constructed plot . . . two very appealing personalities. This is good stuff." —*The Washington Times*

"Southern California's troubleshooting twosome, Fiddler and Fiora, keep the adrenaline flowing."
—*Boston Sunday Herald*

The Art of Survival

"The story is unnerving, mesmerizing and, when relief from fierce tensions is required, blessedly funny."
—*Publishers Weekly*

"*The Art of Survival* is a slick, well-crafted mystery. . . . It's also a sensitive exposé on human nature written with knowing insight as well as humor and wry wit. The Maxwells excel at creating multifaceted, appealing characters."
—*Los Angeles Times*

Gatsby's Vineyard

"The book evokes, with grace, elegance and love, the colors, smells and sounds of Napa Valley wine making."
—*Vanity Fair*

"By far the Maxwells' best, a California thriller with very real characters and dialogue and a violent, unexpected ending you won't soon forget." —*Palo Alto Times Tribune*

A Fiddler and
Fiora Mystery

MURDER
HURTS

A. E. MAXWELL

HarperPaperbacks
A Division of HarperCollinsPublishers

HarperPaperbacks *A Division of* HarperCollins*Publishers*
10 East 53rd Street, New York, N.Y. 10022

Copyright © 1993 by Two of a Kind, Inc.
All rights reserved. No part of this book may be used or reproduced in any manner whatsoever without written permission of the publisher, except in the case of brief quotations embodied in critical articles and reviews. For information address Villard Books, a division of Random House, New York, N.Y.

A hardcover edition of this book was published in 1993 by Villard Books.

Cover illustration by Danilo Ducak

First HarperPaperbacks printing: February 1995

Printed in the United States of America

HarperPaperbacks and colophon are trademarks of HarperCollins*Publishers*

10 9 8 7 6 5 4 3 2 1

For Dominick, inevitably

ONE

Murder hurts.

A bullet leaves a scar. But pain fades with time. Fresh scars cover the old ones.

Uncle Jake had been dead so long that I thought good memories were the only ones left. I remembered him when the desert wind blew in from Sonora. I remembered him when I drank a cold Tecate beer with lime juice on the rim, the way he taught me. I remembered his laugh.

I had deliberately stopped thinking about how he died. I hadn't thought about the two men who killed him, and who tried to kill me at the same time. I hadn't thought about unfinished vengeance.

Some memories are better left alone.

But the names of the killers were still there in the memory bank. Loco and Koo-Koo. Koo-Koo's nickname was the standard Mexican diminutive for his real name, Refugio. Loco—Jorge Cardenas Portillo— earned his nickname by eating beer glasses and shooting people.

I knew exactly where Loco was. In fact, I thought I was the only person on the face of the earth who did know. I had hidden his grave very carefully and let the wind take care of the elegy.

But Koo-Koo was another matter. As far as I knew, he was still alive. He was too cunning to die before his time. He had thrown Loco at me as a distraction, like a smart hunter throws a venison haunch to a pursuing bear. Koo-Koo was a survivor.

I had taken the bait and lost the prize.

It still rankled, long after the pain had faded and the scar smoothed over. Revenge was only part of it. Koo-Koo was the only man in the world who could tell me who knew why Uncle Jake had died and I nearly had.

Old question. Old scar. If anyone had asked, I would have said the juice was gone; Jake was a double handful of good memories, R.I.P.

Wrong again.

All the anger was still alive the way a match is alive, waiting only for the moment of friction to burst into fire.

The strike came when the phone rang on that bright, hot September day. The guy started talking before I could get around to saying hello.

"You still interested in Jake's executioners?"

My response was instant and soul deep.

"Some dreams never die," I said.

I knew the words were a mistake the moment I said them. I was talking when I should have been listening. I clamped down on my impulses and concentrated on the other end of the phone link, trying to still the anger.

The quality of the connection told me the guy was on a speakerphone. There was heavy-metal music crashing in the background. The effect disguised his voice.

I punched the MEMO button on the answering machine anyway. A verbatim record never hurts.

"But men do die," I added.

"You think you got both of them?" the voice asked scornfully.

"I heard that one of them is south of Mexicali under six feet of sand."

The speakerphone made the caller's laughter hollow, eerie, a sound from a sepulcher.

"Yeah, Loco bought it," he said. "What about the guy that shot you? Still looking for him?"

I didn't say anything.

The caller laughed again, knowing the answer.

"Did you know that Loco and the other dude were just gofers?" the caller asked.

"As in going for the five grand in Jake's pocket?"

My tone suggested I didn't care, but I could feel the plastic of the phone's receiver give under the pressure of my grip.

"They were paid a grand apiece, plus what they could steal from the two of you," the guy said thickly.

"Free enterprise in action."

"So how'd you like to put the real murderer six feet under, the one who put them up to it?"

The voice tantalized me. Familiar, but . . . I couldn't pin a name on it. I closed my eyes, trying to visualize a face.

All I saw was Jake sprawled on his belly in the

dirt, his life and spirit blown out by a bullet in the back of his head.

The memory made the skin on the back of my neck crawl.

"It was a long time ago," I said.

"You saying you aren't interested?"

"Did you ever hear of older and wiser?"

"Bullshit! You aren't the kind to forgive and forget. You swore you'd find Jake's killer."

I changed the receiver to the other hand and stretched the cord until I could see Fiora on the redwood deck of the old cottage. She was locked in the extension of Step Back and Repulse Monkey. She wore a black workout leotard, and her hair was tied back with a Day-Glo green shoelace. Her hair seemed darker now, more like good fresh orange-blossom honey than it used to be. I liked the change.

Fiora turned, and the sunlight caught a little trickle of sweat at the base of her throat. She did tai chi chuan like she did everything else, with full concentration.

I'm not like Fiora. I float along until I find something I want. Right now, I had something I wanted.

"Is this a shakedown?" I asked casually.

The hollow laughter echoed again. It sounded even less pleasant the second time.

"It's a straight business deal," he said. "The package will cost you fifty grand."

"Fifty? What have you been smoking, pal? I don't have two thousand to my name."

"Clean out that secret compartment in your belt."

Not good. He knew me well enough to know about one of my old habits. Banks are never open when you need them, so I maintain a kind of safe-deposit box around my waist.

"It's been a bad year," I said.

"If you're not good for it, your lady sure as hell is."

"She isn't a lady," I said dryly, "and she'd scratch your eyes out for calling her one."

The heavy-metal music drowned out most of his response. I caught a couple of words in the middle that sounded like "cast-iron bitch."

The voice and the spewing, spitting anger were so familiar I suddenly saw a blubbery-lipped sneer and a face whose skin burned but never tanned.

I just couldn't attach a name to the face.

The heavy-metal music took a break. The guy shifted his weight in his chair, making the whole thing creak. He wheezed like a fat man. The way he kept shifting made me wonder if the desk chair hadn't gotten a bit tight on his ass.

The music cranked up again. It wasn't KLOS. No ads. No posturing patter. He was probably playing a compact disc, using it the way guys in the movies put a handkerchief over the phone receiver to disguise voices.

"You interested or not?" he demanded.

His breathiness spoiled the tough-guy effect. I wondered if he was just fat or if he smoked, too. He might have, once. A lot of people had.

The fat, burned face in my memory bank stayed nameless.

"Interested in names?" I laughed. "I can get names out of the phone book for free. Now if you've got proof, something that might stand up in a court—"

"Court? Shee-it. When did you give up putting people in holes all by yourself?"

The hair on the back of my neck stirred again.

His question invited the kind of response that a professional informant or an undercover cop loves to get on tape. The kind of response some prosecutor might enjoy introducing in a trial.

I'm nervous about answering that kind of question. It's one of the problems that goes with a past that outlives the statute of limitations.

"I said I'd heard Loco had died. I didn't say I killed him."

"Yeah, yeah, yeah. It will still cost you fifty big ones for names, extra for evidence that would stand up in court."

"How much extra?"

"We'll work something out," he said.

"Everything's got a price, right? Friends, blood, revenge, everything."

"Congratulations, babe. If you've learned that, you'll die smarter than Jake ever did."

Shooting pains in my hand told me I was still holding the phone too hard.

"How about it?" he prodded. "You interested?"

A fast look at the deck told me that Fiora was wrapping up her tai chi workout. I didn't want her to walk into the middle of this conversation.

"I might be," I said. "But I don't front that much bread blind."

"I'll give you a taste for free. Kind of an appetizer. You'll like it."

He made it sound like dim sum or dope, but I wasn't in a position to drag out the conversation with complaints.

"When and where?" I asked.

"Today. Lunch. Venice Beach."

"Any special place?" I asked sarcastically.

"There are a couple of swap-meet style booths

and a hot dog stand next to the Mystery Annex and Small World of Books. Get yourself a frank and some kraut at noon, straight up."

"I don't like kraut."

"Suit yourself. Just sit your ass down on one of those benches beside Oceanfront Walk and wait. Be alone."

"You want yours with or without mustard?"

"I won't be there. But somebody else will be. The appetizer."

The caller's cackle was sharp and abrasive, a comedian supplying his own laugh track because the audience had no sense of humor.

He was still laughing when he hung up.

I stood there for maybe ten seconds, counting silently to myself, trying to shake off the tension that had gathered in the back of my neck. There's a scar there, left after a Mexican doctor dug a .45-caliber slug out of my skull. The slug had been fired an instant after the one that killed Jake.

I know. I heard the shots.

That much I remembered, and not much else. The doctor I saw in the States said head wounds were like that. I might remember in bits and pieces, all at once, or not at all.

So far, I hadn't remembered much except in my dreams. The kind that make you wake up sweating.

Very gently, I hung up the useless phone. As I walked slowly out into the hot sunshine on the redwood deck, I wondered how much to tell Fiora.

The look on her face said she had already pulled some of it out of thin air. She's like that—fey, haphazardly prescient, an irritating Scots witch.

"Did I hear the phone?" she asked mildly.

"Just a salesman."

While I stared out over the Pacific toward the spot where Santa Catalina lurked in the smog like a faint old memory, Fiora picked up the white terry-cloth towel from the table and dabbed at her face and neck.

"Must have been a hell of a salesman," she said. "You usually get rid of them more quickly."

"It was an interesting offer."

My voice was casual. I was still deciding how much to say and thinking about Jake at the same time. Fiora's brain is a mainframe. It can handle multi-tasking like that. But my microprocessor still bogs down.

Fiora lifted her hair and let the air circulate on the back of her neck, saying nothing, letting the silence ask questions for her.

September is usually good for one hot spell. This year's had waited until the end of the month but then had made up for it by turning into a scorcher. Four straight days over a hundred at the Civic Center in Los Angeles. Cracked pavement and rolling brownouts in the San Fernando and San Gabriel valleys.

Even the beach was getting roasted. The marine clouds burned off before breakfast each day. Then the sun bore down on the sand like hell's own kleig light, broiling everything in its reach and throwing a pitiless glare on the imperfections of the world.

Fiora had the skin and the features to stand up to the intense light, but even she had to squint a little in the glare. The effect deepened the tiny wrinkles around her eyes. It made her look more mature and more vulnerable at the same time, like her slowly darkening blond hair. I approved of the change.

"Salesman, huh?" Fiora said finally. "Well, I'm not buying."

"He wasn't selling anything to you."

"No, but you are," she retorted.

I thought it over, cursed beneath my breath, and said nothing more.

"Let me know when you want to talk about it," Fiora said, turning away.

"I'm not sure I ever will."

She paused, ran the towel over her face once more, and turned back to me.

"That bad?" she asked.

But her face told me she didn't have to ask. She knew.

"Shit," I muttered. "The call was from somebody wanting to sell me the name of the other killer, down in Mexico."

For some things Fiora has a long fuse. Business, usually. She had just concluded the deal of a lifetime that had been spent making deals. No matter how difficult or tricky the deal had become, she had been as calm as a clam. In the end, she had sold off the investment banking firm she had spent most of her life creating.

Those kinds of transactions suck energy and emotion like a black hole sucks energy. The sale was complicated by the death of a friend who had not deserved to die, and by the investigation that revealed he died because of the deal.

Together, Fiora and I had done a fair job of restoring the celestial balance, but the job was not without cost. More to Fiora than to me, understandably. Rory's death still weighed hard on her mind. Her emotions had been stripped down to bare bright copper wire, just waiting to arc and throw sparks.

That's probably why she flashed so hard and bright when I mentioned Uncle Jake.

"Sweet God above," she snarled. Her mouth flattened into a thin, tight line. "I hope they weren't asking more than a dime for the information. That's nine cents more than it's worth."

Like the rest of us, Fiora lashes out when she's angry. She lashes out even harder when she's scared.

This was fear talking. She had always regarded Jake as a dangerous influence on me, even after he died. In no way had she ever forgiven him for nearly getting me killed along with him.

I understood how she felt. It was too bad, but up to now it hadn't been impossible.

Up to now.

You see, for better or for worse, I did love my wild uncle. He had always seemed to me to be the kind of man worth admiring. And avenging, if it came to that.

"I told you a long time ago that I'd spend every dollar in that old steamer trunk to find out who did Jake," I said flatly. "I feel the same way now, only the job may not cost that much. This guy is willing to peddle a name for fifty thousand bucks."

Fiora looked at me with eyes that were suddenly the color of the deepest part of a breaking wave, where dangerous riptides wait. She didn't say anything. Then she looked away, searching the sky as though it held some answer to whatever question she was asking herself.

"Money isn't what's at stake," Fiora said in a low voice. "We both know it."

"What is, then?"

She glanced at me quickly, as though not certain my question was serious.

It was.

Slowly Fiora looked out at the ocean again. The expression on her face was more weary now than fierce or frightened.

"I spent the longest week of my life in Mexico, watching you dangle between living and dying," she said.

"I don't remember it."

"I do. How would you feel if I had been the one shot and you the one with fingers on my pulse because you were terrified if you let go I would die?"

There wasn't much I could say to that, but I tried.

"Fiora . . ."

She waited.

I couldn't think of anything to say.

"You really don't remember much of what happened, do you?" Fiora asked. "Is that why you don't talk about it?"

"It's one of the reasons."

Another was that every time Jake's name was mentioned, Fiora got a pinched, tight look around her eyes and mouth.

"You do remember your next trip to Mexico," she said acidly.

"Yes," I said.

It was all I said, too. Nothing had happened during the trip that would bring light to Fiora's eyes.

"You were haunted for months afterward," she said.

I took the white towel from Fiora's hand and smoothed it across her shoulders. There was a sheen of sweat on the skin above the scooped neck of her leotard. Her deltoid muscles were like sculpted bronze, tense and unyielding.

"You don't want to know what happened," I said quietly. "If it helps, nobody else knows either."

Then I realized I was lying. Somebody knew enough about Loco, me, and Old Testament justice to make a good guess as to how the sullen, stupid glass-eater had ended up under six feet of sand.

I looked at my watch. I'd have to hurry to set up the meet the way I wanted it. The caller had been good enough to guess what had happened to Loco.

Which meant the guy probably had guessed what I might have in mind for him.

two

As I stood in front of the locked box where I keep weapons, I should have been thinking about lunch dates and death. But I was thinking about Jake.

To me, Jake was the last truly free man. Free as an eagle, free as the winds of the wild Montana winters, free as sunlight on a summer day at ten thousand feet in the Rockies.

He was the favored child of an indulgent mother and a doting, much older sister—my mother. That gave him a certainty that the whole world loved him, particularly women. He was more right than he was wrong, but he used his charm with a gentleness that made him all the more attractive.

Handsome, physically gifted, and ruthless in his pursuit of freedom, Jake never married any of the women who watched him with hungry eyes. As a young man he shagged cows from horseback long after helicopters and Jeeps came into fashion. He dug for placer gold long after the mining combines and capitalist syndicates took over. He rode the rails and went on the bum when the rest of the world rode Greyhound.

Jake was a man out of joint with his own time. Not surprising for a man with the blood of Scots Highlanders, Norwegian berserkers, and Cheyenne warriors running in his veins.

It was an existential difficulty I understood.

Jake was a smuggler. He loved the game so much he'd smuggle anything. He ran refrigerators, television sets, and Levi's south into Mexico and marijuana north into the United States.

In those screwball days, dope was a kind of sacrament, a political statement, and many smugglers regarded themselves as priests. But Jake never had such illusions. If there had been an illicit demand for violet-scented potpourri in Laguna Beach or Haight-Ashbury, he would have filled his battered pickup with kilo bricks and headed north with a grin on his face.

Jake was in love with the idea of running the border. He smuggled because it gave him an excuse to roam the dry, wild country—the wilderness of the Sonora and the Mojave and the Valle Imperial. Like Edward Abbey, Jake was an anarchist. He needed the freedom of the badlands the way other men need the order and predictability of concrete sidewalks.

Jake was an adventurer, not a criminal. Adrenaline was more important than dollars. To him, money was just a way of counting coup. He was like Fiora in that, although she would violently deny it.

Even though I never knew my own father, Jake wasn't a substitute dad to me. He was my hero, not my role model.

When Jake died, he left me quite a varied legacy: a love of the badlands, a taste for the underside of life, and a steamer trunk full of used, nonsequential twenties, fifties, and hundreds.

He also left me a seasoned Model 1911 .45-caliber Colt pistol.

Fiora had long since turned the trunk of dirty money into enough clean cash that I could spend my life gainfully unemployed. Jake's blue-steel legacy interested me more.

That's why I was staring into the lockbox, trying to decide which of my cold steel friends to take to lunch.

Besides Jake's Colt, I also own a high-tech piece of metal sculpture called a Detonics .451. Hand-machined and so esoteric that it shoots cartridges handmade from .308 rifle rounds, the Detonics is as state-of-the-art now as the Colt was in 1911. Unfortunately, it is also what my friend Benny Speidel, the Ice Cream King of Saigon, calls a "signature weapon."

Unlike Jake's .45, of which there are probably a couple million in existence, only a handful of Detonics ever made it into the civilian population. Benny says the gun can be so easily traced I might just as well engrave my name, address, and telephone number on the slug.

I usually defer to Benny on such matters, but not on the Detonics. Part of me revels in its idiosyncratic nature, and another part of me simply appreciates its efficiency. You never know when you're going to have to put a slug through the engine block of a diesel truck. I don't do that very often, but I like to know that I can if I have to.

As I stared at the Colt and the Detonics in their chamois sacks, I realized for the first time that they represent the two sides of my nature. Like Jake, I appreciate the .45 because it's proven, trustworthy, and anonymous. The damn thing is so old it has a five-digit serial number. The blue steel of the barrel has been worn by decades of contact with leather and denim. The stories that gun could tell would be magnificent.

But I admire the Detonics, too. Like Fiora, the other anchor point in my life, the Detonics is an expression of a restless, ruthless intelligence that constantly adapts itself to the changing world.

I was still trying to choose between the two guns when I heard Fiora start up the Beast. While I had rummaged in the past and in the gun locker, she had canceled a flying lesson and arranged a substitute teacher for the English-as-a-second-language class she taught once a week at the Asian Senior Citizens' Center in Santa Ana.

Fiora didn't know where I was going, but she was going along. Period. No argument.

I had argued anyway.

I lost.

Frowning, I looked at the two very different weapons lying in their chamois bags. Sentiment favored Jake's .45. Besides, the meeting was going to take place in a very public place. The .45 would fit better under a loose *guayabera*.

If I carried Jake's gun, Fiora might not even notice that I was armed. I had enough on my mind without having to match wits with my high-wattage former wife. I put the .45 in its leather holster at the small of my back and went outside.

Fiora had changed into a white cotton shirt and a pair of blue shorts. The shirt made her skin glow warmly, like bread when it begins to toast. She was fiddling with the Beast's rearview mirror when I stepped up onto the chrome-steel running board and slid into the passenger seat.

It was a good-sized step, even for me. The Beast is a Chevrolet Suburban, a four-wheel-drive utility wagon with oversized off-road tires that lift it an extra few inches in the air. Fiora had been so disgusted with her last taste of international finance that she had traded her 750iL BMW for the Beast as part of her personal Buy America campaign.

Frankly, I had really mixed feelings about the deal. I hated to lose the twelve-cylinder star cruiser. Driving a 750iL is like driving a cross between a F-111 fighter bomber and an M-1 Abrams tank. But I still had the Cobra for performance on the pavement; and besides, I figured I'd get to drive the new truck most of the time, once the novelty wore off.

Wrong.

Fiora loved the Beast. Power steering, power brakes, automatic transmission, self-locking hubs, and on-demand four-wheel-drive—all part of what she called the Great Equalizer. When it comes to rough country driving, the Beast makes Fiora every bit as capable as the brawniest macho man. She kind of likes that.

Hell, she likes it a lot. She also likes the added height of the oversized tires and high-lift shocks. It puts her almost at eye level with those cross-country truckers who used to ogle her thighs in freeway traffic jams.

"It's going to be a bitch of a day in the city," I said as I snapped the seat belt into place. "You don't have to go with me."

"I paid an extra five hundred bucks for a heavy-duty radiator, just because you said I'd need it to run both air conditioners at the same time. Today I'll find out if I wasted the money."

"Have I ever steered you wrong?"

"There's always a first time," Fiora said coolly.

She snapped down into gear and rolled onto the little dirt road that threads through the ramshackle collection of century-old cottages that surround the one I rented long ago. On the way in from the Pacific Coast Highway, the road runs past a sign that says WELCOME TO CRYSTAL COVE. PLEASE SET YOUR CLOCKS BACK TO 1947.

The sign works going the other direction, too, reminding me that I'm about to enter the real world again, whether I like it or not.

The traffic on PCH was already bumper to bumper, thousands of sweaty inland residents headed like steel lemmings for the seaside bluffs. Fiora watched northbound traffic. I started south, looking for some kind of a break in the steady flow of hot metal and rubber.

"Here comes a slot," Fiora said.

I looked at the traffic coming out of Laguna.

"You're clear after the white van," I said. "Okay, hit it."

Without looking in my direction, Fiora punched down on the accelerator, taking the big truck across two lanes of southbound traffic and merging into the northbound flow.

It always amazes me that this fierce and independent woman, who is unwilling to trust anyone but herself, will take my word without hesitation. She was angry enough to trade me for a dog and shoot the dog, yet she trusted me.

It was the damnedest thing.

"Put the bloody gun in the glove box where it belongs," Fiora said after a time. "You look like you're trying to hatch a pine cone."

With a muttered curse I dug Jake's pistol out of the small of my back and dropped the weapon into the center console with the map books and the CD player.

"You want to throw your fit now," I asked, "or are you going to make me wait until some time that's really inconvenient, like when I might need to be using the damned gun?"

Without answering, Fiora shifted up into overdrive and let the engine settle into cruising speed.

"I have a right to know when you're armed," she said, after a moment. "We're straight-up partners, or we're an accident looking for a place to happen."

We had been living together as man and wife for a lot longer than we had originally been married but we had been real partners only in one undertaking. It had involved a local banking family whose fine name was being fouled by a son involved in laundering money for some South American "businessmen."

Fiora mousetrapped me into helping her solve that problem. Ever since then, she has regarded us as consulting partners. She claimed it was one of the reasons she had sold off Pacific Rim. She said consulting was more fun.

As I had always resented her fascination with money shuffling, I should have been happy her business was sold. Most of the time I was.

But sometimes I was happier than others. This wasn't one of the happiest times.

"We're only partners in that so-called consulting business of yours," I said bluntly. "This isn't a consultation. It's a personal matter."

"Codswallop."

"You don't feel about Jake the way I do. You never did."

"So?" Fiora asked.

"So don't expect the same consideration from me on this one that you would get in other circumstances."

"Jake first and to hell with the rest of the world," Fiora said neutrally. "Even when he's dead."

"*Especially* when he's dead," I shot back. "Don't get in my way, Fiora."

I expected an explosion. What I got was like watching an eclipse shut down the sun.

Quiet.

Fiora checked the side mirrors, gave way for a Porsche she could have turned into roadkill, and flicked a glance at me. She had never looked at me just that way before.

I didn't like it.

"I never get between you and Jake," Fiora said. "You taught me that a long, long time ago."

"Just like you taught me never to get between you and your brother."

"My dead brother. Your dead uncle. Dead, but not buried."

Fiora didn't say anything else. She didn't have to. Her voice was as ruthlessly matter-of-fact as her eyes.

I blamed myself for her brother's death, even

though Fiora didn't. For the first time I wondered if she somehow blamed herself for Jake's death.

Before I could ask, she was talking again in that cold tone that puts my teeth on edge.

"You're breaking two rules," she pointed out. "Only one of them is important, I suppose."

I grunted. As far as I'm concerned, no rules are important.

"You're trying to work alone," she said.

"You *did* notice, then."

She ignored me. "Working alone is foolish but not necessarily dangerous. Letting personal feelings interfere with your judgment is both."

Nothing irritates a man as much a woman who's right more than she's wrong. I glared out the window at the sun-struck chaparral on the hills.

"Let's go pick up Benny," I finally said. "That way you can stay home and buy Luxembourg or something."

"Benny is in the mountains. He can't get home before tonight."

"How do you know?"

"I called as soon as I knew it had to do with Jake."

"What did you do, ask Benny to come down and hold my hand?"

"Yes," she said succinctly.

"Jesus—"

"Somebody has to—" Fiora said, talking over me.

"—Christ!"

"—If only to keep you from blowing a stranger away for cutting you off on the freeway!"

"What's that supposed to mean?" I demanded.

"Waves of rage are rolling off you like heat off the sun."

I stared at her.

"You've been like that since three seconds after you picked up the phone this morning," Fiora said flatly.

Then she went back to watching traffic.

I sat and told myself she was wrong from the first word to the last. Unfortunately, I'm not real good at lying to myself. Pulling the wool over your own eyes is a great way to die young.

For some reason I thought of Jake, face down in the dirt.

Fiora took the cutoff through the canyon behind Corona del Mar. We were all the way inland and on the freeway before either of us spoke again.

"I didn't really hate Jake," Fiora said.

"Like hell."

"How could I hate someone who looked so much like you? Especially now. You're the same age he was when—"

"I know."

She shivered as though someone had stepped on her grave.

"I was afraid of Jake then, of his hold on you," Fiora whispered. "I still am."

"What would you have to fear from a 'no-account dope smuggler'? 'A walking anachronism'? Someone who 'made Tarzan look like a Fulbright scholar'?"

Fiora smiled oddly. "So you *were* in the motel room with Jake when I called. I always wondered."

"Yeah, I was there."

"Then you heard him laugh at me," she said.

"I heard."

"Jake always laughed at me like that when he was on a smuggling run."

"But that last trip wasn't a smuggling run. He was shooting a cheap thriller, a movie about himself, for God's sake."

Fiora said nothing.

"Look," I said. "Jake knew I'd promised you I would never smuggle anything again. He never asked me to break that promise."

"Yes."

The single word was followed by a silence that made me uncomfortable.

"Were you there during the second call?" Fiora asked after a long moment.

My expression answered for me. I hadn't been there. Hell, I hadn't even known there had been a second call.

"Then Jake never told you what he said to me?" she continued.

"No."

Fiora let out a long breath. "Maybe I should have told you. You might have let him go alone. Maybe . . ."

After a moment of silence, she shrugged.

"Maybe what?" I asked.

"Maybe your beloved uncle would have lived long enough to disillusion you, instead of leaving that dirty job for me."

I opened my mouth, but Fiora was still talking.

"Jake called me. It must have been after you left. He said, 'Fiora, honey, I know you don't give a shit about me and maybe you're right. But I need that boy with me and I need him bad. I won't let him inside, I promise, but I have to have somebody I can trust.'"

The words came easily from her lips, telling me

that she had spent so much time worrying over them they were like old friends. Or enemies.

As the words echoed, I felt something shift in my mind, as though reality were rearranging itself in my memory. I have big gaps in my personal record of going to Mexico with Jake that last time. I had always assumed the gaps were the result of the concussion from the .45 slug in my skull. Now I wondered if there might not have been more than a concussion involved.

Why had Jake needed someone he could trust? Had there been a contract out on him from some Mexican cops who hadn't been paid enough? Or had some rival smuggling gangs finally made good on their threats to take the brash gringo out of the game?

Pulling the wool over your own eyes is a great way to die young.

Or maybe it had been a great way *not* to die young.

Maybe I had decided that amnesia was the better part of valor when it came to avenging Jake.

"Why didn't you tell me then?" I asked.

"Jake asked me not to."

"Since when did you begin taking orders from Jake?"

"Since the instant I realized you wouldn't forgive me for telling the truth," Fiora said.

"What truth? That some *federales* or border bandits wanted Jake's balls for a hood ornament? Hell, there was nothing new in that."

Fiora's hands tightened on the wheel until her knuckles were white. Then she exhaled long and deep, as though getting rid of bad air.

"Jake never told me exactly what was going on," Fiora said.

I waited, suspecting I wasn't going to like whatever she said next.

I was right.

"He just said there are some things that are best left alone," Fiora whispered.

"What things?" I demanded.

"I don't know. I can only guess."

"Do it."

She shook her head. "Some things are too important to guess about."

"Like who wanted to kill Jake," I said flatly.

"Like *why*."

The part of me that preferred the Detonics knew Fiora was right.

The part of me that had kept Jake's gun all these years didn't care.

tHREE

For a while, the drive was as quiet as things can be on the northbound 405. The two of us sat isolated in our steel cocoon, each waiting for the other to speak.

Over the years we have learned about every way there is to come apart. Now we're trying to find one way to stay together. Living with unresolved—and probably unresolvable—arguments from the past was a problem we both wanted to solve.

Even so, we were all the way to Long Beach before a whiff of the atmosphere around the Clean-Air Gasoline refinery at the base of Signal Hill made Fiora wrinkle her nose and mutter dark things about corporate irresponsibility. I muttered something in return that said I agreed.

In a slightly more companionable silence, we

merged with the atonal Sturm und Drang of the postmodern folk opera called Los Angeles. The unsettling thing is that LA may be the most successful city of our age, which is only to say that LA contains all the manic energy and conflicting ambitions necessary to tear the place apart.

All cities are tense, but Los Angeles is like an E-string that's been overturned to play an extra octave. The result isn't music. It's a shrill, penetrating, head-banging, nerve-shattering, mind-bending cacophony; a dull high-speed blade sawing hard steel; a drive-by shooter ripping through a thirty-round magazine on full automatic.

LA is more an imperial capital than a city. It relies on water imported from the Colorado River, on food imported from Chile and Wenatchee, on dope imported from Mazari-Sharif and the Guajira, and on citizens imported from every corner of the world.

LA is illegal Chinese peasants from Fukien and legal Vietnamese warlords from colonial Saigon. LA is hard-working Mexicans from Guanajuato and lazy lowlifes from the urban slums of Tijuana. LA is Okies from Bakersfield and lace-curtain Irish from Boston and poor blacks from Mississippi and the Bronx. LA is Iranians and Iraqis, Kenyans and Brits, Lao Hmong and Brazilians, Belizians and Kurds and Armenians, all shouldering for space and power in a city that was founded by Native Americans, colonized by Hispanics, built by Anglos, and is now populated by every race on earth.

A hundred languages, a thousand ethnic groups, a hundred thousand clans, a million people, all pushing to exit the same freeways, all trying to pass beneath the same golden arches, all tromping across the same strip of devil grass, all trying to occupy the same square yard of broiling sand.

Once, when I was younger, I thought the melting pot was a crucible. I believed that someday an amalgam could be recovered from the bottom and hammered into the new America.

But as I surveyed the candy-apple low-riders and the battered Accords, the silver Mercedes Benzes, and all the rest of the four-wheeled lemmings on Venice Boulevard, I realized I was no longer an optimist. The melting pot will have to bubble for a long time to amalgamate this polyglot sprawl. Blood is too thick, anger too real, and violence too handy.

Los Angeles is what Rome must have been in that brief little moment just after the barbarians breached the walls. In fact, Los Angeles reminds me a lot of ancient Rome, except that LA has landfills instead of vomitoriums.

There is hope for the city, I suppose. There is hope for any place with so much human energy. But lots of human beings will be ground up and lost between now and the time when hope is realized.

Today definitely wasn't going to be that hopeful day. In the relentless heat, Venice Boulevard was hell with potholes.

Though I hadn't said a word aloud, Fiora gave me a wary, sideways look. It occurred to me that I was feeling caged and angry and violent, like Jake used to feel when he had been away from the desert too long. Some people were not meant to live in cities. Jake was one. I'm another.

Fiora was feeling the tension, too. She drove with one eye on the sluggish traffic and the other on the dashboard dials. Every few moments she tinkered with the climate controls, trying to keep the front and rear air conditioners running without overheating the engine. We only needed the front one, but she was being mulish about it.

Keeping both air conditioners going was a losing battle in stop-and-go traffic. Finally Fiora pulled into the parking lot of a shopping center ten blocks from the beach and shut them off.

"You steered me wrong," Fiora said flatly. "Oversized radiator or no, the little needle is going into the red zone."

"Slip it in neutral and rev the engine. Get the fan busy pushing more air."

"Rev an engine that's already too hot? Give me a break!"

I reached over and threw the gearshift into neutral. Then I put my big foot over hers on the accelerator and pressed. The needle on the heat indicator paused in its climb.

Fiora jerked her foot out from under mine and reached for the door handle.

"You can drive or we can walk," she said. "I'm sick of holding my breath waiting for this thing to explode."

My woman does not take surrender easily or gracefully. But she does take it.

I switched places with Fiora and checked the temp again. The needle was still too damned close to the 260-degree mark, which was enough to boil coolant. I could fix it the slow way or I could do it fast.

I wasn't in the mood for slow. I rolled down the windows and turned on the heater full blast. Then I pulled back into traffic. For the next five minutes we roasted while the heater core siphoned off the excess engine heat.

As soon as the needle dropped back toward normal range, I took Fiora's hand and gave her sweaty, elegant fingers a squeeze.

"Don't worry so much," I said. "There's a time for everything. Maybe this is the time to find out what happened to Jake. No big deal, love. It was all long ago and far away. Nothing dangerous now but memories, and we've already survived them."

Fiora squeezed back but didn't say anything.

In those long ago and faraway days, I had spent some time in Venice with Jake. I still remembered its crazy pattern of streets. When I found a side street that looked familiar, I turned onto it. There had been plenty of changes, but the skeleton of the old beach-and-bohemian neighborhood was still there.

After a few false leads, I found an alley whose potholed single lane ran parallel to the beach. The alley wasn't much wider than the Beast. I fought through crowds of sand-encrusted pedestrians and sullen local residents for several miles until I found what I needed.

"Finally," I said under my breath and began digging in my pocket.

The kid was in his late teens. He had been messing around with the engine of a sun-bleached, rusting Beetle that was parked half in and half out of a single-car garage between Thirteenth and Fourteenth streets. Now he was just sliding in behind the wheel to drive off.

I crooked my finger at him and showed him the corner of a green and white United States Federal Reserve note. The kid understood the mother tongue of Angelenos. He climbed out and shambled over to the Beast.

He was wearing the obligatory baggy surfer

shorts. His brown hair was rolled into Rasta-man dreadlocks. His feet had surfer knobs and his eyes were dull, as if he had already smoked the day's first stick of ganja.

I stuck my head out of the open window.

"Fifty bucks to use your garage for a couple of hours," I said.

The kid gave me a look that said he hadn't been born yesterday.

I showed him a portrait of a sour Ulysses Grant.

"Hey, dude, the parking lots only charge two bucks an hour," the kid said.

"Cool. I'll make it a hundred. My lady doesn't like motels."

If you're going to tell a lie, make it one they can understand. The kid walked over, leered at Fiora for a moment, and grabbed the money.

"Close the door when you leave," he said. "And have a nice lay."

The kid came real close to getting a backhand along with the two bills, but I needed the garage. I waited until he left, then backed in and shut off the engine. The rear half of the truck was in the shade. The front half wasn't. Sun beating through glass made it so hot it was hard to breathe.

I didn't really care. On a stakeout, comfort is the last consideration. Field of view is the first. From our slot in the garage, I could see across a commercial parking lot and through the pedestrians on the boardwalk to the bench in front of the hot dog stand.

It was quite enough for us to hear the grinding roar of ocean waves a few hundred feet away. The smell of brine mixed with grill grease from the hot dog stand and the oily stink of the old garage.

Hordes of hot, sandy, surly people wandered on the wide walkway looking for something to do.

Are we having fun yet?

"Now what?" Fiora asked.

She sounded as though the heat—or the weight of the past—had begun to wear her out. When I looked over at her, I saw that my little trick with the heater and the choice of parking spots had put a heavier load on her than I realized. Her face was flushed and streaked with sweat. Her eyes were hollow.

"Now you slide on over to the hot dog stand and buy three of the biggest cups of ice water they'll sell you," I said. "Pour one over your head and bring the other two back here."

Fiora dug a five out of her purse and opened the door.

"While you're at it," I added, "see if you spot anybody looking as suspicious as we do."

"Don't go anywhere without me."

Her voice was casual, but the look she gave me wasn't.

As Fiora walked down the alley toward the crowded sand, I admired the sway of her hips. Then I dug out the Nikon ten-power birding glasses and went to work on the sand dwellers.

Beaches bring out the exhibitionist in people. Too bad more of the bodies on display weren't gallery quality. Much of the skin was pale, overstuffed, and mottled with heat. Most of these folks got to the beach once or twice a year and burned each time.

The locals were already darkened by a full summer of sun. Now their skin was crinkling like cellophane. In a few years it would look like cheap leather.

Through the seething boardwalk screen of roller-bladers, skateboarders, and nervous pedestrians, I spotted the bench the caller had mentioned. It was empty. I scanned the crowds, looking for anyone who was paying more attention to the bench than to the bikinis and French-cuts.

A band of Hare Krishna devotees snaked by on the sidewalk in their saffron robes, chanting and clashing their brassy finger cymbals. The Sixties had a long half-life for some folks.

A few young gang-bangers lounged around on a grassy little lawn near the base of the pier. They were overdressed for the occasion in Levi's and reversed baseball caps, but at least their feet were bare. The boys were paying too much attention to the nubile gringa beach bunnies to be dangerous.

Fiora stood in line at the stand, looking bored but actually giving the crowds a careful study. Two Middle Easterners in codpiece Speedos made a big show of standing right behind her, examining her ass and discussing the rest of her body with suitable gestures.

That kind of rudeness happens often enough in the cultural Babel that is Los Angeles. Too many third-world men think that a woman alone should be flattered by even the crudest male attention. Being blond and frankly female, Fiora came in for a lot of flack from time to time. She ignored it for the most part, even though it goes against her nature to suffer fools in silence.

Fiora bought the cups of water, drank one, and headed back down the boardwalk. A few minutes later she came through the alley from the opposite direction and got in the truck.

"Trouble?" I asked.

"Only with the wanna-bes."

"Healthy male libidos," I said. "You shouldn't take it personally."

"Take it? Love, they couldn't deliver it if they worked in relays."

Smiling slightly, I took one of the cups and drank. The water was straight from the tap. It tasted faintly salty and frankly recycled. Water is another one of those commodities that suffers from importation.

"I walked down to see the big crowd by the base of the pier," Fiora said. "They're shooting a movie or a commercial or something."

"Not Visual Arts Studio, I hope," I muttered. "That would be pushing old times a little too far."

Fiora shook her head. "I didn't recognize the logo."

"Good."

There are coincidences in the world, but damned few of them are as coincidental as they first appear.

Jake had supplied lots of dope to Hollywood types in his heyday. One of his customers, a struggling producer named Aileen Camp, had been swept right off her feet by Jake's gentle outlaw mystique.

It was one of the major mismatches of Jake's life. Aileen Camp turned out to be ambitious, sexually hyperactive, and as compulsive as an addicted chimp in a crack cocaine experiment. She was a user in more ways than one and in every way that mattered.

Aileen was part of the Hollywood generation that grew up in the late 1960s convinced that dope could supercharge the upswings and dampen the downswings of life. She and a lot more like her did crystal meth, coke, LSD, THC, Thai Stick, and anything else that came along, washing it down with alcohol if they were honest or herbal tea if they were into hypocrisy.

Jake sold dope but didn't use anything stronger than Acapulco Gold himself. Maybe that was part of his appeal to Aileen. She bought his cooperation with her body and somehow turned his free-form life into a script. Even more astonishing, she hustled enough production money for a low-budget Hollywood film, a bastard kind of sequel to *Easy Rider*. They had been scouting locations on the desert in Baja California when Jake was killed.

I've never quite decided whether Aileen and her sort were supremely arrogant or desperately frightened. Whichever, drugs killed some of them, destroyed the careers of even more, and accelerated the obscene inflation of movie budgets. A lot of bright stars have burned out in the flames of Hollywood's free-base pipes.

Aileen hadn't been one of the burn cases. She parlayed her talents and her frenetic energy into a solid list of producing credits, including an Academy Award for Best Picture, and finally became chairman of Visual Arts, one of the few remaining American-owned studios in Hollywood.

Aileen's photo now turned up reguarly in the Calendar section of the *Los Angeles Times* and once in a while in the entertainment section of *People* magazine. If photographers can be believed, she was still thin, still striking in a brittle way, and still aggressively ambitious. Unless she had done a successful thirty days at Betty Ford's clinic in Palm Desert, I assumed she still burned all sorts of exotic fuels, too, although if she did she must have had the constitution of a Belgian plow horse.

"I didn't smell sulfur, Aileen's natural fragrance,

if that's why you've got that odd look on your face," Fiora said in response to my unspoken thoughts.

There was a steely edge to her voice. Aileen and Fiora had not gotten along very well. Aileen had a way of letting every man in the room know she might be interested in him, under the right circumstances.

She had taken matters a step further in my case. One night, she had climbed into my bed unannounced and uninvited. She woke me up in a way that was guaranteed to make a male react rather than think.

It was after I had met Fiora, which was why I successfully defended my honor. I was ready and able, but not willing. Not with Aileen. Fiora and I had taken one look at each other and then stopped looking anywhere else.

The intensity and finality of our coming together had baffled Jake. He and I were alike in many other ways, but not in this one. Jake had never looked at a woman with the gut certainty that this one was his.

Fiora had felt the same about me. As soon as she joined me in Mexico, she recognized Aileen for the sexual predator she was. The intelligent blonde refugee from the rural West and the frenetic blonde producer from LA had disliked each other on sight.

From the look on Fiora's face right now, nothing had changed. There was a glacial quality to her hazel-green eyes that I rarely saw. At some very primitive level, Fiora is as possessive of me as I am of her.

"Aileen is long gone," I said.

"But not forgotten. I saw you reading something about her in the *Journal* just the other day."

"She's been dead longer than Jake, so far as I am concerned."

Fiora arched her eyebrows skeptically and said not one word.

"What do I have to do," I muttered, "pull down the garage door and prove my unflagging ardor?"

Fiora glanced over her shoulder and measured the eight and a half feet of space from the back of the front seat to the tailgate. Then she smiled the kind of smile that always brings me to Yellow Alert.

"Why do you think I bought an air mattress?" she asked.

Then she reached over, laid her hand on my knee, and kneaded the muscle just above like a cat kneads an Oriental rug.

"You're trying to distract me from my quest, damsel," I said, glancing off toward the bench, which was still unoccupied. "That's why knights usually leave their fair ladies home in the castle."

Fiora's hand slid a bit higher on my leg.

"Damsels," she said, "learned to pick the padlocks on their chastity belts long ago, just in case some knight happened by their castle on a quest of his own."

Beneath Fiora's fierce and feline independence is a passionate nature that draws me like a moth to a bonfire. I have never gotten tired of finding and releasing the soft and sensuous female that lives inside her tough shell.

I glanced at my watch, trying to decide how much time we had. It was only a quarter to twelve . . . and we had made love in much more unlikely places. . . .

Fiora must have sensed the tension in my thigh muscles. She hung for a moment in midair, trying to decide not whether she wanted to but whether we *should*. I was ready to make up her mind for her when I glanced one more time toward the bench.

A burly man with black hair was just sitting down. There was a familiar set to his thick shoulders. An unhappy memory stirred somewhere back in my mind.

"Rain check," I said to Fiora.

Instantly she looked at the bench.

I grabbed the Nikon glasses from my lap. The man turned as he looked around, giving me a full view of his face. Even without a bushy mustache, I recognized him.

"Refugio Armijo. You slime-licking son of a bitch."

"I take it this won't be a joyful reunion?" Fiora said unhappily.

"It will be for one of us."

"Which one?"

"Me. Koo-Koo was the second gun the day Jake died."

fOUR

I sat watching Koo-Koo for several minutes, learning what I could from his face and manner. He didn't look quite as menacing as he had in the Mexican desert. Then he had been lean, mean, and fast as a snake, a cunning gunsel used to surviving in the violent anarchy of the Mexican Interior.

Today Koo-Koo looked like someone's overweight uncle. The *bandido* mustache was gone. He was clean shaven and sported a gringo haircut, as though he had been living north of the border for a while.

But he hadn't forgotten what he had once been. As he glanced at the *vatos locos* who were sprawled on the sand in their jeans and gang-color sweat bands, Koo-Koo's expression was disdainful—the smart old dog dismissing the young pups with contempt.

Koo-Koo wore jeans, too, but despite the heat he had on a short Levi's horseman's jacket. He was probably using it to hide a gun.

"You're sure it's him?" Fiora asked.

"Would you forget the face of your executioner?"

She made an unhappy sound.

Koo-Koo was restless on the bench. He looked right and left, squinting in the blazing sunlight. Then he shifted just enough to show that something was resting on his knee. A brown manila envelope, as blank and tantalizing as a hooker's smile.

I lowered the glasses for the first time, letting my eyes adjust to images in real time and distance.

"What are you going to do?" Fiora asked.

"I'm going to think about it for a minute."

Fiora let go of the breath she had been holding, then reached for the glasses in my hand.

The realization that she was afraid for me was startling. Sometimes I am amazed at my own effect on her, just as I know she sometimes is amazed at how deeply she can touch me with her anger or her love.

Saying nothing, Fiora stared through the glasses at Koo-Koo for the space of another long sigh.

"You've gotten a better handle on your temper in the last few years," Fiora said finally.

The sound I made wasn't encouraging, but she kept talking anyway.

"There was a time when you would have put Koo-Koo in the ground without a second thought, the way you did Jake's killer. No questions, no negotiations, just enough time for the man to look at you and know why he was going to die."

The hair on my neck stirred. I had never told a soul what happened between me and Jake's killer.

"How did you know?" I asked.

Fiora lowered the glasses and smiled at me. The smile was like her words, bittersweet.

"I know you, love. I always have. It just took some years to cope with what I know."

With that, she picked up the glasses and went back to watching the man who had almost killed me.

"He looks relaxed, almost bored," Fiora said after a time.

"Contrary to popular belief, hit men don't usually walk around looking furtive or vicious."

"I think he'd be nervous, if he knows he's about to meet the victim that got away."

I took the glasses from Fiora and studied Koo-Koo. She was right. He was glued to the bench, waiting for the appointment, but his eyes were more interested in the acres of flesh than in anything else.

"Is somebody setting Koo-Koo up for you?" Fiora asked.

"Could be. He sure doesn't look like he's about to meet a dead ringer for the man he murdered."

I smiled, wondering how Koo-Koo would react when he saw Jake's twin walking toward him across the years.

"I don't like that smile," Fiora muttered.

"Neither will he."

We watched in silence for a few more minutes. Koo-Koo glanced at his watch. I looked at the dashboard clock.

Noon straight up.

The line in front of the hot dog stand snaked out onto the boardwalk and toward the front door of the bookstore. Koo-Koo seemed to have the patience of a vulture waiting for a water hole to dry up. I wondered how long he would last before he decided that nobody was coming.

After another minute, I looped the binocular strap around my neck, like my hobby was sea gulls or beach bunnies. Jake's gun banged against the console as I fished it out. I shoved the soft leather holster down into the small of my back, slid the clip over my belt, and pulled the loose shirt back into place.

"I'm going to let Koo-Koo figure I was a no-show," I said. "If he's fronting for somebody else, he'll lead us back to them."

"Where do you want me to be?"

"Back home in Crystal Cove."

"Try again."

"My second choice is right here," I said.

"Your second choice sucks."

"Fiora, I can't move freely with you hanging on my sleeve."

"I'm not hanging on your sleeve."

"What would happen if I ordered you to stay in the truck?"

"Everything but that."

I looked at Fiora, trying to break her resolve with my most masterful glare.

It didn't work.

"I'm a partner, not a concubine," she said flatly.

I drew a deep breath and tried to think of an escape clause.

No luck.

In truth Fiora is as capable in these circumstances as any human being I know except Benny. Fiora makes up for her lack of physical strength with intelligence, pragmatism, and fast thinking.

"Chivalry *is* dead," I grumbled.

"On hiatus," Fiora corrected with a dazzling smile. "As soon as this is over, you can go back to opening doors for me and hauling out the trash."

"Such a deal."

"And seducing me in strange places. Did I mention that?"

"Sold."

Fiora smiled. "What do you want me to do?"

"Circle around this block and slip into the bookstore from the other direction. Keep an eye on Koo-Koo through the window. The pedestrians on the sidewalk will screen you."

"Where are you going to be?"

"I'll find some cover down the boardwalk where I can still see the bench. That way we have him covered, no matter which way he leaves."

She gave me an odd look.

"You're the one he's likely to recognize," Fiora said. "Wouldn't it make more sense for you to take the bookstore?"

"He came from the other direction. When he finally leaves, he'll probably head back the same way. That's—"

"My point exactly," Fiora interrupted. "Koo-Koo doesn't know me from guacamole dip, so I'll be in no danger from him. If he spots you, he's likely to do something macho and stupid."

There was impeccable logic to Fiora's argument, which didn't make me any more eager to accept it.

"I'll watch him carefully," she said. Then she added, "No matter what he does, I'll stay put until you join me."

Fiora would, too. She is very careful of the few promises she makes.

That should have made me feel better than it did.

On the other hand, how much trouble could Fiora get herself into while fifty thousand half-baked, mostly naked Southern Californians watched?

As we got out, I flipped the electric lock on the Suburban's doors. Fiora already wore that bland, blank smile she puts on when she wants to reassure the world that she's nothing more than a well-built blonde with the IQ of chewing gum. She gave me a quick kiss in passing and touched my mustache with her fingertip.

I circled in the other direction and walked down to the spot where the street dead-ended against the beachfront walk. A short block away, Koo-Koo sat with his back to me and to the sidewalk. Apparently he was transfixed by a pair of bikini-clad volleyball players who were throwing themselves around on the sand like tryouts for a Bud Lite commercial.

A knot of pedestrians came along. I used them as a moving screen all the way to the Small World of Books and Mystery Annex. The bookstore is shielded from the sidewalk by a patio restaurant. I found a spot inside next to the magazine rack where I could look through the windows. I had a clear view of Koo-Koo. Fiora was out of sight somewhere down the boardwalk.

Koo-Koo watched the volleyball game as if it were a striptease show. If he was worried about his luncheon date, he didn't show it. The way he shifted from one haunch to the other without leaning against the back of the bench told me I had guessed right. There was a gun under his jacket.

The store was like the heat wave, warm and sticky. Damp beach air curled the covers of the paperbacks and magazines. I thumbed through a couple of New Age journals, a feminist monthly, and two art magazines.

Koo-Koo glanced at his watch. Suddenly he seemed to notice that I was twenty minutes late. He looked around, making sure he was sitting on the only bench on the block. Then he went back to ogling the sweaty female flesh.

He looked like he was having a great time. Probably the only thing that would have pleased him more was a cockfight or an execution.

At twelve-twenty-five the Krishnas made their shuffling return from the south end of the boardwalk. The leader was a pale kid with a long red topknot and a face to match. Heatstroke wasn't far away, but he thumped the drum and chanted like the faithful metaphysical tape recorder he was.

Showing a surprising interest, Koo-Koo turned to watch Krishna's devotees. Maybe they reminded him of a procession of *penitentes* following plaster saints to a Mexican church. Maybe he was finally bored.

Even without the glasses, I could see sweat on Koo-Koo's face. The bench must have been getting more and more uncomfortable. He shifted around like a drop of water on a hot griddle.

At twelve-thirty-five Koo-Koo gave up. He stood, glanced around once more to be sure, then shrugged and trudged across the sand to the sidewalk. The way he moved made me think his boots pinched. Once he reached the concrete, he lurched along with rounded shoulders, a man who was hot, bored, and irritated at being sent on a fool's errand.

He was headed directly toward Fiora.

When Koo-Koo was twenty yards ahead, I eased out of the bookstore. He was easy to follow. His blue jeans and jacket made him stand out like a hellfire preacher among the G-string-and-pasties set.

I kept as many people as I could between us while I looked around for the shine of Fiora's golden hair in the sunlight. I saw the two Middle Eastern lechers first. They stood shoulder to shoulder on the sand beside the sidewalk with their backs to me. Between them, I caught a glimpse of Fiora's face.

The two men made a perfect screen for her. In the manner of strangers at a bus stop, she seemed to be chatting vaguely with them. Actually she was looking past their shoulders at Koo-Koo and watching for me at the same time. As soon as she saw me, a change came over her. She had just spotted her bus.

Koo-Koo walked past Fiora and the two Arabs without a second glance. He was moving like a man with a destination now. Fiora continued mostly to ignore her admirers until I drew abreast. Then she started toward me, leaving one of the men in mid-sentence.

The two men looked surprised, then unhappy. Undoubtedly they had assumed Fiora was enthralled by the shape of their Speedos. One of the men grabbed her arm to keep her from leaving.

It was a mistake.

"Let go," Fiora said distinctly.

He tightened his grip.

Fiora's free hand moved in a quick chop that caught the nerve in the man's wrist. He dropped his grip as if he had just gotten a thousand-volt shock. He yelped phrases in a language I didn't understand.

It was just as well I didn't. I might have been even more unhappy with him than I already was. I gave the yelper a look that shrank his codpiece.

"Say 'goodbye,' dear," I suggested to Fiora.

"Goodbye, dear," she said.

Before we walked away, Fiora gave the two men a knife-edged smile.

"First lesson in cultural sensitivity," she said clearly. "American women aren't camels in the marketplace. If you remember that, you won't have to spend so much money on whores."

"Or camels," I said.

Fiora gave me a sidelong glance and stroked my wrist with soothing fingertips. Only then did I realize that my hand was a fist. Slowly I relaxed my fingers and allowed Fiora to take my hand and lead me down the sidewalk after Koo-Koo.

"Smile," Fiora said. "You look like you want to kill something."

"I do. It's wankers like that who give men a bad name."

"They would give shit a bad name."

Hand in hand, we fell in behind Koo-Koo. He was half a block in front of us. He hadn't looked over his shoulder once. Either he was oblivious or he was leading us the way a Judas goat leads slaughter-house lambs.

When Koo-Koo turned left into a cul-de-sac, I began to feel edgy.

"Wait until I signal you," I told Fiora.

I left her and eased up to the cul-de-sac, half expecting to find Koo-Koo waiting for us. All I saw was his back disappearing around the corner. I gestured to Fiora. We both got to the next corner in time to see Koo-Koo turn inland between a row of duplexes.

He still was acting like the last thing on earth he expected was to be followed. The brown envelope was carried openly in his left hand.

Memory shifted again. I remembered that Koo-Koo was left-handed, like me. That's was why he hadn't succeeded in killing me. He had expected me to move one way and I had moved the other.

"Live and learn," I muttered to myself.

Or die dumb.

The sound of the shot that killed Jake came back to me as though it had just happened. The rage that followed was old but had lost none of its strength. For an instant I was younger, looking down the barrel of Jake's .45 at his executioner.

Reflexively I reached around to the small of my back and touched Jake's pistol. The handle felt cool despite the heat of the day. The weapon was there, ready, waiting.

"Remember the plan," Fiora said in a low voice. "Let's see where he leads us before you do something you can't undo."

"Quit reading my mind."

"It's a dirty job, but somebody has to do it."

"Koo-Koo could be headed for a car," I said. "If he is, we're up Shit Creek without a canoe."

I looked back up the alley. A block and a half away, the truck's nose stuck out beyond the garage door. I hesitated but couldn't think of any other way.

"Get the rig, quick," I said as I dug the keys out of my pocket. "Come south to here, then cut inland one block and turn south again. If you haven't seen me after three blocks, go inland one more block and double back going north. I won't be hiding, even if Koo-Koo is.''

For once Fiora didn't argue. She grabbed the keys, turned, and sprinted up the alley toward the garage.

fIVE

It was the cowboy boots that had made me decide Koo-Koo was headed for a car. No man hobbles very far on high heels. I tagged up for a second before I moved to the mouth of the new alley.

Still unaware of me, Koo-Koo was walking on packed dirt between cars in one of those small vacant lots that offer overpriced beach parking on hot summer days. As I started down the alley, Koo-Koo stopped, unlocked a car door, and disappeared inside. Not once did he look over his shoulder.

Fiora was still a block from the truck, sixty seconds from being in position. A man can start a car and cover three blocks in sixty seconds. If Koo-Koo took off in a cloud of dirt, I'd never find him again.

That had happened to me once before. I was damned if it was going to happen again.

Koo-Koo was out of sight in his car, which meant he couldn't see me either. Slouching a little to lose a few inches of height, I sprinted the length of the alley. Then I straightened up and tried to look nonchalant as I slid between the two cars at the back of the lot. The coffee-grinder noise of an old starter came from Koo-Koo's direction.

American automotive families have distinctive sounds. This one was a Chrysler. The starter ground again, clashed, then stopped. A badly tuned large-bore engine came to life. It sputtered and muttered before it finally caught. A cloud of bluish smoke blossomed behind the familiar tail fins of a late 1960s Dodge Charger, 426 hemi, four on the floor, and shackles on the back springs.

Koo-Koo must have seen *Bullitt.* His car was a carbon copy of the one the hit men drove. Like Koo-Koo, the black Dodge had once been dark, sleek, and dangerous. But like Koo-Koo, the car had lost a lot of its sting. The hubcaps were rusty chrome. There was a deep dent in the rear bumper, as though he had smacked a telephone pole in the parking lot of a beer bar.

Aw, Koo-Koo, you've had a tough life, haven't you?

The voice in my head sent cool ripples down my spine. It sounded like Jake's when he was mellow and rather savagely amused at the same time.

Koo-Koo rolled down the window to let the heat escape from inside the car. Then he peered carefully over his shoulder and started to back out. The crease in his bumper must have taught him something. He drove like my maiden aunt.

Though I was making no attempt to hide, my presence still didn't register. Koo-Koo shifted into first and started forward.

"Hey, man, you got a flat!" I called.

The brake lights came on as Koo-Koo stopped, turned, and looked at me blankly, as though he didn't understand. Maybe he didn't. I had never heard him speak a word of English.

"Your tire," I said loudly, pointing to the left front of the car. "It's flat. Savvy? El flat-o."

Along with the exaggerated gringo-speak, I brought my hands together like a tire deflating.

Koo-Koo got the message. His face darkened. He slapped the shifter into neutral and jabbed down on the foot brake. He still hadn't looked at me closely. He was more worried about having to change a tire.

I moved to where I blocked his view. Hands on my hips, I stood looking down at the tire, shaking my head sadly over his misfortune and hiding my face at the same time.

The driver's side door popped open. Koo-Koo stuck out his head to assess the damage, but I was still in the way. I wanted him to get out of the car. As long as he was behind the wheel, the big car was as dangerous as a loaded gun.

He growled an intricate, obscene Spanish oath about whores, scrubwomen, and goats, turned off the engine, and hauled himself out of the car to get a better look. Though he moved more slowly than he used to, there was still plenty of muscle beneath his gut.

I suspected that what he had lost in reflexes he made up for in sheer meanness. It was a common tactic among those of us lucky enough to survive our thirtieth birthday.

A single look told Koo-Koo the tire was round and fully intact. His big head swung toward me like a bull toward a matador. His eyes fixed on my face. I stared at my executioner for a long, cold moment.

"*Hola, Koo-Koo,*" I said softly. "*Hola, pendejo.*"

"*¡Madre de Díos, Jake!*"

Koo-Koo swallowed hard and clung with both hands to the car door that stood open between us. He shook his head once, sharply, as though trying to orient himself in a world where he had grown older but the dead hadn't.

"*Digame,*" I demanded in my best border Spanglish. "*¿Quién es su jefe?* Who sent you to kill me and Jake?"

I took a step forward. I was so close I could smell him, stale beer, old sweat, and fear mixed with the machine odors of hydraulic fluid and gasoline leaks from the car.

There was an instant's warning when Koo-Koo's shoulders shifted, but I didn't leap far enough backward. The stop on the door must have been broken, because he shoved the heavy metal panel way past its normal stopping point.

The door weighed as much as the blade of a small bulldozer. Its lower edge caught my shins. Hot sunlight shattered into fierce stars as pain overloaded my brain.

I stumbled back and caught myself on the front fender. Reflexively I twisted around, trying to face Koo-Koo and clawing for the gun in the small of my back at the same time.

He let go of the door and took off, running like a bull with tender hooves. I rolled off the fender to follow. My knees buckled on the first step and my palms dug furrows in the dry dirt. The ocean roared in my ears for a moment while my stomach tried to decide what to do with the breakfast it no longer wanted.

The sound of Koo-Koo's boots thudding down the alley was a call to arms, but I responded like a man in a vat of glue. Finally I managed to roll over on the ground, pull out the .45, and drag myself upright on the car that had been parked next to the Charger.

Braced across the top of the car, I got one clean bead on the back of Koo-Koo's Levi's jacket.

There was a time when I would have pulled the trigger and let God sort out the rest. But that time was past. The shot was too long and the background was too full of people.

Shit.

Rage is a good painkiller. I dragged myself around the car and hobbled down the alley after the fleeing executioner. Somewhere in the fog, I heard Jake screaming at me.

Get going, you lazy son of a bitch! Kill that bastard! He's getting away!

The bleeding gashes on my shins had gone mostly numb by the time I got to the far end of the alley. I lurched into the street right in front of the Suburban. Fiora jammed on the brakes and stuck her head out the window.

"He's got a gun!" she said.

"Which way?" I demanded.

She hesitated, reluctant to tell me. Then she looked at my eyes and pointed down the cul-de-sac toward the beach.

"He turned left at the sand," Fiora said.

I went after him, but I wasn't setting any speed records. My legs seemed to have lost all feeling from the knees down. It was an improvement.

Just before I got to the sidewalk, I shoved the gun into the front of my waistband and dragged the shirt over it. The last thing I needed was a panicked herd of sunburned tourists or some local muscle freak looking to be a hero.

I jogged unevenly across the sidewalk onto the sand, searching for Koo-Koo's indigo jacket ahead of me. After a few moments I found it.

Fear had made Koo-Koo a sprinter, but he was in lousy shape. A hundred yards down the beach he had slowed down to a fast walk. The gun must have been stowed under his coat again, because his hands were empty. He kept glancing over his shoulder, searching for a past that hadn't been buried deeply enough.

I looked both ways, hoping to see a lifeguard Jeep or an LAPD beach unit, anything that might give me options beyond the one I felt hard against my belly. I didn't want to use the gun.

Not with Fiora just behind me.

Not with kids building sand castles in the sun.

Not now.

But now was the only time I had, and there wasn't a cop in sight.

Jake's laughter rang in my ears. *You're getting soft, kid. Don't you think you can take him yourself?*

The sand was deep and loose, like running on a treadmill. In spite of that, I made up half Koo-Koo's lead before he saw me and started running again.

My legs felt like sticks. I kicked up my pace anyway, pretending I was a middle-distance runner at the beginning of the bell lap.

The cowboy boots and the extra forty pounds began to take their toll. Koo-Koo started floundering in the soft sand. When I cut the lead to thirty-five yards, he quit looking over his shoulder and tried to sprint again.

That dash lasted about ten seconds. He stumbled, went to one knee, and lurched back to his feet. Then his hands went to his waistband.

Reality shifted to slow motion as adrenaline flooded through me. When Koo-Koo came around toward me, I caught the burning flash of sunlight on a chrome barrel.

Mexicans do love flashy guns.

Jake's fierce laughter washed through me as I reached for his worn old blue-steel .45.

Koo-Koo's weapon was a heavy-barreled revolver, a .357 by the looks of the ribbing. More than enough muzzle velocity to punch a slug through me and several more people on the beach behind me.

Off to the right, someone screamed in shrill recognition of Koo-Koo's gun.

As he swung the Magnum toward me, I stopped and brought the .45 up, two-handed. I heard more shouts, warnings, Jake's and the others all mingled with my own.

"Throw down your gun, Koo-Koo!"

The Magnum's bore was like a mouth just starting to yawn.

Now, Fiddler! He's bought and paid for. Take him!

"No. ¡Digame, Koo-Koo, digame!"

But it was too late to talk and I knew it. Even as I yelled at him, I slipped the thumb safety on the .45 and pulled the trigger twice.

I heard the shots, felt the heavy recoil pass through my hands and up my arms. The sunlight was so bright and the adrenaline so fierce I swore I could see the big, fat, slow-moving slugs leave the muzzle of Jake's gun, travel the forty feet, and knock Koo-Koo sprawling before he could fire a single shot.

Then all I heard was the roar of the ocean waves and my own blood. I saw open mouths but I didn't hear the screaming tourists who had just figured out this wasn't a movie.

Koo-Koo tried to cry out. I saw his lips move but I heard nothing, felt nothing, as I crossed the sand and approached him warily.

Sunlight burnished the chromed weapon that had come within an instant of putting me where Koo-Koo was, on his back in the sand, two red splotches growing on the plaid pattern of his pearl-button cowboy shirt, the toes of his boots pointing obliquely toward the sky.

I watched over the sights of Jake's gun as I kicked one of the boots hard, looking for reaction.

Nothing.

Jake laughed manically, somewhere in hell.

I circled to one side, watching Koo-Koo's trigger finger. It straightened slowly, unwillingly, like the reflexive extension of a dead frog's leg. I kicked the gun out of his hand and knelt beside him.

Koo-Koo's eyes were open, unfocused.

"Who sent you?" I asked softly.

He stared straight into the overhead sun.

"Tell me, you bastard, or I'll leave you to die."

But Refugio Armijo was beyond threats, his soul slipping away, taking a piece of my own, leaving something cold in its place.

Abruptly I heard the ocean's roar again and, with it, a woman's voice, sharp and commanding.

"Freeze! Police officers! Drop the gun!"

I dropped Jake's gun into the hot sand.

"Raise your hands! Put them behind your head and lock your fingers!"

I did.

A familiar hollow sound came from behind me. Heavy pistol sliding back into hard leather holster. The cold ratcheting noise of handcuffs.

A small, firm hand snapped one bracelet on my right wrist, then dragged it around and down to meet the other wrist. The second bracelet bit and held.

"Face down and stay there."

The cop shoved me forward. The sand was soft and burning hot against my cheek. From the corner of my eye, I saw a wiry woman wearing a dark blue uniform. She had on Bermuda shorts instead of trousers, but her gun was full length. Mouse-brown hair, dark eyes, and a wary look.

Part of me felt a little sorry for her. She didn't have the faintest idea what was going on.

I was going to do my best to see it stayed that way.

"Get good statements from everyone," I said.

She shot me a look that told me I should begin exercising my right to remain silent. Then she pulled out her walkie-talkie and described the scene in cold coplike terms. Backup was already en route.

I lay there and prayed that Fiora would stay the hell away.

S|X

The lady cop and her male backup both looked good in shorts, even though he didn't shave his legs. Working together, the officers took care of the basics, calling for a field supervisor and the coroner and moving the crowd out of the way. Then the woman—the brass tag above her left boob said her name was Spurlock—and her partner hauled me to my feet. She read me the litany of Saint Miranda without consulting the pocket card.

"Do you want to make a statement right now?" Spurlock asked when she had finished warning me of my rights.

"You couldn't have been more than ten yards behind me," I said, "so you know it was self-defense."

Spurlock didn't say anything, which pissed me

off. It wasn't hard to do; I really hadn't wanted to shoot Koo-Koo.

"Too bad you weren't quicker," I added. "You could have shot him yourself and gotten a gold star. I don't need the hassle."

"Should I take that as 'yes' or 'no'?" Spurlock asked.

"No. I don't want to make a statement right now."

When I said those magic words, both cops lost interest in me. I was suddenly a piece of garbage inside a pair of handcuffs, and they cared more about the handcuffs than about me.

For the next hour, the entire Los Angeles Police Department pretended I was a stray piece of furniture. They didn't want my name, rank, or serial number. They didn't want to answer my questions. They didn't want to ask me anything.

Miranda has certainly cut down on the idle chit-chat.

Finally the cops stashed me in a holding cell at the West Los Angeles station. I settled in to get good and bored.

Jails are like hospitals. They're frightening only if you believe you'll never get out. As long as you're healthy, patient, and in good odor with God, you'll be freed as soon as the paperwork is filled out.

I reminded myself of my indelible innocence about a hundred times over the first three hours. The rest of the time I lay on my back on the concrete cell bench and told myself I was glad my shins had finally thawed out, because that meant the damage was more apparent than real.

I wished they were still numb anyway. The skin hadn't been broken badly, but both legs sported spongy, blood-filled bruises the size of surfer's knobs.

Every five minutes the grizzled drunk-tank veteran in the cell on the left side of me asked if I had a cigarette. Every five seconds later I told him I didn't.

On the other side of me was an old Armenian pirate who owned a service station in Culver City. He had punched his wife in the right eye and broken a few of her ribs. I knew all about it. I also knew he intended to black her other eye and break the rest of her ribs just as soon as he got out. I told him if he kept beating the old lady he would wake up dead some day and the jury would let her off with probation.

Things got real quiet in the fourth hour, except for the drunk. I had plenty of time to polish my half-truths and carefully choose my lies.

The fifth hour began to drag, but at least the drunk shut up. I began to breathe more deeply. Nobody had offered me a phone call, which was a good sign. If LAPD is going to charge you with murder, they tend to observe the obvious rules to the letter.

The less obvious rules are a different matter, which is why I worried about Fiora. She had been nowhere in sight when the black-and-white took me away. I hoped she had enough sense to remain invisible. Cops love to have two versions of the same story to compare. Other than Koo-Koo, Fiora was the only human being within reach whose statement might be used to impeach mine.

As the sixth hour began, the drunk on my right went into withdrawal. The sound of his retching and the stench of his agony filled the stale, cramped lockup. I banged on the bars with an empty soda can until the turnkey shambled back and made a note of the situation in his log.

"How about a hose or something to clean him up?" I asked.

The turnkey looked at me like I was stupid. Maybe I was.

"Chill out," he said. "You won't be here much longer. Your lawyer's out front right now."

"A small blonde?"

"In your dreams, asshole."

The door slammed shut.

Ten minutes later the turnkey came back and unlocked my cell. When he stepped backward and opened the door, he pulled a Maglite from a loop on his belt. Machined from aircraft-grade aluminum, these flashlights can throw a tight beam at fifty yards. They can also fracture a skull at arm's length.

The jailer wasn't planning on lighting my personal darkness. He held the Maglite loosely in his right hand, ready to parry with the backhand and club with the forehand in case I wanted to dance.

I came out of the cell slowly and went where he pointed like the docile, sweet-tempered creature I am.

The interview room smelled better than the lockup, but it wasn't as cool. Two minutes after I sat at the table, the door opened again. A middle-aged man with a rumpled suit and a rumpled face walked in.

I whistled silently, impressed.

Ray Bently was the most expensive honest criminal defense attorney in Los Angeles. Some of his colleagues charged more, but they were the kind who took grocery sacks full of small unmarked currency as retainers. They were also the kind who charged more to obtain continuances than they did to try a case.

Ray loved the practice of criminal law, but mostly from the other side of the courtroom. He had spent twenty productive years as a top-level prosecutor in the Orange County District Attorney's office. Then he ran into a new DA who was more interested in headlines than he was in law.

Very soon Ray was working for the defense. It wasn't as much fun as prosecution, but it did beat drawing up living trusts and probating estates.

Ray was a cracking good lawyer if you were innocent and a conscientious one if you were guilty. I was innocent, at least in my own mind, but considering what I had decided to do, I wasn't entirely sure I was happy to see Ray's hangdog face with its round, wire-rimmed glasses and drooping walrus mustache.

"So, boy, you think maybe you finally dug yourself a hole you can't climb out of?" Ray asked.

We had become drinking buddies for a couple of weeks while he defended one of Benny's friends. That, and Ray's age, must have made him feel he had the right to call me "boy."

Normally, I would have shrugged the matter off. I wasn't normal at the moment. I was still filled with a burning cold rage.

"I haven't seen a booking slip yet, so I don't know," I said.

"You *do* know what you did?" Ray asked sarcastically.

"Yeah," I said. My tone was a dead match for his. "I shot a man in self-defense. Clear-cut. Open and shut. So open and shut I'm surprised Fiora bothered to call you. You're too damned expensive for routine stuff."

Ray scowled as he set his briefcase on the floor, sat down on the chair opposite me, and took hold of the edge of the table as though he were testing its strength. He leaned forward on stiff arms and stared at me with sober, cold eyes.

"The law treats the taking of a human life very seriously," he said. "And if I were you, hotshot, I'd treat it seriously, too."

"I'm in jail, old man. That's as serious as it gets."

Ray tilted his head to one side and nodded, as though confirming something.

"Fiora told me you would be as cold as dry ice and about as much fun to take on bare-handed. She told me you're like that if you have to shoot someone. You don't like it, do you?"

"Not one fucking bit."

He grunted. "That's reassuring."

I bit down hard on my temper. Then I stood up, walked over to the door, and walked back as though I had just entered the room.

"Let's start over again, Ray. It's good to see you," I said through my teeth, offering my hand. "Too bad you've wasted a trip. Until LAPD pulls their thumb out of their ass and finishes the paperwork, I don't know if I'll need a lawyer."

Ray shook my hand, returned my toothy smile, and waited until I sat down before he began shuffling through his briefcase.

"Your missus said it was clear self-defense," Ray mumbled as he rustled papers. "I couldn't get any of the investigators to flatly contradict her. God knows there were plenty of witnesses."

"Like I said. Open and shut."

"What nobody seems to know is why it happened in the first place."

Ray had a way of cutting through the fat, the muscle, and the sinew, right to the bone. It was a talent that made him both valuable and dangerous.

"What did Fiora say?" I asked.

"She said to ask you."

I couldn't hide my surprise. I hoped to hell I hid my satisfaction.

"First of all, Fiora didn't have any part of this, not even as a witness," I said. "She was waiting for me a couple of blocks away, where our truck was parked."

Ray nodded and said smoothly, "There's no reason to think the cops believe otherwise, if that's what's bothering you."

I waited.

He let the silence expand invitingly until he realized I wasn't going to spill my guts.

"All right, Fiddler. We'll do it your way. As direct as a bulldozer. Why were you chasing Refugio Armijo?"

"Are you on retainer?"

"I'm not going to talk out of school whether I'm retained or not," Ray said coldly. "But yes, I'm on retainer."

"Okay," I said, "this is precisely what happened."

For the next few minutes I described, in great and accurate detail, everything that happened from the moment the crazy Mexican stranger in the battered Dodge almost clipped me as he backed out of a parking spot to the moment I pulled the trigger. It was an unhappy, unsettling story of random urban violence between two utter strangers.

Ray listened like a tape recorder, quiet and utterly

efficient, until I stopped talking. Then he tilted his head to one side, tugged thoughtfully at the drooping tip on one side of his mustache, and sighed.

"Just like that, huh?" he asked finally.

I nodded.

"Just a day at the beach that went terribly wrong," Ray said slowly, his face as expressionless as his voice.

I nodded again.

"A chance encounter that leads to an argument between two men, both of whom happen to be armed," he summarized neutrally.

"My gun came with a permit," I pointed out.

"Yes. The police mentioned that."

"I didn't pull my gun until the other guy—"

"Refugio Armijo," Ray slipped in.

"—pulled his. The shooting was his call, not mine. What was I supposed to do? Let him kill me and a few other innocent folks on the beach?"

Ray growled deep in his chest, like Kwame does when he's warning the neighbor's cat to stay away from his food.

"Shit happens in LA all the time," I said. "This time it happened to him and to me. I'm not proud of it, but I'm not going to fall apart over it either."

There was silence while Ray worked the story over in his mind. Then he asked the crucial question.

"You ever see this guy before?"

And I had a lie ready that people would believe.

"He was a Mexican. They all look alike to a white boy like me."

Ray's shrewd old eyes stared at me through the round little glasses that made him look like an old-time circuit-riding preacher.

"Not bad," he finally said. "Not bad at all."

I raised my left eyebrow in the way that irritates Fiora.

"You realize," Ray said, "that if you tell it to the cops just once—and it turns out not to be the truth —they can and will use it as a club. They could chase you right into the gas chamber with it."

He was right, of course.

"Can I get out of here without making a statement?" I asked.

There was another thoughtful silence. Then Ray shook his head.

"I doubt it," he said. "If you don't make a statement, you'll spend the night in jail while the cops finish the paperwork and dump it on some prosecutor's desk."

"Then what?"

Ray shrugged. "Luck of the draw, Fiddler. If the prosecutor is a kid marking time until he goes into private practice defending rich dope dealers and weenie-wavers, you're home free."

"And if he's a smart, shrewd prosecutor like you were?"

"If the prosecutor is a hard-assed lawyer—and there are a few left—you'll be charged with manslaughter."

"How? The witnesses all agree he drew first and I shot in self-defense."

"If I were the prosecutor, I'd keep sending the investigators back until they found something to punch holes in your story about random urban violence."

"Even with a beach full of witnesses?"

"Given your record—" Ray shrugged. "Face it.

There's more than one cop who would love to give you a bad time."

"What you're saying is I can keep my mouth shut and cool my heels for a day or a week in a cell, letting matters take their course, or I can tell the cops outside what happened and take my chances on getting out right now."

He nodded.

"Bring them in," I said flatly.

Ray looked surprised for the first time since he had walked in the door.

"Hell, boy. There are worse things than a few nights in jail, and you know it."

"Yeah. And some of those things will happen unless I get out of here. Now."

SEVEN

The cops came into the interview room: two Dobermans and a streetwise mongrel, everybody on their toes and guarding their balls. The two suits—Jernigan and Blair—were part of the first team to hit the beach. They were homicide dicks, squared away and sure of themselves in their blue shirts and striped ties. Both men had empty loop holsters on their belts.

The mongrel wore jeans, Birkenstocks, and a Hawaiian shirt loose around the waist to hide his gun. Family: Peace officer. Genus: Undercover narc. Species: Miami Vice cowboy. His name was Dugger. He didn't care for the two suits worth a damn. Mangy and aloof, he wandered off in a corner while Jernigan set up the tape recorder on the table.

"Okay. For the tape machine," Jernigan said,

"you've been advised of your right to remain silent and you are represented by counsel."

I looked over at Ray.

He nodded wearily, as though glad lawyers couldn't be held responsible for the lies their clients told.

"My lawyer's here and I know I don't have to talk to you, but I want to set things straight," I said.

"So go ahead," Blair suggested in a bored voice. "Set things straight."

That told me who was Mutt and who was Jeff in this act. Blair was the designated skeptic, the mean cop whose job was to drive me into the arms of his understanding good-cop partner.

Earnestly I launched into a recapitulation of random bad luck and urban violence. It was a convincing story because it was absolutely true.

As far as it went.

You see, I had been cutting through the parking lot, headed for the beach, when this guy almost backed over me. I yelled something at him. He stopped, said something back, and called me some names. I didn't like that. So I went and stood by the car door. Only I was so mad that I stood too close. He gave me a shot with the door that damn near broke my legs.

With that I stood, pulled up the legs of my jeans, and showed them the impressive knots and livid bruises. Jernigan looked at them, then got up and left the interview room.

I turned to Blair. "You did find his car, right? It was a block and a half from the beach in a little dirt lot."

"We found it."

Good. Nothing like physical corroboration. It makes cops feel much more comfortable.

"Well, then I got really mad," I began.

"Hold it," Blair said. "Wait for Jernigan to get back with the camera."

When the other half of the partnership returned with a Polaroid, I displayed my shins again. They showed up real well in the photograph.

While Jernigan snapped another round of photos, I wrapped up my half of the story, all about how mad I had been and how the guy had gotten out of his car for a fight but must have lost his nerve because he took off running. I hobbled after him, caught up, and was shocked beyond belief when he pulled out a gun. Luckily, I just happened to have one of my own.

Bang, bang. That was it. And what was his name, anyway?

Nobody answered, although I caught Blair and Dugger exchanging the kind of look that said they weren't happy campers.

"Your pistol permit seems to be in order," Jernigan said, "even if it was issued by the sheriff of some cow county I didn't even know California had."

I nodded and made a soothing noise.

"But what I don't understand," Jernigan concluded, "is why the hell you had the gun with you at the beach."

Way to go, Jernigan. I didn't think of that until the second hour you had me in the cell.

"I didn't remember it was in the glove box until we got to the beach," I said.

Blair looked at the ceiling.

Dugger looked at the floor.

Jernigan looked sympathetic. It wasn't his fault. He was born with that kind of face.

"I decided it was safer to carry the gun with me than it was to leave it in the car," I said.

"Safer?" Jernigan asked.

I shrugged. "Yeah. You guys know better than I do how many cars are clouted every day in Venice Beach parking lots."

Blair bridled at the implicit criticism of LA's finest.

Jernigan shrugged it off. He knew I was right about Venice and auto burglaries, whether I was telling the truth about the rest of it or not.

Dugger had found a toothpick somewhere, maybe on the floor, and was chewing it. He took it out and spoke for the first time.

"You got a record, pal?"

"You've run me," I said. "You tell me."

He shrugged. "Sacramento, yeah, but that's not the only place there are records. I just wanted to see if you'd save us the trouble of querying every other state in the union."

"Save the taxpayers' money," I said. "I'm a law-abiding citizen."

Dugger looked like he didn't believe me, but he had worn the same expression since he walked in the door. In his case it was acquired rather than hereditary.

"How about Mexico?" Dugger said. "You ever in any trouble down there?"

Good thing I wasn't wired to a little black box. I can control my face but not my heart rate. I would have pinned the needle on the paper.

"When I was younger, I spent the night in jail in Ensenada," I admitted a little sheepishly.

"Drugs?" Dugger asked.

"Pulque. You know, booze."

Dugger chewed down on the toothpick hard enough to split it. He spit out a splinter and watched me with eyes the color and clarity of shucked oysters.

"They don't lock up gringos for drunk and disorderly," Dugger said.

"It took me a while to figure out that they were after twenty bucks, not me. Like I said, I was young." I shrugged. "So I gave them twenty, and they let me out."

The undercover narc shifted the broken toothpick around on his tongue and looked at the floor, watching me out of the corner of his eye without seeming to.

"Does the name Bobby Soliz mean anything to you?" he asked.

Dugger was good. The question was so casual it took a moment to sink in.

"Was that who I killed?" I asked, not looking in Ray's direction.

Jernigan and Blair looked irritated, which suggested to me that all the cops were fishing but Dugger wasn't using the same bait.

"No," Jernigan said. "The guy you killed was Refugio Armijo."

Dugger gave the cop a cold look.

Jernigan ignored him.

"What was the name again?" I asked Dugger.

"Robert Medrano Soliz."

"Wasn't there a boxer by that name?" I asked. "I think maybe I saw him fight at the Forum, years ago."

It was a good answer to Dugger's question, but it

wasn't the one he wanted, so he went fishing some more.

"Did you ever meet Soliz? Personally or professionally?"

I shook my head.

That wasn't good enough for Blair, who pointed at the tape machine and said, "Speak up. The sound of an empty head shaking doesn't register on tape."

"I don't remember ever meeting a boxer named Robert Medrano Soliz," I said distinctly. "Got it?"

I wasn't the first man to develop a bad memory under cross-examination. I wouldn't be the last.

Blair shot me a dirty look.

"What the hell does this boxer have to do with the guy I shot?" I asked.

"Dunno," Blair said. He looked over at Dugger. "Do you?"

The narc glowered back and said not one word.

"Okay," Jernigan said after a moment, "let's go back over it again, just so we can be sure we understand everything. You were coming from where?"

Nice touch, that. I hadn't told them in the first version because I wasn't sure whether any of their eyewitnesses had seen me on the boardwalk earlier. To answer, I had to take a chance.

"I had gone over to Pacific Avenue to get a beer," I said. "I was cutting back to the beach through the parking lot when this Mexican damn near ran over my feet."

"Okay. Then what happened?" Blair asked.

He might have asked the question, but he didn't look interested in the answer. Nobody did.

And so it went for the next seventy-three minutes. By then we were all running on autopilot, phoning it in, doing it by the numbers because no one wanted to do it at all.

I told them the same story over and over again, varying a little here and there with a fresh detail but keeping the essential thrust intact. Jernigan and Blair picked a few loose threads out of the weave, but neither of them was able to find a thread long enough to make the whole piece unravel.

My scenario sounded all too plausible to seasoned Los Angeles homicide cops. At least there had been an argument involved in this shooting—lots of people get killed for being on the wrong street corner when one of the chickenshit gangs drives by and starts shooting.

Dugger was a different matter from the homicide cops. He didn't entirely buy my story, but he seemed reluctant to bring in the rubber hoses and bright lights. The suite for four dancers was getting ready for yet one more reprise when Ray finally intervened. It was the first time he had said a word.

"Look, gents, my client has given you the same story six or seven times by now. I've lost track. So have you."

Nobody argued.

"You've been cutting bait for more than an hour," Ray said. "It's time to go fishing or find a better brand of bait."

Dugger looked sour and ready to argue. "Look, just because a dirtbag has a—"

"Dugger," Blair said, cutting across him, "let's you and me and my partner have a little chat. Outside."

"Shee-it," muttered Dugger, but he followed the others outside the interview room.

Jernigan and Blair must have known Ray from

his days as a deputy district attorney. They knew he could be real trouble. While the cops filled in the narc, Ray and I waited. Finally Jernigan came back in.

"You're free to go," he told me in a matter-of-fact voice.

The tight spring of tension between my shoulder blades begin to unwind.

"That means you're not going to file?" Ray asked.

"Not at the moment."

"At the moment," Ray repeated neutrally.

"Hell, Ray, I don't have to tell you how it is," Jernigan said. "You've been around a long time."

"Memory is the second thing to go," Ray said in a dry voice. "So tell me how it is."

Jernigan gave a crack of laughter.

"Your client looks pretty clean, as shootings go," the cop said. "I might want to recommend some lesser charge later, but right now it sure doesn't look like murder to me, or even manslaughter."

Ray nodded soberly, doing a good job of hiding his reaction behind those round glasses.

"What about Dugger?" Ray asked. "That go for him too?"

Jernigan grimaced as though his authority had been challenged. "What makes you think Dugger would say anything different?"

"He had a different agenda."

"Catching crooks is everybody's agenda."

Ray made a growling sound low in his chest. This time it might have been laughter.

"I've seen Dugger before," Ray said. "He's from Administrative Narcotics. Those guys have been known to go their own way in the past."

"Dugger doesn't make the call. I do."

"I'm reassured."

I shot Ray a look, wondering why he was pushing.

"Oh, hell," Jernigan said, disgusted. "Dugger should be nominating your client for a good citizen medal and he knows it. Dugger's just pissed at the moment."

"Huh?" I said, trying to sound surprised rather than interested.

Jernigan smiled at me as only an old cop can smile.

"You were lucky. Koo-Koo Armijo was some kind of big-time Mexican doper once. There's been a conspiracy case pending against him and this guy Soliz for so many years the warrant's gotten yellow."

In the back of my mind, I heard Jake's voice.

Well, damn. Who'd have thought that of Koo-Koo? I thought he was just some waiter at a ptomaine restaurant in Puerto Peñasco.

Yeah, Jake. Who'd have thought it. But you should have. You paid for that oversight with your life.

And damned near with mine.

"So that's where Dugger came in," Ray said.

"Yeah." Jernigan never looked away from me. "But don't think you can go around wasting anybody who knocks you on your ass in a parking lot. You got lucky, that's all."

"I hear you," I said.

And I did.

I had been lucky in more ways than one. Before today I had known a bit about Koo-Koo and a lot more about a Mexican welterweight named Bobby Soliz. I hadn't known until now that there was a connection between the two.

How about it, Jake? Did you know?

Nothing answered in my head but silence.

I turned and followed Ray out of the interview room. After a few more formalities, I was free to go to Fiora while Ray rounded up everything the cops had taken from me.

Fiora was sitting alone on a wooden bench in the lobby of the West LA station house, watching the currents of urban misery swirl by. There were smudges under her eyes that made the rest of her skin look pale. She had her knees drawn up in front of her as though cold from more than hours of sitting beneath an institutional air conditioner.

When Fiora saw me, she came off the bench and gave me a hug as though I were the one who was cold. Then she tipped back her head and measured the new shadows in my eyes.

"Thanks for calling Ray," I said. "Without him, I'd probably still be back there doing laps."

"Does that mean they're letting you go?"

"There may be some problems down the road, but for now I'm free to go on doing whatever it was I was doing."

The darkness at the center of Fiora's eyes expanded.

"Haven't you learned to leave well enough alone?" she asked in a husky voice.

I looked around for Ray.

"Jake's dead," Fiora said. "Are you going to keep pushing until you're dead, too?"

"Leave it alone."

Neither one of us liked the sound of my voice, but there wasn't a damn thing to do for that either.

When Ray found us, we were still picking our way in silence through the mine field of the past. Ray handed over a big envelope that contained my wallet, belt, pocket change, and the laces from my deck shoes. I sat down on the bench and began to thread one of the laces. Fiora took the other shoe and went to work on it.

"There's one piece of your property missing," he said.

"I noticed."

"They want to run ballistics tests. They'll compare a bullet from your gun with any stray forty-five slugs they might have recovered from dead people. It's standard procedure these days."

I kept lacing.

"That doesn't give you any problems, does it?" Ray proded.

"Nope."

I didn't add that I would have felt differently if the cops had managed to confiscate my Detonics. There was a new barrel on the gun, so ballistics matches would have been inconclusive, but a careful check of the exotic brass might have raised questions about an incident that had been written off as a typical gang-bang shooting involving a crack merchant named Freeway Ricky.

Even as I made a mental note to get Benny to change the firing pin on the Detonics, I felt cold and worn out. Some people are born shooters. I'm not one of them.

But sometimes I've had to do it anyway.

As the three of us stood on the front steps of the

station house, Ray scribbled something on the back of one of his business cards and handed it to me.

"That's my home phone," he said. "I have this gut feeling you're going to need it."

eIGHT

Fiora sat wedged against the far door of the Suburban all the way home. I tried not to take it personally. I wasn't feeling very lovable at the moment anyway. I looked forward to Crystal Cove's rundown, ramshackle embrace.

Crystal Cove is what is called "inhold" land. It's the residue of the nineteenth century, when the owners of Irvine Ranch let good friends sign long-term leases on beachfront cottage sites.

In the past decade, Irvine has been forced to donate much of its coastal holdings to the California State Park people, in return for the right to develop the rest as resorts and high-ticket homesites. Just about the only land that's left in private hands is the leased land in the cove.

The resorts have been slow in coming. The closest

lights are still a mile away on either side of Crystal Cove. So is the kind of wealth that marks—and mars—the Gold Coast beaches. Crystal Cove is an island in time, an island with seventy-year-old cottages and eucalyptus trees as big around as a water tank.

I was looking forward to my own personal, peaceful time machine. The stench of urban humanity in the jail had been enough to put me off cities for some time to come. My pores felt clotted. The taste in my mouth was right off the drunk-tank floor.

While I made something to cut the taste, Fiora stripped messages from the answering machine, sorted the mail, and changed into a light cotton caftan. I heaped a plate with sandwiches made out of Tillamook, dry salami, and sourdough. By the time I sliced up some new apples, opened a St. Stans Amber for myself, and poured a glass of soft sauvignon blanc for her, Fiora was out on the deck waiting for me.

"Anything?" I asked, referring to the phone and the mail.

"Nothing worth mentioning."

She took the glass of wine, left the food, and walked over to the railing. Silently she stared out into the night, as though she preferred it to whatever she might find in my eyes.

The air was so clear I could see a few lights around the isthmus on Catalina. Closer to home, the brightest stars barely managed to burn through the dome of city light up the coast.

The natural textures and peace of night have been banished by man-made light. Only in the desert can you look up at midnight and see all the way back to the beginning of time.

I ate half a sandwich in a single bite. As the taste of jail gave way to the clean flavor of cheddar, I settled back on the chaise and sipped at the sharp, bitter ale.

After a few minutes of silence, Kwame deserted his post guarding the sandwiches and walked over to stand beside Fiora. His broad, lion-colored head nudged her hand in a silent bid for attention.

I knew just how he felt.

When Fiora reached down and absently stroked Kwame's head, I was a little jealous.

"What now?" she finally asked without turning around.

I didn't answer, because anything I said would only make her more unhappy.

She read my silence perfectly.

"You can't leave it alone," Fiora said.

"No." Then, "I doubt you really expect me to."

Fiora sidestepped that double-edged truth with another question.

"Is there anything I can say to stop you?"

I thought for a while. Very carefully.

"I don't think you'll force that kind of choice on me," I said. "It's not your style anymore."

That touched a nerve.

Fiora spun around and looked at me. In the light reflected from the living room window, her expression was all angular shadows and slashes of anger.

"Keep pushing," she said flatly. "You'll get there."

"I've been there. We both have. Neither one of us liked it. That's why we're here."

"Here isn't much fun for me."

"It isn't something I chose," I pointed out.

"Bullshit."

"Fiora—"

She talked right over me, her voice vibrating with anger.

"You love it," she accused, "you and Jake both. Revenge! *Jesus!* It's just the thing to make you feel old-fashioned and manly and virtuous."

I drank some ale. Its bitterness was sweet by comparison to Fiora's tone. At one time that tone had infuriated me. After a lot of painful years, I had finally understood it was pain driving her, not scorn.

But it still pissed me off.

I took another drink, watching Fiora the whole time, trying to quench my temper. No one, but no one, can reach me like she can.

"Pretty lady," I finally said, "you have no room to lecture me about vengeance and other outdated virtues. You've diced up plenty of folks over transgressions so morally arcane the rest of the world would have overlooked them."

Fiora took a drink of wine. And watched me. She hates being called pretty lady.

"So don't tell me you object to vengeance on religious principles," I continued. "You and I are members of the same church."

"I object to anything that threatens your life."

"Koo-Koo is history."

"So is Jake. So tell me why I'm dreaming again, Fiddler. And while you're at it, *tell me why I'm dreaming when I'm wide awake.*"

I had opened my mouth to say something, but that stopped me cold. Fiora is a very bright, very modern female who happens to be prescient at inconvenient times. Not who, what, why, when, and where prescient. Hell, no. That might be useful.

But when I'm in danger, she knows it.

She knew Jake was dead and I was wounded but alive before I knew it. She called a lawyer and got him to work ransoming Jake's corpse and my slightly more lively body from Mexico.

And she did it from California, at almost the exact moment the first shot was fired.

Neither one of us is particularly comfortable with Fiora's unpredictably fey turn of mind. We used to deny it existed. We still try that approach occasionally. Most of the time we simply don't talk about what her dreams are or aren't like . . . and when her gift or curse of vague foresight appears, I listen. Carefully.

I took another drink of ale and thought about asking just what Fiora's dreams had been like: if she had seen a face, a time, a place, a weapon, anything.

"No," Fiora said. "Nothing useful. Just the dead-cold certainty you're in danger."

Her words gave me a chill. I know Fiora can't read my mind, but the longer we're together, the closer our thought processes become.

"I'd be more threatened by leaving this alone," I said, "particularly now that I've got blood on my hands because of it."

Strangely, that seemed to make sense to Fiora. Her expression softened in the dim light.

"You're sure?" she asked. "No questions and no regrets, no matter how it turns out?"

Her voice made me uneasy, yet there was only one possible answer.

"Yes."

Fiora drew a deep breath and let it out slowly. Then she went past me into the house without a word. I heard the front door open and close.

For an icy instant I thought she had walked out on me. Just like that. Gone.

She had done it before.

I had done it to her.

But this time it didn't make sense.

I sat there waiting, trying not to think or feel, wondering what the hell was going on. Kwame came over and sat on his haunches beside me, looking through the glass door into the house, watching the front door.

The sound of the Suburban's door slamming came through the damp salt air. I was halfway out of my chair when I heard the front door of the cottage open. With a sound that was half curse and half sigh of relief, I sat down again.

Fiora snapped on the deck lights, ruining the intimacy of darkness. With one hand she snagged the wine bottle from the kitchen counter. As she came back out on the deck, I saw a large brown envelope in her left hand. She stood over my chaise for a long time, watching me with eyes that were as enigmatic as night. Without a word she held out the envelope.

"What's—" I began. Then realization hit. "Is that the envelope Koo-Koo had?"

"Yes."

"Jesus Christ. I wondered why the cops hadn't sprung it on me."

I inspected the envelope in the light. It was blank on both sides.

"Your mistress is a bad dog, Kwame," I said with deep satisfaction. "She has been obstructing justice."

Kwame caught the part about "bad dog." He lowered his ears and gazed at me uncertainly. I stroked his head, reassuring him that all was well.

"You found the car before the cops did," I said.

"I don't know what you're talking about. I just happened to see a car abandoned in a parking lot, a beat-up old muscle car of the sort a Mexican killer might drive."

Fiora poured more wine and sipped. Her face was like her voice, expressionless.

"The door was open," she continued. "The envelope was on the seat. I'll turn it in to Lost and Found as soon as I can figure out who is lost and who is found."

I turned the envelope over again. No marks. No stamp. No sign of origin or destination.

"Did anybody see you?" I asked.

"What do you think?"

"I think I have a thief for a consulting partner. A damned good one."

I hefted the envelope. It was quite thin, almost as though it were empty.

"Did you look inside?" I asked.

"Why would I do a dumb thing like that? I don't want to know. If you do, open it yourself."

I thought about Fiora's warning. She seemed to be uneasy about something more complex than my own physical safety. I wondered for the space of several breaths why an envelope so thin could trigger such a feeling in her.

Then I bent the metal tabs up and ripped open the flap.

With a whispering sound, two pieces of paper slid out. One was a photographic blowup, the other a sheet of plain paper that looked like a child's paste-up project—words made of letters cut out of newspapers and magazines.

JAKE'S KILLER IS HERE
GET THE MONEY
TOMORROW

"Somebody has seen too many bad movies," I said, handing Fiora the note. "I wonder if they let Koo-Koo in on the joke."

I kept the photograph. As I looked at it, my stomach went hollow. Jake jumped out at me like a bearded, long-haired outlaw prince. He was dressed as he had been the day he died.

The only other photo of Jake I had was in my mother's family album. It had been taken when Jake was a teenager. It had none of the hawklike handsomeness his face eventually acquired.

This new picture caught Jake's tough humor, his weathered squint, and his unruly smile. It was a portrait of the free-spending outlaw chieftain throwing money around, making sure everybody had a good time. It was the thing Jake loved best to do.

The setting was familiar, too, a ramshackle seafood restaurant in Puerto Peñasco called Mariscos Californios. Jake loved to eat spiny lobsters, thumb-sized shrimp, and seviche there, washing it all down with a dark Mexican beer from a brewery that didn't survive him by many years.

There were a dozen other people in the picture. Mexicans and gringos, men and three women around a table that was littered with the remnants of the kind of epic pagan meal Mariscos Californios was once known for.

The picture must have been taken on Jake's last trip south, when he was spotting locations for his life story cut down to celluloid size.

Leaning back in his chair with a bottle of Mexican beer in one hand, Jake looked completely at ease. Judging from the empty bottles, trashed lobster shells, and flattened wedges of *limón* on the newspaper-covered table in front of him, he was probably mildly drunk and certainly well fed.

Relaxed, but not disarmed. The blocky shape of his .45 showed in the waistband of his pants, just over his hip, where he always carried it butt forward, cross-draw style. The gun, like his go-to-hell smile and pagan good looks, was so much a part of my memories it made me ache.

I had never seen Jake look happier than he did at that moment. When I could bear it no longer, I looked away.

Fiora stood to one side of me, out of the light, staring over my shoulder at the picture. She must have felt the sadness as keenly as I did. Her eyes glittered in the light, magnified by unshed tears.

"I never hated him," Fiora said finally. "He looked too much like you."

"Jake got the looks in the family. I got the meanness."

Laughing, crying, shaking her head, Fiora threaded her fingers into my hair as though hungry for living warmth. We held each other hard for a moment before we went back to studying the painful fragment of a past that wouldn't stay buried.

After a while I could see beyond Jake to the other faces. Some were familiar. Aileen Camp, next to Jake, looked uneasy, out of her element in the Mexican dive. But she smiled aggressively into the camera and clung to Jake's arm as though she thought he was going to get away. He would have, too. He always did.

Next to Aileen was her producing partner, Barry Franklin. He was a theatrically handsome man with flawless teeth and dark, curly hair. Next to him was Jeff Wilbur, the director of Jake's life story. Then there was a budding starlet named Marcia something-or-other, who had been flat-backing her way into the movies. All but one of the rest of the people were gofers and groupies, without which no film production is complete.

The man who didn't fit was sitting on Jake's left, watching the camera lens as though it were a coiled rattlesnake.

Bobby Soliz.

"Small world," I muttered. "Too damn small."

"Meaning?"

"The undercover narc asked me about Soliz."

"Who?"

"This one," I said, flicking my fingernail against Bobby Soliz's grim face.

"What does he have to do with Koo-Koo?" she asked.

"I don't know, but I'm going to find out."

Fiora frowned down at the photo, staring at the face.

"He looks more Chicano than Mexican," she said slowly.

"It's the haircut. He's a homeboy from East Los Angeles. He used to be a pretty good boxer on both sides of the border, but he was a better doper."

"Was he Jake's connection?"

"And a friend. Jake and I had a couple of wild

nights with Bobby down in Mexicali, back in the old days."

"Meaning that you don't think Bobby Soliz would have killed Jake."

I shrugged and thought it over.

"Yeah," I said after a bit, "I guess that's what I mean. Bobby was a nasty piece of work, but he and Jake were pretty close."

"How close is pretty close?"

"So close they shared the same bottle of pulque. And some other things, too, now that I think about it. They liked the same kind of women."

"Sorry I asked," Fiora said.

"That was before we met." I smiled up at her. "It's one of the reasons you looked so good, as a matter of fact."

"For your exclusive information, you aren't the first half-curried outlaw to notice that I'm prettier than a Tijuana whore."

There was no laughter in Fiora's voice. She was looking at the picture. At Jake.

Uneasiness snaked through me. I waited for her to say more. She didn't.

"Bobby had this old-fashioned Mexican outlook about lots of things, including friendship," I said. "He wouldn't have betrayed Jake without good reason. And Jake wouldn't have betrayed him."

"An honorable gangster?"

"Uh-huh."

"Sweet God. I suppose you believe in Santa Claus, too."

"It's a male thing," I retorted. "You wouldn't understand."

"For these really tiny things, I'm grateful."

Ignoring Fiora, I stared at the ex-boxer's face.

Even with bad light, the photographer managed to catch some of the shrewdness in Bobby's eyes. There was a faint cobwebbing of scars around his brows, legacy of his time in the ring.

I had seen Bobby fight once, when he was California state champion. He had knocked out a promising young fighter from Salinas. But the challenger had cut Bobby up so badly the fight was almost stopped. Until that night, I hadn't known how badly a man could bleed.

I had never seen a man grin while a doctor stitched him without novocaine, either.

When they finished closing the cuts, Bobby stood in the shower in his trunks, while hot water ran red off him and he laughed and drank beer like it was lemonade. That was probably the night he decided to give up boxing and become a full-time dope smuggler. A fighter with thin skin will never win a world championship.

Absently I wondered whether Bobby was still alive, and, if he was, what other scars he had managed to acquire.

Fiora took the picture from me and held it in the light. I closed my eyes and lay back against the chaise.

"These other people are all Hollywood types," she said after a moment. "Do you really think they're stronger suspects than your friend the boxer?"

"You're the one who's always telling me that Hollywood is a cutthroat place."

"Too bloody right."

"You've been hanging around Benny too much."

"I like variety in my slang."

I almost smiled, but it seemed like too much effort. Maybe Fiora had been right. Maybe I shouldn't have opened that damned envelope.

"The Hollywood variety of cutthroat is usually too chickenshit to do the job himself," Fiora said.

"That's why there are the Koo-Koo Armijos of this world."

"Lovely thought."

"Lovely? You have a weird mind," I said, yawning.

Fiora tugged on my hand, silently urging me to my feet.

"Come on," she said. "Tomorrow is another day."

We went to bed, but both of us slept badly. Jake kept popping out of an envelope, looking ghastly and gory, trying to explain in crazy block letters how this had happened to him, but I couldn't read the print by the light shining off the muzzle of his .45.

I'm not sure what Fiora dreamed. All I know is that she clung to my hand all night no matter how restlessly she slept, as though she was afraid if she let go of me for an instant, one of us wouldn't make it to sunrise.

I didn't have to ask which one.

nINE

I was up just after dawn, tired of Jake's monologues in my head. The day broke clear and headed for hot again. The duty agent at the San Diego DEA office sounded irritable already, but he took my phone number and passed it on to Special Agent Matt Suarez. I settled in by the phone to wait.

Uncle Jake would have liked Matthew Suarez, even though he was a cop. Jake certainly enjoyed Suarez's father, Aaron Sharp, even though Sharp had worked on the opposite side of the line. Sharp was a customs agent whose experience reached back to the time when cops weren't bureaucrats. In those days cops and smugglers were more like one another than they were like the rest of the world.

Sharp had kept Fiora—and me—from being executed by a fast, clever sonofabitch called Volker. Unfortunately, I hadn't been able to return the favor.

Volker doubled back later and killed Sharp in the shadows of a railroad tunnel that starts in the United States and ends in Mexico. No one knew whether Sharp died in Mexico or the U.S.

Sharp left a widow in the United States who collected his pension and cursed his memory. Sharp also left a common-law wife in Mexico who grieved for him desperately and raised his son to honor the border lawman's memory.

Matthew Suarez was his father's son in every way that mattered. He grew up in that shadow world where the border doesn't really exist except as an inconvenience or a means to make money smuggling. Suarez still lived on the border, but these days it was from choice rather than necessity; he had joined the U.S. Drug Enforcement Administration.

Suarez was a different cop from his father, in some ways a better one because he was more gentle and less given to quick violence. That made him one of the most effective border cops I've ever met. Sometimes I think the only real cultural assimilation is the kind that takes place when human bloodlines become so hopelessly blended they no longer make much difference.

The border ran right down the middle of our friendship, but not in a divisive way. Suarez liked knowing at least one man who had understood that Aaron Sharp was more than just as ass-kicking thug. For my part, I liked knowing at least one border rat who understood how a free spirit like Jake could have been an honorable man as well as a marijuana smuggler.

Early in his career, Suarez had lived undercover south of the border, playing the *traficante* and gathering information about the smuggling organizations that ran northern Mexico as though it were a separate nation. I had enjoyed traveling with Suarez from time to time, recapturing the adrenaline of my youth. Now Suarez was the DEA border liaison agent in San Diego. If anybody knew what had become of Bobby Soliz, Suarez did.

Four minutes after I hung up, the phone rang. It was Suarez.

"Getting up or just going to bed?" I asked.

"I was sleeping at home, for once."

"How've you been?"

"Fair."

His English was laconic and had a kind of Okie twang to it, for his gringo grandparents had come from the Panhandle. His Spanish was crisp, almost continental, thanks mostly to the Jesuit priests in the Mexicali school where Sharp had enrolled him.

"You sure I didn't get you out of bed?" I asked, hearing him yawn.

"Just tired. I've been working double shifts."

"I thought the smuggling action moved over to Florida."

"The reporters moved over to Florida," Suarez said dryly. "Not the same thing."

He yawned again.

"One fast question and I'll let you go back to sleep," I said.

"Shoot."

"Do you have any idea how I could get in touch with an old-time smuggler named Bobby Soliz?"

For a moment the silence was so complete I thought the line had gone dead. But Suarez was still there. He was just trying to figure out how to respond. Finally he lit a cigarette to buy a little more time.

"I might," Suarez said, exhaling heavily, "but I'd have to know why."

It was my turn to clam up and think. Suarez was not the kind of man to make his friendship or his favors conditional. The primitive, reptilian part of my brain started sending out danger messages. Something was rustling out there in the bushes, hidden, tensed, waiting for the right moment to spring.

"Bobby's name came up in connection with a guy who tried to blow my brains out yesterday," I said.

Suarez waited, as though it was up to me to fill the silence.

"I think everything all goes back to Jake's time," I said. "So I'd like to talk to Bobby about the bad old days."

There was a silence followed by the sound of Suarez exhaling, taking a drag, and exhaling again.

This time I kept quiet.

"Is there more to it?" Suarez asked.

"I don't know. I could bullshit you with wild guesses, but I get the feeling you'd rather go back to bed."

Suarez smoked and thought for a while longer.

Finally I offered to let him off the hook.

"Look, Matt, if this gives you any trouble at all, just say so and I'll go at it another way. If Bobby is still alive and in Mexico, someone knows it. You were just first on my list of people to ask."

"Oh, I know where he is, all right," Suarez drawled. "I don't even mind duping you in to him, if that's what you want."

"That's what I want."

"Yeah. Well, maybe you can tell me if this has something to do with LA."

"LA and Bobby?" I asked.

"Yeah."

"LA, Bobby, and a dude named Koo-Koo Armijo, too," I said.

"The name's not familiar."

"He used to be part of Bobby's drug operation, according to somebody in LAPD," I said.

"When?"

"Years ago, maybe all the way back to Jake's time. So far as I know, neither he nor Bobby figures in anything current."

Suarez drew so hard on his cigarette that I could hear the sizzle of dry paper and tobacco.

"Even if it was something current," I added, "you can forget about Koo-Koo."

"Why?"

"He was the guy who tried to kill me yesterday."

" 'Was,' huh? I take it you planted a tree in his memory."

"Yeah. Frankly, I would rather have talked to him."

"Well, life's a bitch and then you die."

Suarez fell silent. Then he laughed once. It wasn't a comforting sound.

"I'll take you to see Bobby," he said, "but I go in with you."

"You don't have to. I could just—"

"With me or not at all," Suarez interrupted flatly. "I've had about all the razzle-dazzle bullshit I'm going to take from the big-city types."

"Should I be insulted?"

"You're not a big-city type. That's why you're going to pick me up at the Otay Mesa port of entry at one o'clock today."

Suarez hung up before I could agree or disagree. I hung up and turned to the doorway. Fiora was standing there, already dressed in sweats for her workout.

"Who was that?" she asked.

"Matt Suarez."

"What? You just blabbed your whole life story—including the real story of what happened yesterday—to a cop?"

Fiora speaks her mind without civilized filters for the first few minutes of the day. That's why I usually let her get up alone.

"Suarez is a federal agent, not a cop," I said.

"They're both on the same side of the law, which in this situation you're not."

"I need information I can get quickest on Matt's side of the law."

"Why don't you just turn yourself in right now and save me all the suspense?" Fiora asked sarcastically.

"I have better things to do than sit in jail."

"Then you better do them quick," she retorted. "When LAPD finally figures out you've been jerking them around, they're going to slap your smart ass in jail."

"Yeah," I said. "That's why I'm going to Mexico right now."

Fiora's eyes widened, showing me clearly the fear and shadows, legacy of a sleepless night.

"What about the phone?" she asked.

"What about it?"

"What if the guy who set up Koo-Koo calls?"

"That's why you're staying home, *partner*."

Otay Mesa is five miles east of the Pacific Ocean and just north of the mythical line called the U.S.-

Mexico border. The mesa top used to be some of the finest dry-land barley ground in Southern California. Now the major crop is smuggling.

The land is crisscrossed with a drunken spider's web of dirt trails and footpaths left by *coyotes* leading hordes of illegal immigrants north to the Promised Land. Some of the smuggling routes are as old as the boundary between Mexico and the United States. Some are as new as this morning's sunrise.

I've seen Otay Mesa on cold moonlit nights when it looked like the loneliest place on the face of the earth—and one of the most beautiful. That was before San Diego and Tijuana developed urban overload and exploded up onto the flat mesas east of Interstate 5. Today Otay is an unwilling bridge between both cities, both nations, both cultures: a grubby rainbow stretched between poverty and the chance of wealth.

The nightly stampedes of illegal immigrants have pretty well flattened the barley crops. What isn't flattened is paved over by the new eight-lane port of entry that has been built to accommodate traffic from the *maquiladores* plants around Tijuana International Airport.

When I arrived at the port of entry, black vultures were circling in the hot updrafts over the mesa, a reminder that the dirty little arroyos and cactus-studded canyons regularly yielded up all kinds of festering remains to be scavenged.

I shut off the air conditioner and rolled down the Suburban's windows, trying to acclimatize myself. The third-world ferment of Mexico takes some getting used to, even when you live only a hundred miles away.

An Aeronaves de Mexico DC-10 was on final approach to the airport when a rumpled *aduanero* spotted me. He started toward me immediately, wearing a dark green peaked hat that looked like it once belonged to a Texaco pump jockey. The man's expression said he might enjoy shaking down a rich gringo in a shiny new truck.

Matt Suarez came out of the Mexican Customs Office and waved off the *aduanero*.

''Es mi amigo,'' Suarez called out.

The Mexican official was philosophical about the lost opportunity.

''Sí, mi jefe. A sus órdenes.''

Proving once again that it's who you know that counts, especially in a world run by poverty and *patróns*.

Suarez made a show of inspecting the truck's cast aluminum wheels and the shiny bull bar on the front. He opened the door and stepped up on the polished running boards.

''And they say Mexicans like chrome,'' Suarez said. ''You sure you want to take this thing south? Somebody's liable to steal those wheels at a traffic signal.''

''I promised Fiora I'd get some steer horns for the hood and a little dog with red flicker eyes to put on the dashboard.''

Suarez grinned. ''Don't forget a skunk for the radio antenna.''

I laughed and shook hands as Suarez slid into place with a lean, whiplike grace that reminded me once again of his father.

The Mexican border guard stood aside and waved us into Mexico like a matador grandly passing a bull.

''Where to, *jefe*?'' I asked.

Idly Suarez pointed down the road toward town.

I gave him a sideways glance. He smiled again and said nothing. For whatever reason, he wasn't going to tell me our destination until we got there.

Ten feet south of the border, Los Estados Unidos disappeared behind us as though it had never existed. We rolled past vendors peddling cheap serapes, bullfight paintings on black velvet, and plaster puppies with eyes made of glass marbles. Suddenly, we were deep in the third world, where roads were potholed and children were as numerous as they were poor.

Despite the cultural differences, Tijuana reminded me of every overgrown city from LA to London to Tokyo: too many people, not enough room, a frenetic air of hustling and con games and more violent pursuits as humanity turns and devours the only thing that is left on the landscape—itself.

Tijuana's maze was inhabited by more than a million residents, many of them utterly dependent on the wages of *norteños,* the illegal immigrants who swarm over the border every night. Looking at Tijuana's Colonia Libertad and Colonia Independencia, you can understand why the hopeful and able-bodied head north. It's only surprising that they ever return. No matter how rank LA has become, it is still better than what these folks leave behind.

For the next ten minutes Suarez gave cryptic directions that led us twisting and turning through some of the harshest *colonias* of Tijuana. The streets were totally random, unplanned. I would have been lost in five minutes.

Suarez seemed to have gotten a city map along with his mother's genes. He never hesitated in giving directions. I began to suspect that he had been this route before. Often.

What I couldn't figure out was why.

"You want some *carnitas*?" Suarez asked.

We had just drawn abreast of a little cart at a crowded intersection. In the shade of a tattered umbrella, a woman with skin like rough dark leather cooked anonymous shreds of meat on a grill that was fired by tightly rolled sections of newspaper. She offered a handmade burrito wrapped in greasy paper to passersby.

" 'I don't eat tacos with claws in 'em.' "

"Yeah." He smiled, remembering. "Another piece of my daddy's advice."

The Indian woman approached us with the greasy package. Suarez waved off the food but handed her a thousand-peso note. She rewarded him with a toothless grin and mumbled thanks in a language that wasn't Spanish. Suarez nodded, smiled slightly, and we crossed the intersection.

"Somebody should tell you about your taste in women," I said. "You're supposed to get them before they grow teeth, not after they lose them."

Suarez gave a crack of laughter and lit up another cigarette.

"She's a lookout," he said, blowing smoke out the open window. "One of the local *narcotraficantes* has a stash house somewhere around here."

I lowered my own window to help the rest of the smoke escape. Fiora is allergic to the stuff, and technically this was her truck.

"The doper pays her to keep an eye on things," Suarez continued. "If we had turned the other way, down that little dirt street, she'd have rung hell out of the little copper bell on her cart."

"How come you slipped her the bill, then?"

He shrugged. "She's a Yaqui, from a village over toward Yuma. The Mexican government has been trying to assimilate or annihilate them since the turn of the century."

"Who's winning?"

"Who do you think?" he asked sardonically.

"The folks with the cities where vultures circle."

Suarez smiled thinly. "The Yaquis are Mexico's version of the Australian Aborigines. Yaquis know more about living on the Sonoran desert than any other humans on earth."

"Deserts aren't what they used to be," I said. "Canals, superhighways, and trash blowing in the wind."

"Yeah. Yaquis can live on a swallow of water and a handful of cactus thorns. What they can't do is keep their heads above the flow of crud from so-called civilization."

"Some of them will. People are resilient."

"Somehow that doesn't comfort me," Suarez said. "Some things just shouldn't be adjusted to. The two-legged sewage pouring out of cities is one of them."

"You're getting morose, Mateo," I said. "Is that your Mexican blood or the gringo?"

"Both. The funny thing about blood is that it all looks the same flowing down a gutter."

I knew how Suarez felt, the gut-sick certainty that there was nothing more to the world than concrete and corruption. It comes from being in a city too long.

"You ever think about getting a transfer?" I asked. "Maybe some nice quiet place like Lochiel, Arizona."

The Lochiel Valley east of Nogales had been Jake's favorite place in the whole world. Aaron Sharp's, too.

Suarez shook his head. "Animas, New Mexico. Two hundred miles west of El Paso, two hundred miles east of Phoenix."

"Sounds good to me."

"It is. When somebody shoots at you in Animas, you know why." Suarez flicked his cigarette out the window. "Around here, who can tell?"

I thought about a night Suarez and I had spent in Spring Canyon, only two or three miles from the spot where the Yaqui lookout stood her watch. There had been a lot of shooting that night. Suarez had liked it more than I had, and God knows adrenaline has always been my drug of choice.

"You've been in Tijuana too long," I said. "It's soured you."

Suarez lit another cigarette and didn't disagree.

"Damn," I muttered. "Dead end. You steered me wrong, *compadre*."

Suarez shook his head. An odd hard smile spread across his face.

"I steered you exactly right, Fiddler. Welcome to hell."

I looked up at the tall blank brown walls of what might have been a fortified Moorish city. Two blank-eyed soldiers in khaki were watching us carefully, their trigger fingers curled around the trigger guards of well-polished G-3 assault rifles. Above them was a sign that told me where I was, but not why: PENITENCIARIO NACIONAL LA MESA.

tEN

I looked at Suarez.

"I thought you said Bobby was still in the dope business," I muttered.

Suarez grinned, enjoying some delicious irony.

"That's what I said," he admitted. "I just didn't say where Bobby keeps his office."

"You telling me he's set up shop in jail?"

"You got it. Bobby's been behind these walls for about five years."

"Must cramp his style."

"Not really."

Suarez waved to the guards on the wall.

The two gate guards still watched us, but they took their weapons off full auto.

"In some ways," Suarez said, "Bobby's safer here

than on the streets. These days he has a lot of competition, and they're all snake mean."

"Nice to know things haven't changed much in Mexico."

"Things never change, not in Mexico, not anywhere."

Behind the gate's metal grillwork, a crowd of prisoners milled in the open courtyard, staring sullenly at the world outside. Another pair of guards faced inward from behind a razor-wire barricade, assault rifles at the ready. On the walls, two-man crews sat in heavy machine-gun emplacements, their weapons trained on the several hundred men shuffling around below.

Most prisons are exercises in limited control. La Mesa's control was more limited than most, and the guards knew it.

"Bobby isn't the only connection who's operating from here," Suarez said, lighting another cigarette.

"Somebody in the administration must be getting rich."

"The superintendent gets a grand a week from each connection."

"For protection?" I asked.

"Nope." Suarez blew a hard stream of smoke. "Just to make sure the customers can come and go."

"What about deliveries?"

"They're made outside, but all the arrangements have to be made inside."

I gave Suarez a sideways look and said, "You sound pretty sure."

"Hell, yes, I'm sure. I've been buying smack from Bobby for six months."

"Jesus. You must have cast-iron balls. There are maybe five hundred inmates in there who'd kill you for breathing, much less for being a gringo dope cop."

Suarez drew on his cigarette and looked at the walls.

"The assistant warden *es mi compadre*," he said after a moment. "He figures he'll be warden the day I make my case."

"How long will that be?"

Suarez shrugged. "I've only been doing ounces of brown. I'd like to do a kilo, just for the impact, but Bobby claims he's having a hard time getting one together."

"Is he jobbing you?"

"I don't know."

"That's not good enough," I said flatly.

With a muttered curse, Suarez looked away from the prison walls.

"Bobby lost a big load at the border about a month ago," Suarez said.

"So?"

"So maybe he doesn't have the cash to put together a kilo for me right now."

"Maybe, huh?" I made a disgusted sound. "And maybe you have bean dip where your brains ought to be. What's the rest of it?"

Suarez smiled narrowly. He had never reminded me more of his father than at that moment.

"Maybe Bobby's got something else going on," Suarez said. "My wire into the warden's office says some LA cops came in to see Bobby the other day."

"Who?"

"If I knew who, I wouldn't be hanging around with lowlifes like you."

Suarez pulled out his leather credential wallet

and a matte-black P-38 Walther and dropped them into the console between us.

"You can be my new partner in the kilo deal," he said.

"That might be a bad idea. I'm a dead ringer for my Uncle Jake."

"That's a problem?"

"Bobby may be the guy who hired Jake's killer."

"Bobby won't recognize you," Suarez said.

I started to object, but he cut me off.

"Trust me, for once in your life."

As we climbed out of the car, he palmed some ten-thousand-peso notes and slipped them to one of the gate guards as they shook hands.

Welcome to Latin America, where the lobby guards in apartment buildings carry Uzis, where the parking attendants hold military rank, and where every government official is his own tax collector.

We passed through the gate and into the inner sanctum of hell. Except for the automatic weapons on the walls, it was like walking into the Dark Ages. The air stank of corruption. Raw sewage ran down the gutter in the middle of the yard and into an underground cistern. Dirty men in tattered rags showed open sores as they begged us for pesos or scraps of food. Well-fed thugs in clean jeans and expensive haircuts watched us. They would have cut our throats to test the edges on their knives.

The inside guards didn't carry guns. They made do with lead-weighted billies. One of the guards, a pale Hispano with pop eyes like a plaster dog, led us through a sally port into a side yard. This place was less crowded but still stank of stale piss and drying excrement.

The yard was lined with ragged ranks of shacks

that made the prison look like an old-time auto court gone to ruin, or a fishing camp for poor folks. But by the standards of Mexico, the place was clean and neat. In the open area, a dozen men were playing soccer on rough, raw dirt that had scuffed all the color off the leather ball. Rancho music keened on a tinny radio somewhere.

"A man can do all right in here, so long as he makes his rent payments," Suarez said.

I grunted.

Over the smell of human waste came the odor of food frying somewhere nearby.

"It's not even corruption," Suarez said. "Private quarters are legal in the Mexican prison system."

"Talk about enlightened penology," I muttered.

A group of men had gathered in the shade of the only tree in the yard. A makeshift weight-lifting area was set up there. The inmates were focused on the man in front of the fork-shaped stands that held the bars. The man was naked except for a pair of long-legged workout trunks. He stood bowlegged under a two-hundred-pound load of steel discs at both ends of the bar.

Bobby Soliz had changed little since I had last seen him. He had a bit of a belly now, but he was still hard and flexible. His body had kept its wedge shape. His arms looked well-proportioned and muscular rather than pumped up and overblown with steroids.

As we approached, Bobby snapped off six quick lifts. The effort cleanly defined the muscles of his shoulders and legs. He had picked up some jailhouse tattoos over the years, but otherwise he looked as though he could still go seven rounds with a kid from Salinas.

Half a dozen spectators stood around in the shade, watching the *jefe*. They huffed and grunted along with him, getting the vicarious, if not the aerobic, benefit of the workout. When Suarez and I approached, the men moved aside to make room. Some of them nodded and slapped hands with Suarez, a sign that he was their equal. One of them sniffed at me like a skeptical dog, but nobody challenged me.

When Bobby finished his lifts, two of the groupies stepped in to spot for him while he shifted the bar back to its rack. Once the bar was in place, they fell to work removing the keepers and adding weight discs. Bobby bent at the waist and blew hard, catching his breath.

When Bobby straightened up, Suarez took a towel from one of his seconds.

''Hola, señor. ¿Qué tal?''

"What's happening, Mattie?" Bobby replied. "Who's your pal?"

Bobby stared in my direction, dark eyes hooded and hidden beneath heavily scarred brows. My pulse rate jumped. I waited for a whistle to blow, an alarm to go off.

Then I realized Bobby didn't recognize me. Not now. Not ever again. He was as blind as the prison walls.

"This is my money man," Suarez said casually. "He's got enough in his hip pocket to buy a kilo. You know anybody who's got one to sell?"

Bobby kept staring at me, waiting for me to speak for myself.

"You look like you're in better shape than you were when I saw you fight at the Forum," I said.

Like most athletes, Bobby was vain about his

body. He ran the towel across his glistening chest and straightened his back, popping his pecs like he was trying to intimidate an opponent.

"You saw me at the Forum?" he asked.

"Yeah."

"No shit." A look of genuine emotion showed around Bobby's dead eyes. "Man, the Forum. That was the good old days."

He spoke in the faintly accented English of a Spanish kid raised in East LA. A lot of folks in Tijuana have that accent. A lot more are acquiring it the hard way.

"Talking about the old days," Suarez said, "have you been listening to the LA news?"

Bobby shook his head.

"Big shooting up there," Suarez said. "Some guy who used to be from around here got wasted. Dude by the name of Armijo."

Bobby scowled and spat deliberately.

"That sonofabitch," Bobby said. "Somebody should have put him down a long time ago. He was a real *pendejo*."

"What did he do to you?" Suarez asked, acting surprised.

"Ripped me off for—"

The outburst dried up in mid-sentence, as though Bobby had remembered there was an utter stranger standing nearby. He rotated his head slowly, trying to break the tension in his heavily muscled neck. Then he looked in my direction again.

"They still fighting at the Forum?" Bobby asked.

"They're playing hockey, if you like to see white guys go at it, but they don't do the big fight cards anymore."

"The fight game ain't what it used to be."

"Nothing is," I agreed.

"The system always favored black fighters over Mexicans, and now look at what they've got," Bobby said. "This rapist Tyson and a fat old man named Foreman."

The seconds and hangers-on muttered, echoing their agreement, spitting in the dust and nodding their heads gravely.

Bobby held out his right hand. One of the men dropped a ten-kilo barbell into it. Bobby lifted the weight overhead as if it were Styrofoam. He did some curls as he walked around, trying to keep the rhythm of his workout.

When Bobby turned, I caught a glimpse of a dark indented scar just in front of his left temple, as though he had been whacked with a hammer. Small black flecks peppered that side of his face. Classic powder burn marks. Whoever had tried to do him had been in real close.

"So you're still trying to find your kilo, Mattie," Bobby said. "What makes you think you're going to find it around here?"

Suarez's expression told me he was surprised. Bobby's pals watched him out of the corner of their eyes, waiting to see what he would do next.

I stepped in.

"Look," I said, "if you want me to take a hike while you talk, Matt—"

"Stay put, man," Bobby said.

I looked at Suarez, shrugged, and stayed put.

Bobby shifted the barbell to his left hand and cocked the weight behind his ear to isolate new muscles.

"No need to take a hike because there's nothing to talk about," Bobby said coolly. "I might have done Mattie here a favor or two in the past, but a kilo is a lot of dope. Where the hell am I going to get that much in La Mesa Penitentiary?''

Suarez's face was blank, obviously more for the benefit of the groupies than for Bobby.

"My mistake," Suarez said softly. "I thought things were different than they are."

His voice was devoid of rancor and all the more dangerous because of it. It was like seeing Aaron Sharp come to life again.

Bobby heard the difference. He quickly straightened and handed the barbell to a spotter. Wiping his hands on the towel, he moved toward Suarez with a conciliatory smile on his face.

"Don't worry," Bobby said cheerfully. "There are lots of dudes around here who can do your kilo. I'm just not one of them. Okay?"

Suarez grunted. It wasn't a happy sound.

"Hey, homeboy, don't be mad," Bobby said in an earnest voice. "Nothing personal. I just don't want any more trouble right now than I already have. So let me buy you and your friend a beer, just to show there's no hard feelings. ¿Está bien?''

Bobby must have had some sight left, enough to let him hook a muscular arm around Suarez's shoulders and give him a powerful *abrazo*, It was as though he was trying to temper his insult.

One of the groupies dug three cold cans of Tecate out of a grimy ice chest in the shade. Somewhere he found a wedge of *limón* and rubbed it on the rim of each can. Then he delivered them to Bobby, Suarez, and me.

"*¡Salud!*" Bobby called out.

He knocked back half the can in one draught. Suarez and I echoed the toast and drank a little out of courtesy. Then Suarez cuffed Bobby's bare shoulder lightly.

"Look, *vato*," Suarez said, "I can see how things are, so we're out of here, okay? No harm in trying and no bad feelings."

"You bet," I agreed. "It was worth the drive just to see Bobby again after all these years."

Bobby tilted his head as though listening to me and to something in his own head at the same time. He stared at me, trying to see me through his blind eyes.

"That voice," he muttered. "I know it. . . ."

I tried to look uninterested, but I knew I resembled Jake in more than looks. On the phone, it had been impossible for anyone but Fiora to tell us apart.

Bobby muttered about my voice a few more times, then pointed to the dark scar on the side of his head.

"I have a helluva time remembering people since this happened," Bobby admitted. "Do I know you from the joint?"

"Nope. I never did time."

He started his behind-the-neck lifts again, but slowly. He was still trying to remember why he thought he should know me.

"Hollywood," he said finally. "Maybe that was it. You ever have anything to do with the movies?"

"I go to them, once in a while. Other than that, no."

He nodded and pumped more iron while he talked. "I had a bunch of big-time Hollywood producers down here trying to buy my life story, a long time ago. I thought maybe you was one of them."

I took a swig of beer, thinking about the picture

Koo-Koo had been carrying. Suddenly I knew what had been discussed at lunch the day it was taken.

"My story's still for sale," Bobby said, prowling around as he spoke.

"Sorry. I've got no connections in Hollywood."

"Well, that's too bad," he said, joking. "My story's still for sale, even if the ending's a little different than it was back then."

I glanced at Suarez. Bobby was getting a little close to the truth, even if he was more caught up in who he was than who I was.

We started the round of handshakes and good-byes. Bobby's grip was very Mexican, soft and gentle for a man who could bench-press his own weight.

Suarez and I left the residential compound and were back in the main yard, headed for the gate, before either of us began to relax. He flung away his nearly full can of Tecate, triggering a small riot among the dirty, ragged main-liners.

"Christ," Suarez muttered. "There goes about five grand worth of Uncle Sam's buy funds."

"You mean you don't chalk Bobby up as a success for the Mexican criminal rehabilitation system?"

"Bobby couldn't draw a straight breath through a straw."

"Some things don't change," I agreed.

"He should have jumped at the chance to sell a kilo. He's two months behind in his rent payments to the warden."

"Maybe he wants to get back into the prison mainstream."

"No way. That's where he got shot in the first place. They won't miss twice."

The guards passed us out through the gate and back to the street. Two urchins had just finished polishing the chrome wheels on the truck. They came over, chattering excitedly about what a wonderful job they had done and what a beautiful machine it was after their hard work.

"You better pay the little *buitres*," Matt advised.

"What's a *buitre*?"

"A buzzard," he said. "Bad luck to make them mad. They'll follow you for weeks."

I didn't need that kind of karma, so I gave them a dollar bill each, almost three thousand pesos.

When Jake was alive, a dollar was worth less than a hundred pesos. No wonder the barley fields of Otay Mesa have been beaten flat.

"Bobby didn't act like a man who needed money," I said to Suarez as the little vultures ran off.

"Yeah. I wonder where he's getting his protection."

As Suarez and I got in the truck, the cellular phone in the console began to ring. I picked it up.

"Yes?" I said.

"Your friend called again," Fiora said flatly. "He wants to meet you. Soon."

eLEVEN

Ninety-five minutes, port of entry to home port.

The Suburban isn't as much fun as the Cobra, but double-nickel vigilantes do jump out of the way when the chrome bull bar appears in their rearview mirrors. Fiora said I was a road bully the first time I pulled that stunt. I felt real bad until I remembered that she ordered the after-market bull bar in the first place.

Like she said, her car is a Great Equalizer.

Everything looked normal at home. Kwame lay flat out in the thin shade of the lemon tree, his tongue lolling from the heat. He lifted his head and looked at the truck when I pulled in. His ropy tail wagged twice. Then his head flopped down again, too hot to move anymore.

When I came into the bedroom, Fiora was wandering around fresh from the shower, wearing only a towel and the fragrance of her soap. She looked edible, among other things.

Fiora took one look at me looking at her and shook her head.

"Oh, no, you don't," she said.

I looked hurt. "What do you mean?"

"You know what I mean. I just got cool for the first time since the sun came up, and you come along with a look in your eyes that says you want to make me all hot and sweaty."

The woman knows me too well.

"It usually happens after you've been to Mexico, too," Fiora said. "What is it about the place? Are the streetwalkers such a turn-on?"

"The only streetwalker I saw was a Yaqui woman about a hundred years old."

Fiora lifted her dark blond eyebrows skeptically.

"And I resent your implication," I said. "I was only responding to the sight of your beautiful bare shoulder and the faint smell of lavender on your skin."

As I spoke, I reached out to tease the spot where the end of the terry cloth was tucked over itself to secure the towel around Fiora's body. She locked her arm over the cloth, holding it in place.

"I can't think when you do that," she said, "and right now I need to think."

"I know you can't think when I do that. That's why I do it."

I stroked the back of her arm with my index finger, trying to ease through her guard. I thought I detected a tremor in the clenched muscle so I stroked a little more thoroughly, probing the warmth where soft skin pressed against soft skin. Her breath caught with a small ripping sound.

"Don't get me wrong," I said. "I like the way you think. But I also love to turn the thinking Fiora off and turn the sensual Fiora on."

"Uh-uh."

To demonstrate her invulnerability, Fiora presented me with a calm, composed face in the mirror.

I stroked a little lower, running my finger down the terry-cloth covering until I found the place where her hip flared.

"You know the Fiora I'm talking about," I said. "She's the one who forgets for the moment all those important thoughts that fill up her brain. . . ."

Fiora stared at me in the mirror, showing nothing of her response. Her expression seemed like a deliberate challenge. I fished for the edge of the towel and slid my hand between the two layers of cloth.

"The one who loves to respond to the sensation of having her skin touched. . . ."

"Fiddler, damn it," Fiora said, but there was no real anger in her voice.

I pushed a little farther, almost to the inside edge of the towel, just short of the taut bare belly beneath.

Fiora's eyelids flickered and she lowered her face, as though suddenly unable to meet my eyes in the mirror any longer. I laughed softly and nuzzled the damp tendrils of her hair that had stuck to the back of her neck.

"Thank God," I said. "I was beginning to think I had lost my touch."

"In other words, this little exercise wasn't for my pleasure at all," Fiora said without lifting her head. "It was just a display of your mastery over me."

I brushed my fingertips very lightly against flesh still cool from the shower.

"Maybe," I said against her nape. "But from where I stand, it was more a display of your mastery over me."

I pulled Fiora fully against me, so she could have no doubt about the meaning of my words. A faint shiver went through her. She raised her head and looked at me in the mirror. Her expression was a mixture of sensuality, anticipation, and the faint irritation of a bright woman who finds herself deflected from her course by her prowling mate.

"I like your version better," Fiora said.

She turned into my arms. The motion broke the flimsy grip of the towel. It fell to the floor in a damp heap.

The feel of Fiora made my breath stop, then come out in a groan. We are so completely different, yet each time we meet as man and woman, we rediscover that our differences are much less important than the ways we fit together.

The second time Fiora came out of the shower, she didn't bother with the towel. The desert wind known as the Santa Ana had begun to blow. The air dried her body very quickly. She looked at me lying on the bed and smiled.

"What else did you do today?" I asked, stretching.

"Sat around all day, fielding telephone calls for you and taking messages like a good little secretary."

With that, Fiora disappeared into her dressing room.

"Good little secretary," I mimicked beneath my breath, "my ass."

"What about your ass?"

"What are you up to?" I demanded.

"What could I possibly be up to? I was so busy spinning on my thumb waiting for you that—"

"Here we go," I muttered.

"—I only had time to handle one call."

"Who?"

"Your extortionist friend."

"What did you do?" I asked.

"Exactly what you told me to do."

"That will be the day," I muttered.

"I told him you were interested in his proposal," Fiora said, "and that you would be ready to do business tonight."

So far, so good.

"Did he give you a bad time?" I asked.

"No."

It was like pulling teeth. If I hadn't been feeling like a well-fed lion at the moment, I would have growled at her.

"What did he say?" I asked.

"The usual."

"I don't get all that many phone calls from extortionists. What the hell is 'the usual'?"

"How much money. When. Where. With or without escort. The usual."

I could hear Fiora rustling and shuffling but I couldn't see her. It was just as well.

"So what did he decide?" I asked a bit curtly.

"He didn't. I did. He must be new at the game. He hadn't even thought about how to handle the exchange. I had to give him pointers."

Oh, shit.

"Pointers," I said neutrally.

"Yeah. The guy is a terrible negotiator."

"Compared to you, most people are."

A black backpack arced out of the dressing room and thumped onto the floor.

"What's that?" I asked.

"The twenty-five thousand."

Every bit the thoughtful little secretary. Fiora had even gone to the bank for me and gotten the cash.

Why did that make me so nervous?

"Wait a minute," I said. "I thought he was asking fifty."

Fiora came out of the dressing room in tight white shorts and a white shirt that showed her black bra beneath. I had seen the hooker look in fashion magazines but didn't know Fiora had gone in for it.

"He *was* asking fifty." She shrugged. "Like I said, he knows from nothing about negotiations."

I looked Fiora up and down. The combination of thin white shirt and black bra was downright, blatantly sexy. When a woman dresses to please you and herself, you sometimes forget that she also is capable of dressing to catch the eye of other men in the world.

"You aren't planning on wearing that outfit outside the house," I said.

"Of course I am." She looked at herself critically in the mirror. "It's the latest word in bad taste."

"It isn't your usual—uh, style."

"Usually I'm not delivering twenty-five grand in a black backpack to a crook."

"*What?*"

"It's just one more negotiating tactic," Fiora said calmly, tucking in the flimsy shirt. "If he's looking at me, it will be easier for you to sneak up and stick a gun in his ear, right?"

"Wrong! Absolutely, totally, completely—"

"Better get dressed," she interrupted, "or he'll be looking at your bare ass instead of mine."

A transvestite hooker undulated across Highland Avenue in front of the truck, then stopped and looked through the windshield.

"Which one of you wants me?" she asked. "If it's both, I'll work out a special rate."

"You need a closer shave," I said.

He flipped me off and took up a position in the gutter, watching the approaching traffic, waiting for a trick. He was maybe seventeen. The needle tracks on his arms were as inflamed as his eyes.

Welcome to Hollywood. The town itself is the last great illusion. Movies aren't made here anymore—deals are. What's left of the glory days of old is a Hollywood Boulevard lined by "adult" bookstores and "adult" movies for the unimaginative. For the people who couldn't manage their own dreams, hookers and pushers worked every street corner. The price was disillusionment, but there were plenty of buyers.

Hooray for Hollywood.

We were an hour early for the exchange. As I turned west on the boulevard, the last light was fading in the sky ahead of us.

The street of dreams was *Blade Runner* without the acid rain. The bitterness of the place was almost palpable. The illusion had worn through, leaving nothing but the false-front scenery of unfulfilled ambition.

The sidewalks teemed with a world of extras, a casting call for a Kafka film starring Madonna in drag. Hustlers and pimps, punkers and unemployed musicians, Iowa hopefuls and junkies who never had any hope: all of them trying to catch that magic moment when the smog dissipates and the night has not yet eaten the day.

I glanced over at Fiora again. It was hard not to. I had never seen her in an outfit like that before.

"You want me to duck into one of those curio stands and buy you a Def Leppard T-shirt to cover your underwear?" I asked.

"Why bother? I fit right in this way."

"The hookers are paid for it."

"So are secretaries."

"Shit."

"Think of it as a bathing suit," Fiora said. "On the beach I'd be overdressed."

"We're not on the beach."

We cruised past Musso & Frank's Grill. Once it had been Hollywood's fanciest restaurant. Now it was reduced to feeding nostalgia junkies, tourists, and extortionists. The stucco façade was badly faded. The windows looked greasy and dark. Except for the lights on the neon sign, it was hard to tell that the place was still in business.

"Worship at the booth where Clark Gable stroked the inside of Carole Lombard's thigh under the linen tablecloth," I muttered. "View the spot on the carpet where William Faulkner, Raymond Chandler, and F. Scott Fitzgerald all lost multiple Manhattans on the same night in 1946."

"I tried to talk him into someplace nice and deserted, but—" Fiora shrugged.

"Don't do that. It's distracting."

She gave me a sideways glance.

We circled the block a few times over a ten-minute period, trying to look like lost tourists. The restaurant parking lot had barely a handful of cars in it. Nostalgia was out of style.

Shadows cast by fifty-year-old streetlights had begun to deepen, giving the place a dangerous aura. Fiora studied the lot uneasily. Urban darkness can be daunting, even to women as confident as she is.

"You still want to go through with this?" I asked.

"Want? No. But I'm going to do it just the same. Comes with the territory."

"It wasn't my idea to be partners. Not like this."

"Let's go back to arguing over my underwear. It's more interesting."

We made one more pass to burn the layout in my mind, then headed for a stop-and-rob market on Highland. Fiora bought herself dinner—Fig Newtons, Cheetos, and a big bottle of Evian—while I worked on the vehicle.

General Motors has had its problems over the years, but they have managed to keep their heads about the Suburban. Basically it's a truck, straightforward and functional. I appreciated that accessibility as I unhooked the interior lights and oiled the latches on the cargo doors so I could slide in and out soundlessly.

Fiora sat in the front seat, watching the nightlife and alternating sweet and salt fast food. She only does that kind of trash eating when she's nervous or when she's on the road.

"You've got the Beretta, right?" I asked.

"Uh-huh."

She started to dig the little black gun out of her purse to show me.

"Leave it for now," I said. "Waving a firearm around on the street in Hollywood is likely to draw a black-and-white."

The thought of cops did not cheer Fiora.

"If we should come across a cop," I said, "drop the purse and step back from it. Street cops in LA have lots on their minds these days. You twitch and you're liable to get shot about thirty times."

"Thanks," she said sarcastically.

"You're welcome."

The air mattresses from the truck's cargo box were the kind that inflated themselves. I stretched one out on the flat load bed and unfolded the survival blanket that was one of the hundred things I had put in the box. The silver side of the blanket would show up too well in the dark, which meant I would have to keep that side against my skin. I was going to be one hot puppy.

As blinds go, the Suburban wasn't as good as the trunk of an automobile, but it would do. Through the smoked glass of the truck's side windows, I'd be all but invisible in the dark.

In the shadowy interior I checked the loads on both the Detonics and Fiora's little purse pistol. Then I went inside the market, bought my own dinner—a prepackaged microwaveable chili dog and a Granny Smith apple—and climbed in the back.

Fiora drove around for a while, letting the last of the light fade while I finished my meal. At five minutes before ten, we parked in the darkest corner of the lot behind the old landmark restaurant.

"Now what?" she whispered.

"Now you'll follow directions," I said softly from beneath the survival blanket, "or I'll turn you over my knee."

"Mmmm. Sounds twisted."

"Serves you right for wearing your underwear in public."

It was hot under the survival blanket, which was dutifully reflecting my body heat back to me. I lay on my belly where I could see between the high backs of the two front seats. The truck was parked with its nose aimed at the back of the restaurant. The lot still was almost empty.

The sounds of traffic on the boulevard mixed with domestic sounds from the residences just off the commercial strip. A television played a Spanish soap opera through an open window. Another set nearby was tuned to a preacher or a used car salesman; in Korean, it's hard to tell the difference. From beyond the darkness, two cats screamed with sexuality and violence, the mating call of modern Hollywood.

At ten o'clock straight up, a swarthy busboy wedged open the restaurant's back door with a plastic pail. Then he began trudging back and forth with big white plastic bags of trash which he threw in a dumpster. When he was finished, he left the back door open to air out the kitchen.

Los Angeles has a real advantage over other cities. Garbage doesn't stink quite so much in dry climates. In New York, the summertime smell of an alley behind a restaurant could gag a skunk. Not that this dumpster was any bed of roses. The smell of rancid grease mixed uneasily with the night-blooming jasmine. Exhaust fumes from the boulevard and the dusty odor of dead palm fronds completed the olfactory feast. Decay is slower in a desert city, but it happens just the same.

At four minutes after ten the cellular phone made

its funny little chirping sound. Fiora switched it to internal speaker so we both could hear it.

"Hello," she said.

"I see you're punctual," the man said.

Cautiously I lifted my head and looked around. If he could "see" that Fiora was punctual, he must be watching the truck. The best vantage point nearby was the four-plex with the Spanish soap opera blaring out.

"Of course I'm punctual," Fiora said coolly. "This is business."

"Where's the money?"

He had dropped the heavy metal background. Even so, his voice was no more familiar this time than it had been before.

"In a black nylon backpack, just as you requested."

Fiora flicked a glance in the rearview mirror that told me she was losing patience with this clown.

"Oh, yeah," he said, "backpack. Good."

Fiora looked at the phone as though she had a bad connection.

"Now listen," he said. "For your own good, I don't want you to be able to identify me. It's better for you that way."

"Really? How sweet of you."

"So take the money and put it in that trash container in front of you," he concluded. "Got it?"

"Not quite," Fiora said crisply. "I haven't seen the kind of proof that would put Jake's killers in jail."

I did another full 360-degree head check, still trying to spot him.

"I've got a picture," the extortionist said, "taken

from the same roll of film as the one you already
have. Three men. Jake's killers.''

''Where is this picture?''

''It's . . .'' He hesitated.

''We've been over this before,'' Fiora said. ''No
preview, no payment. Where is the picture?''

Silence.

We had reached that delicate moment in any illicit transaction when somebody has to take a
chance. He wanted us to do it. We wanted him to
do it.

Fiora was right. The guy wasn't much of a negotiator. He gave in after nine seconds.

''Okay,'' he said, ''listen. There's a brown envelope, just like the other one, on the ground underneath the end of the dumpster in front of you. It's a
picture of the men who killed Jake. Put the pack
down, shove it under the dumpster, and take the
envelope.''

''Pictures can be doctored. We need proof.''

''I have proof. Bank records. After I've collected
the money and counted it, I'll call you back and tell
you where to look for it.''

Fiora glanced at me in the mirror. I gave her a
slow shake of the head. I was still trying to locate the
caller.

''No, thanks,'' she said. ''My twenty-five thousand against two photographs and your word to call
me back with the good stuff. No deal, babe. I
stopped believing in the Easter Bunny a long time
ago.''

The guy was silent for a while. The sound of his
labored breathing was loud over the speaker. There
was the crinkle of paper and the ratcheting sound of
a cheap plastic lighter.

A small yellow light flared in the darkened hallway inside the restaurant. There probably was a pay phone on the back wall, next to the door of the men's room.

"Oh, all right," the guy finally said, exhaling heavily into the receiver. "The document will be in another envelope. I'll leave it when I pick up the backpack. You can come back in ten minutes."

Fiora looked me.

I nodded, figuring I could take him the moment he came out to collect the backpack. I was more interested in him than I was in the so-called proof he was offering.

"All right," Fiora said. "But the goods better be as advertised. Fiddler doesn't believe in turning the other cheek."

"Yeah, yeah. Just leave the money the way I said or the cops will get a call about Fiddler's past relationship with a doper called Koo-Koo."

Checkmate. He hoped.

"Got that?" he asked.

"Yes."

The connection broke at his end.

"Now what?" Fiora asked unhappily.

"He's inside the restaurant."

"Where?"

"In the hallway by the back door," I said.

"How do you know?"

"I saw the flare when he lit his cigarette."

"Bloody hell," Fiora said, chewing her bottom lip. "How are you going to get past him?"

"I've decided I love your underwear. It's really distracting, especially for a man who pants while lighting a cigarette."

"What do you want me to do?"

"Get out, go around to the rear of the truck like you had the money back there, and then leave the door ajar while you walk over with the backpack and make the swap."

"High jiggle factor?" Fiora asked, rubbing it in.

"Not too high. Smokers have bad hearts."

Her smile flashed for a moment. "So I distract him just a little. Then what?"

"When you've got the picture, take the truck around the corner onto Hollywood Boulevard and wait."

"Be careful."

"Count on it."

tWELVE

Fiora's new look was sensational. I almost forgot the rest of the job as I watched her hip-swinging glide across the parking lot in those short shorts and gauzy top. She played to the silent watcher magnificently, moving into the pools of light like a lithe swimmer, drawing his eyes away from me.

I eased out the cargo door Fiora had left ajar and slid along the right side of the truck. Ducking low, I peered around the front fender.

Fiora stood like a street-walking angel, her body positioned so that the light outlined her breasts and the flare of her hips and turned her hair molten gold. A smart blonde gone naughty for the night.

I don't know about the guy waiting for his cash, but I could barely take my eyes off her. That's the problem with working women; they're a helluva

distraction to working men. Mother Nature is a sex-
ist from way back.

Once Fiora was sure she had the watcher's attention, she strolled toward the dumpster next to the
back door of the restaurant. While she moved, I cat-
footed through a narrow gap in the oleander hedge
that screened the back portion of the parking lot
from the street. In black jeans and a dark T-shirt, I
was just one more anonymous wedge of darkness.

The white flare of Fiora's clothing was at the far
end of the dumpster as I slid between the rough
brick of the restaurant's wall and the dusty hedge.
Her back was toward me as she knelt, retrieved the
envelope, and slid the backpack into place. The light
over the back door of the restaurant was perfectly
placed to show her off.

Then Fiora turned slightly, and I saw that the
damned filmy blouse was unbuttoned halfway to
her shorts. She straightened up and walked back
toward the truck, the envelope visible in her hand,
her part done all too well.

Unfortunately, that was as far as my luck went. I
had hoped to be able to circle around behind the
dumpsters and wait until the guy came to collect the
backpack, but the bins were parked flush against
the back wall. There wasn't room in back for a fat
rat.

The sour smell of grease and decaying food was
stronger now. The backpack blended into the shadows beneath the far end of the second dumpster, the
one closer to the restaurant door. From my position,
I couldn't control the situation. That left only one
other way to go—into the dumpster.

Fiora was almost at the truck when I glanced into
the smelly interior of the closer dumpster. It was full

of white plastic refuse bags, the kind that rustled and sighed if you breathed on them. Someone my size would sound like a heavy-metal band in a tin closet.

I slid along to the second bin and looked in. It was filled with what looked like lawn cuttings but smelled like garbage left too long in the sun. I braced myself on the slippery rim of the bin and levered up and over.

The Suburban's door slammed as Fiora got in. I swung around and lowered myself slowly into the garbage. The smell got worse, and then got seriously awful as I settled down on a pile of salad trimmings and plate scrapings.

The first fifteen seconds were the worst. I gagged on the stench, swallowed, and breathed lightly through my mouth, waiting for my sense of smell to overload and cut out. While I waited, I pulled out the Detonics and hunkered down so that my head was below the top of the bin.

Honest to God, Jake. The things I do for you.

The Suburban's engine fired up immediately. Fiora must have been waiting for me to get into position. I closed my eyes just before the headlights came on, flooding the back of the restaurant in hard, white light.

Working with someone as smart as Fiora can be a real pleasure at times like this. I had my night vision intact, and the guy on the telephone had just been jacklighted.

I heard a *thunk* as the transmission shifted into gear, *wheeze-buzz* from the fan belt and alternator as Fiora started off, and the moist sound of all-terrain tires rolling across asphalt softened by the hot day. Then the parking lot was silent except for some kind of hip-hop number blaring from a car cruising the street.

When that noise faded, a muffled sound came from the direction of the open restaurant door, like the shifting of feet on tile. I drew as deep a breath as I could, considering the stench, and prepared to dive into the garbage if the guy got too close.

I really hoped he wouldn't.

No more sounds of movement came from the restaurant. Very slowly I lifted my head above the rim of the dumpster to look around. No one was in sight. Nothing moving but a bluish veil of smoke drifting out of the hallway into the glare of the naked light bulb above the back door. The guy must still be inside, smoking and waiting for whatever stupid people waited for.

Come on, turkey. Come get the corn.

The smell of garbage was thicker than the night. Something wet had soaked through the lower part of my left pants leg. It felt slimy against my skin.

There was another muffled sound from the dark doorway. He must have been well back in the hall, where he could see the corner of the dumpster and not much else. I played with the idea of going in and dragging him out, but I wanted to catch him with his hand on the backpack, no chance for denial and lies about innocent bystanders.

Then again, I could always hammer the truth out of him, but that wasn't the sort of thing I wanted to do on a public street.

Lights cruising by on the other side of the oleander hedge caught my eye. A dark car was pulling up to the curb. I could only see the front of the car, but the sound of two-way radio traffic was loud and clear: a police car on the prowl.

Unhappily I sank down a little farther into the reeking garbage, trying to listen in both directions at the same time. More shuffling sounds came from the restaurant. The extortionist must not have been able to hear the cops, because he was breaking cover and heading toward the dumpster.

I shrank a little lower, waiting. The patrol car moved ahead a little, changing the pattern of light and darkness above the dumpster.

I stayed put. Somebody in the four-plex could have called the cops to check out prowlers in the parking lot. After my recent run-in with LAPD, I couldn't afford to be caught within ten miles of anything fishy.

And that was definitely the smell in the dumpster. Fishy.

Listening, breathing shallowly through my mouth, I waited. Sounds came: an idling engine, a door slamming in the four-plex, a call of greeting or derision, approaching footsteps. . . .

I stopped breathing and listened hard.

A shoe scraped on the dirty pavement in front of the dumpster. He was so close I could hear the faint wheeze of his breathing. He grunted as he bent down. The nylon backpack scraped over asphalt, pulled by an invisible hand.

I could see him in my mind's eye, bending down at the other end of the bin. Five feet from me. So close and yet so far away.

When he straightened up again, he must have noticed the idling squad car. He sucked in harshly. Then he panicked and ran back toward the restaurant doorway.

The prowl car started up and turned into the parking lot. Headlights swung across the front of the bin, past the spot where the extortionist had stood just a moment before. After the lights swung past I stole a quick peek.

The black-and-white was making a slow, sweeping turn in the vacant parking lot. The driver wore aviator glasses. His partner was hunched over a clipboard writing something down. Strictly routine. Looking bored, they idled out of the parking lot and headed back toward the boulevard.

The cops took their sweet time about it. When they were finally out of sight, so was the guy with the backpack.

I vaulted out of the bin and almost fell on my ass. Something slippery and disgusting had coated my running shoes. My pants were stinking and soaked. My shirt looked like splatter art.

Stamping my feet cleared the treads of my shoes. I headed at a run for the door that still stood open. The guy had dropped the other envelope in plain sight at the end of the dumpster. I grabbed the paper on the way by, folded it in half, and shoved it into my waistband between the Detonics and the small of my back.

The dank little hall led to unmarked swinging doors. I shoved them open enough to look around. The hallway forked. In the kitchen a pair of busboys were toking on a joint while they sucked up the dregs of some diner's wine. No one else was in sight.

I pushed through the door and headed down the other hallway. It led to another set of doors that opened into the dining room. I hit them hard and fast.

A long cherrywood bar went down one side of the room. The only occupant was a round-bellied man wearing a cut-away jacket and a pleated shirt.

He glanced at me over the row of glasses he was polishing. He had a Charlie Chaplin mustache and mean, piggy little eyes. He looked as if he had been sampling his high-octane wares.

The barkeep couldn't see the gun in the small of my back, and he was too far away to smell me, but he took in the food slime on my clothes and pegged me quick.

"Get out of here," he snarled. "You want scraps, you wait in back with the rest of the garbage."

A real charitable guy.

"I've eaten, thanks. Did a fat guy hauling a backpack come through here?"

The bartender took two steps to the right. His hands disappeared below the level of the bar.

"Goddam street people are taking over the world," he muttered.

He straightened up, showing me the leather sap in his hand.

"I bet you never used that on Ray Chandler," I said.

"Huh?"

"The guy with the backpack," I said. "Did you see him or didn't you?"

The bartender lifted a hinged section of wood and stepped out from behind the bar. Looking at me, he patted the palm of his hand with the head of the sap.

"I warned you people what would happen the next time I caught someone in the dumpster, throwing garbage all over the parking lot for decent people to pick up."

"Yeah, life's a bitch."

I took one more look around the empty place and headed for the front door.

"Go out the way you came in," he ordered. "The front door ain't for bums."

I still didn't want to show him the gun, not with LAPD cruising around. I kept walking toward the front door.

The bartender must have been used to hitting drunks or cripples. His overhead stroke was slow and sloppy. I blocked it with a forearm, stepped in, and barred his wrist, levering just hard enough to let him know I could break his arm.

Sudden pain turned the sullenness in his piggy eyes to fear. He dropped the sap. The small shot-filled club dangled loose and useless from the loop on his wrist. I changed my grip, took the sap away from him, and stepped back.

"That's your free one," I said, releasing him. "Get out of my way."

The bartender stumbled backward. I shoved the sap into my hip pocket and walked out the front door at a speed just short of a run. Not a single fat man was in sight.

I had lost him.

Vehicles of every description prowled up and down: pick-ups, low-riders, blue-collar sedans, and white-collar station wagons, all cruising back and forth in pursuit of hookers or crack or meth or weed, every street corner an open-air vice market, each dark side street a trysting spot for strangers. The boulevard was hot and stinking of sweaty desperation and the kind of decay that is more psychic than organic.

I wondered if this was the result Jake had in mind when he became an outlaw.

Aw, come on, kid. Things are never that simple. Any-

way, you've lived off the cash in that steamer trunk, and I've never heard you complain about it before.

True enough.

But not that simple.

Maybe that's why I spent so much time chasing other people's troubles, just to prove that I myself was pure, that I hadn't been tainted by whatever karma clung to that trunk full of dirty greenbacks.

The high profile of the Beast showed in the purple glow of an iodine streetlight half a block away. Fiora was waiting for me. There was no question of her loyalty to me, but her feelings about my Uncle Jake were . . . complex. I wondered if Jake's karma was why this particular quest had made her so uneasy.

Fiora started the engine when she saw me approaching in the rearview mirror. When I slowed to a walk, she honked once, impatiently. I picked up speed and stepped into the truck.

"Someone came out the front door of the restaurant about sixty seconds ago," Fiora said, pulling down into gear with a quick motion. "Looked like he was carrying the backpack, but I couldn't be sure."

I slammed the door as Fiora pulled out into traffic. Then it hit her.

"What is that smell?"

"Me."

"Good God. What happened?"

"I joined the ranks of the dumpster diners, right up to my knees. Where are we going?"

"He had a dirty white Mercedes, maybe ten years old, parked at the curb."

"Anything else?"

"He was so fat he waddled. Dressed casually, with longish hair in a ponytail."

A ponytail and a Mercedes. Middle-aged crazy, Hollywood style. Trash with flash, intent on proving he was still young and hip and with it. Whatever *it* was.

Fiora was doing close to fifty on the boulevard, weaving quickly in and out of traffic despite the Suburban's bulk. While she drove, I told her about the cops and the bartender. Then I showed her the sap.

"That's an ugly piece of business," she said, lifting her lip at the sap in distaste.

"Tools are useful, not pretty."

I dropped the sap into the console next to the flashlight and the other gear.

"I don't suppose we got lucky enough to come up with a license plate?" I asked.

Fiora shook her head.

She drove on another fifteen blocks. The exercise was useless and we both knew it. The Mercedes had vanished into the rank Hollywood night.

Fiora slammed the steering wheel with the palm of her hand in frustration.

"Relax, love," I said. "Don't blame yourself. It was my fault. Or bad luck. Or both."

Fiora backed off on the accelerator and slowed down to match the traffic. The lights of the Hollywood Hills were looming up in front of us. She pulled over to the curb and stopped.

"And I thought I was doing so well, too," she said in disgust.

"You did fine."

"I cost us twenty-five thousand bucks."

I shrugged. "Water under the bridge."

She pulled the second brown envelope from beside the seat and handed it to me.

"Don't hold your breath," she said. "I've already looked."

"And?"

Fiora shrugged.

This envelope was a little thicker than the first one had been. There were three photo blowups instead of one. I snapped on the overhead lamp and adjusted it so the light fell on the photos.

She was right. They weren't much.

I fanned the numbered sequence of three shots that had been taken through a long telephoto lens. The images were foreshortened and grainy, as though they had been enlarged from originals taken at great distance, like police surveillance photos.

All three showed the same thing, a dirt street in a small town somewhere in Mexico. It looked like the close of market day, with peddlers and street vendors knocking down their stands and packing up. A battered old International Travel-All was parked in the shade of a building.

Jake's truck.

I was looking into the past, Puerto Peñasco, the little fishing and smuggling village at the head of the Gulf of California. Just beyond the truck, three men stood with their heads together in conversation. They were too far away to be identified.

I went to the second shot. The overhead light shone on the glossy surface of the print, hiding everything in a white glare. I shifted the photo.

It was grainier than the first, as though it had been blown up from an even smaller negative. But the faces of the three men were clear: Jorge Cardenas Portillo, Koo-Koo Armijo, and Barry

Franklin, the Hollywood producer, Aileen Camp's partner. The two Mexicans were listening. Franklin was talking.

I brought the third photo into the light. That one had been taken shortly after the others, for little of the street scene had changed. The three-way chat must have pleased everyone involved. Franklin was handing Cardenas a grocery sack. The sack was half full but it didn't look heavy. Money, probably.

The contents of the bag must have pleased Koo-Koo. He was grinning like a kid who has just been promised his first piece of ass.

Or like a wanna-be hit man who has just gotten his first contract.

"What do these men have in common?" I asked Fiora.

"Now?"

"Yeah."

"Two of them are dead," she said.

I nodded.

"What about the third one?"

I smiled. "Let's try for a clean sweep."

tHIRTEEN

The single sheet of paper in the third envelope wasn't a paste-up extortion note. It was a photocopy of a Bank of America monthly account statement. I shifted the paper in the light and studied it carefully, letting Fiora read over my arm.

The monthly closing balance was a healthy $572,465. Across the bottom of the copy someone had scrawled *Barry's signature account.*

I stared at the paper for a few more moments before I turned it over, looking for more.

"What's the opening date on the statement?" Fiora asked.

I looked. "Two weeks before Jake died."

"Closing date?"

"Two weeks after."

Instantly Fiora looked back to the top of the page.

So did I. The opening balance on the account was $42,198.

"Looks like Franklin had a hell of a month," I said.

Light flashed and rippled over the pictures as I picked them up again.

"You're assuming there's a relationship between the pictures and the bank balance," Fiora said.

I grunted.

"You can't be sure," she said.

"I can ask. He can answer."

"You do know who Barry Franklin is, don't you?"

"He was the co-producer on the film about Jake's adventures."

"Long ago, far away, in another country," Fiora said flatly. "Now Franklin is one of the most powerful men in Hollywood."

"Doing what? Selling coke?"

"He's an agent."

"Lord," I muttered. "How the mighty are fallen."

"Franklin isn't your generic agent. He's a packager, a middleman, one of the guys who pulls all the strings together for a piece of the gross."

"Nice."

"Not really," Fiora said. "Franklin has a reputation for being a total monster. One of the Valley Vipers. What he wants, he gets, and to hell with what anyone else wants. He's a tough man to bully."

I shrugged. "How is he at catching jacketed forty-five slugs with his teeth?"

"For the love of God," Fiora said impatiently. "Sometimes your headlong charm wears a little thin. Barry Franklin is powerful. You aren't. Keep it in mind."

With that, she stared at the pictures again, using them as a focus while her mind free-wheeled and she told me the shape of modern Hollywood as seen through the eyes of a world-class money shuffler.

"Hollywood is like the palace at Beijing during the Ch'in dynasty or the White House at almost any time," she said quickly. "Everything is access and facilitation. The people who get rich are the gate-keepers, who take ten percent of every piece of action in town."

She flicked a naked fingernail against the photos.

"Don't misjudge men like Franklin just because they seem effete by your retrograde standards. To Franklin, politics is a blood sport. Your blood, not his."

There was a time when I might have been offended. Angry, even. But I've learned to listen to Fiora closely and to take into consideration not only what she says but what she does. There's no point in putting up with a ferociously bright, high-maintenance woman unless you are smart enough to put her to use in other than the obvious, retrograde ways.

"Okay, so maybe Barry Franklin is a hard nut to crack," I said. "So what? I don't believe crimes should go unpunished just because the law is slow to solve them. If that makes me retrograde and macho and all the other modern buzzwords for someone with teeth, so be it."

Fiora kept on staring at the pictures, thinking hard. But while she thought, she put her hand on my leg and kneaded gently. It wasn't calming, but it did make me listen.

"Men like Franklin have a way of insulating

themselves from reality, particularly in Hollywood,"
Fiora said slowly.

"Cocaine."

"That's part of it. Power is most of it. That's one
of the reasons I left Century City. Nothing is real in a
place where bodies and souls are bought and sold
like used books."

"Money makes everything cheap."

"Yes," she said.

There was bitterness in Fiora's voice. She had
worked in Century City for much of her adult life,
wheeling and dealing and eeling around with the
venture capitalists and risk brokers who have fastened themselves onto the great cash cow called the
entertainment industry.

Fiora's ambition to make her own mark had worn
out before her moral sense did. She had retired to
Newport Beach. Newport's riches were vast and
nouveau, but the barracuda quotient was a bit lower
there.

All through Fiora's Century City years we lived
apart, although we saw each other often enough to
keep the fires smoldering. Only after she left the LA
basin did we really recapture the ground that was
common between us. Maybe that's why the place
always made me so jumpy.

For more years than I wanted to remember, I
really thought I had lost Fiora to the city's deadly
glitter. Now she was warning me about territory she
knew better than I ever would. Or could.

I would have been a fool not to listen.

But Jake was just beyond my peripheral vision,
his murder unpunished, invisible scales unbalanced. . . .

"You have to ask yourself," Fiora said quietly.

" 'Is a burned-out hippie doper really worth all this?' "

"Blood on blood," I said. "I couldn't save Jake's life. I can at least send his executioners to hell for him to enjoy."

I looked from the pictures to Fiora's troubled, shadowed eyes.

"It's important to me," I said simply.

Fiora closed her eyes and let out a long, ragged sigh. Her hand slid from my leg, leaving me feeling cold.

"Promise me one thing," she whispered finally.

"If I can."

"Go slow. Hollywood may look effete to you, but it killed your renegade look-alike before he ever knew what happened."

There are certain advantages to life in the fast lane. For one thing, you can always find a place to stay on short notice. Fiora had kept a suite at the Chateau Beverly back in her Century City days. She had paid the bill on time and tipped well when a tip was earned.

People remember that. When Fiora walked into the lobby of the Beverly that night, looking like a streetwalker and accompanied by a guy who smelled like one of the homeless, nobody offered to throw us out.

"Hello, Ms. Flynn," said the night manager, smiling with real warmth.

"Hello, Luis. How is your wife?"

"Still in Argentina with the little ones, thank God." He bowed elegantly to Fiora. "What a pleasure to see you again." He turned to me. "And you, sir."

The guy had class. He didn't even flinch when he caught a whiff of me.

"Luis, can you get me some clean clothes?" I asked.

"My pleasure," he said instantly, measuring me in quick glances. "Thirty-four waist, thirty-six inseam, sixteen neck, and thirty-five arm, yes?"

"Close enough. It doesn't have to be fancy. Just something to keep me from getting arrested for littering the streets of Beverly Hills."

"Consider it done, sir. And might I suggest shoes?"

"Sold."

The Chateau is a quiet little fifty-suite hotel that takes up an entire block on a side street north of Wilshire Boulevard. The hotel makes money by charging outrageous prices and by making sure it can always find room for an old friend. Since it was late in the evening and the Presidential Suite hadn't been booked yet, Luis let us have that.

At regular room rates, no less.

Fifteen minutes after we hit the front desk, I was in a shower that was big enough to hold the Rams offensive line and half the Embraceable Ewes to boot. The marble walls and floor were a little too Roman-decadent for my taste, but the hot water supply was endless.

I came out wearing the huge terry-cloth robe I had found in the bathroom. Fiora was just signing for a supper tray that included a roast chicken, three kinds of cold salad, a loaf of fresh sourdough bread, and a bottle each of Jordan chardonnay and cabernet. By the time we had finished the chardonnay and half the chicken, a bellman appeared with a full set of clothing for me and a cute little nightshirt for Fiora.

"Luis says he's sorry but he can't get you a computer until morning, ma'am," the bellman said. "You're free to use the one in the accounting office until then, if you wish."

"Thank you. I'll be down shortly."

"Computer?" I asked, when Fiora returned from tipping the bellman.

"You have your tools, and I have mine."

She stretched out on the overstuffed couch in the suite's sitting room. The expression on her face was distracted. Most of her high-wattage brain was busy elsewhere.

"Bring me a Grand Marnier and some ice, will you?" she asked absently after a time.

The room's bar was well stocked. I muddled some ice, poured a jolt of Grand Marnier over it, and opened a Heineken's dark for myself.

Fiora was propped up on her side, watching me without really seeing me. I handed over her drink, found the channel changer for the big Sony, and played cable roulette until Fiora came to.

"Wait. What was that?" Fiora asked.

"Don't ask."

She took the changer away and backed up to one of the pay-per-view feature channels.

In silence I watched a blond actress of great celebrity and dubious talent trade ersatz tongue thrusts with a rat-faced actor who had made fifty episodes of a television series and ten feature films playing himself. Her boobs were spectacular but coyly covered. His self-conscious grin made me think of a pool-hall hustler with a bad mouth.

"I thought so," Fiora said. "This was one of the films Franklin packaged. His agency represented the male and female leads, the director, and the screenwriter. The whole picture cost a shade over fifty million."

"It was a real bow-wow, right?"

"From the audience point of view, yes."

"Don't tell me the critics liked it," I said.

"So-so reviews, bad word-of-mouth, no attendance. The picture grossed less than five million in three months before going from the theaters to cable."

"Sounds like a disaster to me."

Fiora smiled her remote smile, the one she uses to irritate me.

"Not for the first pigs at the trough," she said succinctly. "The stars, the director, and the writer got paid up front. That means Barry Franklin got paid up front, too. He and his clients made more money, cash in hand, than the film grossed."

"Christ. Aren't there laws against that sort of thing?"

"Depends on who your lawyer is."

Fiora punched the OFF button on the controller. The tongue-thrusting and fake ecstasy imploded.

"And that, my renegade love, is why I want a computer," she said. "It helps me strip away the glitter and take a look behind it."

She stood up and shed her filmy blouse, black bra, and the rest of her street outfit. Then she took me by the hand and led me toward a bed that was as big as a small aircraft carrier. She didn't even try on the cute little nightshirt.

"Come on," she said sleepily. "The hotel spends

two thousand bucks each on these mattresses. The least we can do is give them a full tryout."

The frolicking was fine, but it didn't prevent Jake from rousting me at midnight to do a few laps with him around the track called motivation.

What did Barry Franklin have to gain by killing us?

I stared at the ceiling for a while, listening to Fiora snore softly somewhere on the other side of the flight deck. After a while, I reached the tentative conclusion that Jake wasn't telling me everything he knew.

Maybe Fiora could shake out the rest of the truth on her computer.

Just about the time the mockingbirds and mourning doves were turning up in the palm trees by the pool, I fell asleep again. I didn't awaken until almost nine.

Fiora was already up, wrapped in a terry-cloth robe and hard at work on a Macintosh LC with modem. She talked softly on the telephone and tapped away madly on the keys, operating what I finally decided was an on-line link with one of the proprietary data bases designed for business types like her. A little more eavesdropping told me that Fiora was talking to some of her old buddies on the East Coast, the ones who made their fancy livings in corporate analysis.

I showered, dressed in the new black denims, blue oxford-cloth shirt, and black linen jacket Luis had picked off the rack of the men's shop in the lobby. The breakfast table was covered with fresh fruit and muffins. Between phone calls, I caught some of Fiora's attention.

"How long are you going to be tied up?" I asked.

"A couple of hours. Maybe more."

Fiora didn't even look up from the list of phone numbers she had compiled. She checked one off and reached for the phone again.

"I'm going out to talk to somebody," I said. "I'll be back by noon. Why don't you see if Benny can come up and join us for lunch?"

That got Fiora's full attention.

"You aren't going to do anything foolish about Franklin, are you?" she asked. "I've got a line on something that might help us."

"I'm not going to go anywhere near Franklin. I'll leave that pleasure for later."

The phone rang, someone in New York returning Fiora's call. She launched into a conversation that was heavily laden with money-manager mumbo jumbo. She waved good-bye to me without looking up.

Sometimes I feel guilty about taking Fiora away from something she obviously loves and does so well.

Then she shifted position, and the white robe fell open just enough to give me a tantalizing glimpse of the woman beneath. I took a deep breath and knew I'd done the right thing.

Selfish, but unquestionably *right*.

I was still congratulating myself on my cleverness when I came smack up against the Forbidden City reality of the Visual Arts Studio. It reminded me of La Mesa Penitentiary. A fortress. A walled city within a city.

The Dream Factory, indeed. A half-section of

prime West Los Angeles real estate surrounded on all four sides by reality but very carefully defended against it.

Like La Mesa, Visual Arts' battlements looked a little rundown at the edges. Tile had begun to fall away from the top of the ten-foot brown stucco walls surrounding the half-section of land that was the studio lot. The barn-size sound stage buildings looked faded and sunstruck, lacking even the bold logo of La Mesa prison.

Only the studio's landmark water tower was bright and shiny. That was probably because it had to be repainted every few years with a new corporate logo as the studio was passed from one conglomerate to another like an aging courtesan.

Long in the tooth, faded glory, over the hill, declining. . . .

The terms all fit. Yet once every few years, a single strip of celluloid emerged from behind those walls that generated several hundred million bucks in revenue. The odds of financial success were better in Vegas, but that didn't stop people from making films.

Basically, Hollywood is driven by the same urge that makes people in search of a relationship strike up conversations in singles bars. Hope wins out over common sense more often than not.

A full circuit of the lot revealed that while the walls were faded and peeling, they were still ten feet high. There were three gates. Each was guarded by a platoon of professionals who lacked G-3 assault rifles but looked pretty formidable just the same.

Fiora was right. The Hollywood types have managed to insulate themselves from the rest of the world. Prisoners of celebrity or of their own arrogance, it makes little difference. They exist in a hermetic little world. Maybe that's why their movies are so badly out of sync with the audiences.

I did another circuit, looking for an opening. If I had been in Mexico, the problem would have been a lot simpler. A handful of ten-thousand-peso notes, a smile, a gesture, gates opening.

Unfortunately, American security guards are more steadfast than sworn police officers south of the border. Better paid, too.

I thought about taking the direct, unsubtle approach: walking right up to the gate to announce myself. Then I thought of Fiora's warning and took the approach that always seems to work in Hollywood.

I bought a ticket.

fOURTEEN

Studio tours are some bean counter's idea for profit maximization. People want to see how movies are made. People will pay to see how movies are made. Therefore, we'll take their money. Only we won't show how movies are really made. That's too complicated, like working a jigsaw puzzle upside down in the dark.

Instead, we'll put on a little show for the folks. We'll throw up a phony sound stage somewhere on the back lot. Then we'll install a couple of ersatz special effects and hire some stuntmen, and we'll pretend that's all there is to making a picture.

We'll have a nice little profit center, in case we never make another nickel from the reeking films we're putting out for oversexed teenagers and their long-suffering dates.

Ten bucks, ladies and gentlemen. Just ten bucks to see sausage-makers at work. Never mind that the real work is so unappetizing that people would pay *not* to have to watch.

It's showtime!

I laid down my ten bucks and joined the fifty other marks on the trams lined up just inside the gates of Visual Arts. There was an empty seat next to a young mother with two energetic house apes in tow. I took the seat and struck up a conversation with one of the boys, trying to look like maybe I was his dad.

Security people, politely dressed like ushers, were stationed at the head and tail of the tram, just to make sure Joe Six-Pack didn't wander off the approved paths. At the second stop I waited until the guards were looking in opposite directions. Then I stepped behind a false front on Frontier Street and vanished like a special-effects ghost.

The hardest part was not laughing out loud.

Matt Suarez's father taught me the secret of stealing elevators: do it in the daytime. Don't waste time dressing like a repairman. Don't bother to have a fake work order in your hand. Just look like you know exactly what you're doing and nobody will ever think otherwise.

I ditched the oh-wow expression and wandered around the lot trying to look like a screenwriter between meetings. Except for my hair—most of the screenwriters had foreheads as high as their ponytails were long—I fit right in.

Twelve big German cars were lined up like a Panzer motor pool on a parking lot next to the main gate. A pair of Latin kids in jeans and T-shirts worked under a portable awning, performing an out-call detailing job on a Mercedes 560SEL. The entrepreneurial spirit at work. Anybody who makes enough to afford a 560 Mercedes can't be bothered to drop by the car wash. Somebody has to bring the car wash to him.

God, it must be awful to be so-o-o busy.

In Spanish, I asked the rag jockeys where the car's owner worked. One of them pointed toward an elegant smoked glass and steel structure rising above the barns.

I should have figured. It was the only building on the lot that looked as though it had modern plumbing.

Interior security was a little lax. Acting like I was late for a meeting, I breezed past a chesty receptionist and on up the stairs. The green wool carpeting got even deeper on the second floor, telling me I was on the fast track to the stars.

The top of the stairs gave me a choice. Left or right. To the right, the brass letters on the mahogany doors got smaller as the titles got longer and more inconsequential.

I went left and hit paydirt at the far end of the long, silent corridor. Double doors with big bold letters: AILEEN CAMP, CHAIRMAN.

No explanations, no qualifiers. The Boss.

I pushed the door open. Unlike the rest of the studio, the door was exactly what it appeared to be —solid wood. The secretary behind the big walnut desk was real solid, too. Middle-aged, sharp dresser, competent, and sophisticated. If I had been in the market for a door dragon, I'd have hired her in a hot second.

"Hi, is Aileen in?"

"Yes."

As the woman spoke, she glanced over her shoulder at the big office door on the left. It was an unconscious gesture, made before the secretary realized that she had never seen me before in her life. The alarm went off when I walked past her desk, headed for the door.

"Excuse me, but who are you?"

Polite, firm, and five beats too late. The inner door swung open smoothly. Aileen Camp looked up over a pair of half-glasses she had been using on a thick, formidable, single-spaced document. She gave it a very nice, rather convincing two count before she reacted.

"Jesus . . . Christ!"

There was so much emotion in Aileen's voice that I forgot she was a famous agnostic.

"Hi, Aileen. Long time and all that."

The secretary appeared in the doorway behind me.

"Security's on the way," the secretary said tightly. "You'd better leave."

Aileen was as pale as the carved ivory elephant that decorated her gleaming desk, but she was tough.

"It's okay, Pat. Hold my calls."

Pat was a real gem. Without a word she bowed out of the office, closing the door as she went.

"Don't be too hard on her," I said. "She's used to gofers and power groupies."

Aileen stood and straightened her shoulders with the unconscious gesture of a woman to whom standing tall and looking good is second nature. She wore a gold silk jacket over a scoop-neck black bodysuit and loose black slacks. Comfortable, expensive, understated, and just tight enough to show that her figure could hold its own, even in Hollywood.

Still lean, firm, tanned, and toned—although she had begun to frost her hair and was going to need a neck tuck before too long if she kept on showing so much clevage.

Tinseltown is tough for women. Beauty is a drug on the market; brains are the kiss of death; and you'd better be short, because the powerful men top out at five foot two.

Aileen was attractive but not gorgeous. She was five foot ten, and she was almost as smart as Fiora. Three strikes against Aileen, but somehow she had managed to carve out a niche for herself in Hollywood. From her appearance, she intended to hold on to that niche against all comers.

It wouldn't be easy. Hollywood is full of folks like Aileen—fractured and smart, talented and ruthless, and, above all, driven. They keep their noses above the cesspool as long as they can, making huge gobbets of money with one hand and spending it with the other.

Hollywood isn't a town, it's an addiction. Nobody ever retires; nobody gets out alive.

"Hello, Fiddler."

Gracefully Aileen came around the desk and crossed the room toward me. With each step, her legendary self-possession closed around her like an invisible suit of armor.

"You used to knock," she said.

"I forgot the code."

Aileen offered up her cheek for the obligatory social kiss, but her lips brushed the tip of my mustache at the last moment.

Good old Aileen. Never miss a chance to make a

guy feel special, right? Maybe that's how she con-
quered Hollywood.

Just beneath her fragile perfume, I caught a whiff
of something else, something on her breath. It could
have been the residue of a Bloody Mary breakfast.

Her pale eyes went over me, from my big feet to
my dark hair, lingering on points in between. When
she spoke again, her voice was husky with emotion.
Her narrow hands clung to my forearms, testing
their strength and prolonging our physical contact at
the same time.

"Do you know how much you look like him?"
she asked.

"Yes."

"Not that many years ago, he and I, we—"

She cleared her throat. Her hands lifted as she
stepped back from me.

"But time only runs one way, doesn't it?" She
smiled rather savagely. "So tell me, Fiddler, why did
your elevator stop at my floor today?"

I looked at Aileen's eyes and saw only the cool
calculation of a woman who has made it in a man's
world. No chinks. No crevices. If she could have
waved her hand and made me disappear, she would
have.

In fact, she was thinking about doing just that.

"I came about Jake," I said.

"He's dead. Dead and buried and forgotten."

"I thought so, too. Then I ran into one of the guys
who killed him."

"What? When?"

Aileen's voice was clipped, staccato, and her lips
were pale beneath their artificial layer of pink.

"Day before yesterday," I said. "Venice Beach."

"Mother of God. How—what happened?"

"He shot at me and missed. I shot at him and didn't."

Aileen stared at me in disbelief. "You killed him?"

"Yes."

She shivered and rubbed her arms as though she were chilly beneath the expensive clothes.

"You're just as cold and crazy as Jake was," Aileen whispered.

"I'm just as retrograde. It's a survival trait brought on by overcrowding. If you don't believe me, read your newspaper. LA is Rome, and the barbarians are already tearing down the gate."

An elegantly manicured hand waved in dismissal of the world beyond the studio walls.

"I suppose," Aileen said vaguely. "I don't have much to do with the city anymore."

She circled back behind the desk and sat down. Control visibly returned to her. The queen was on her throne, and all was well with the world.

"Please sit," she said.

The nearest chair was across from her desk. The supplicant's chair. Before I got to it, the door behind me slammed open. A hard-faced blond man in a tan summer suit stalked into the room. His coat was unbuttoned.

Someone who knew where to look would immediately spot the butt of the small pistol on his belt. Most people wouldn't even suspect that the well-dressed man was wearing a weapon.

Very nice, very discreet—and not very far from his hand.

"It's all right, Ned," Aileen said, leaning back in her chair a little. "This man's an old friend. Fiddler, this is Ned Bishop. He's head of security for the studio.''

Ned Bishop had a blond's pale skin. Though he was fit enough for a man in his early forties, either sun or alcohol had given his face a bit of a flush. His breath was clean and his reflexes were quick. If he drank, it wasn't on the job.

Bishop looked too physical and competent to have come up through the ranks of the gate guards. At first I thought he might be retired FBI. Then I thought better of it. There was something about his stance that suggested the hard-shouldered arrogance of a street cop. LAPD, maybe. Used to mean streets and proud of it.

''Fiddler?'' Bishop said, nodding minutely. ''How did you get on the lot without a pass?''

I grinned lazily. I couldn't help it. Street cops bring out the worst in me.

The flush on Bishop's skin deepened. He took a step forward, getting in my face. He was close enough now for me to see the miniature LAPD badge that he wore as a tie tack. It was the law enforcement equivalent of a Masonic ring, an instant icebreaker that probably got the studio special protection from overworked cops.

''Listen, mister,'' Bishop began in a hard voice.

''Thank you, Ned,'' Aileen said distinctly. ''It was good of you to come so quickly when Pat called. But as you can see, everything is fine. You can go back to whatever it is that you do.''

Whew.

Clear, quiet, and able to peel skin at twenty paces. Aileen had learned to use her voice like a lion tamer uses a whip.

Bishop's color deepened another shade. He didn't

like taking orders from a woman. But it came with the territory, and he was plenty bright enough to know it. He took out his irritation by glaring at me rather than at his boss.

"If you say it's okay, it's okay," Bishop said without taking his eyes off me. "But if it turns out not to be okay, I'll be close by. Real close."

Bishop backed away a step, turned, and stalked out. When he closed the door, I sat down in the chair.

"You might think about giving him a raw knuckle bone," I said. "Guard dogs need to work out their meanness. Otherwise they go sour."

"Ned's a good security man," Aileen said.

I made a neutral sound. It seemed to irritate her.

"A few years ago, we hired him away from a very promising career at LAPD to work for the studio," she said in her lion tamer's voice. "Neither of us has regretted it. Ned knows every policeman in this town."

"Useful."

"Precisely."

Aileen's smile suggested she wasn't particularly upset by Bishop's manners. Guys like Bishop were rough by the standards of the boardroom, but they were polished by the standards of the station house. As private cops, they were valuable not because they could carry guns and badges but because they had contacts who still did it for real.

It must have been entertaining for Aileen to watch while her tame lion kept surly stars with dope problems on their best behavior.

Nor was Aileen alone in her preference for private security men seasoned at public expense. The entertainment industry is full of Bishop clones who walked mean streets long enough to learn when to lean and when to wink. Then they took retirement to become high-priced private muscle for various industries.

I wondered if Bishop had waited for retirement or if he had jumped ship when Aileen waved more honest money at him than he had ever seen before.

"Was there anything else?" Aileen asked me.

Her pink-tipped fingers rested loosely on the desk, silently telling me that she was very much under control again.

I put on a surprised look. "What? No 'How've you been?' No 'Gosh, but it's been a long time, hasn't it?'"

Aileen's expression didn't change. She looked at me with polite interest and little else.

"Jake is the past," she said. "I live in the present."

So much for chitchat.

"Right," I said. "In the present, somebody's been offering to sell me information about Jake's killer."

Aileen's mouth thinned at the reminder of recent violence, but she didn't say anything.

"The salesman even sent me the surviving trigger man the other day as a gift. But this guy is asking a big price for the information."

She waited.

I wondered what it would take to get inside Aileen's armor again. Bishop had shown up at exactly the wrong time.

"So I thought I'd ask if you knew anything that might help me to save the investment."

A slight frown narrowed Aileen's pale eyes.

"Me?" she asked. "All I know is that Jake was killed by one of the—"

"Two," I interrupted.

"What?"

"There were two hit men."

"Whatever. So he was killed by two of the sleazy border bandits he used to run with." Aileen shrugged. "Tragic and all that, but what can you expect? When you lie down with dogs you get up with fleas."

"You should know."

The look Aileen gave me wasn't very friendly. I gave it back with interest.

"Sorry," she said tightly. "I thought you would have gotten over your hero worship by now."

I let it go by.

"The guy who called me said there was more to it than a case of bad friends," I said.

"Really? What?"

"That's what I came to ask you. You were as close to Jake as anyone ever got."

"Except you."

Resonances of old jealousy rang just beneath the cool surface of Aileen's words. Of all the women who had chased Jake, she had been certain she would be the one to catch him.

"Except me," I agreed. "And I don't know who would have paid for Jake's death, or why. Do you have any ideas?"

It was half the truth. I had a bank statement with Barry Franklin's name on it, but I hadn't the faintest idea why.

Aileen spread her hands on the desk, palms down, and looked at the four rings on them. None of them appeared to be a wedding band. She sighed and shook her head.

"I'm as much on the outside looking in as I ever was," she said finally.

"I wasn't there. You were. What do you remember of those last days?"

"Mexico was a bad dream. An acid trip in a shooting gallery."

Aileen's voice was like her eyes, flat and hard.

"How so?" I asked.

"Macho idiots with guns. Violent men strutting for one another, shoving and shouting and swaggering."

I shrugged. "Parts of the border are like that."

"Jake was different down there. I didn't like it at all. I wasn't surprised when somebody got killed. I'm only sorry it was Jake."

A shudder went through Aileen.

"But as for knowing why any of it happened"—she sighed—"I don't. I'm a nice Jewish girl from New York City who went to the wrong school on the wrong coast and never went back home."

"Jake didn't confide in you?"

Aileen gave me an odd look. "Confide in a woman? Jake?"

"Just a thought."

"Just a joke," she retorted. "I don't even speak Spanish. Whatever Jake did to piss off his playmates is a complete mystery to me. Hell, I barely remember what I did down there, much less what *he* did."

"Not too surprising. Uncontrolled use of controlled substances tends to screw up your mind."

It was a nasty crack, but Aileen was well on her way to pissing me off. I didn't like the way she dismissed a man who had spent his last months on earth in her bed.

"Everybody is young and stupid once in their

life," she said coldly. "Jake was the beginning, middle, and end of my drug experience. Period."

Aileen reached for the cut crystal glass on its tile coaster beside her telephone, as though to underline her point.

"Sorry," I said. "I'm nobody's angel myself. Neither was Jake."

For a moment I was afraid Aileen wasn't going to let herself be soothed. Then she sighed and relaxed against the tall back of her chair, accepting my apology.

"It's okay," she said. "It's just that this town runs on gossip. There are people who can kill you with one rumor, if it's planted in the right circle."

I looked around the office. High ticket, top drawer, all the perks except a live-in masseur, and for all I knew Aileen had him stashed in the executive powder room.

"It looks to me like you're at the top of the heap," I said. "I'd think you'd be bulletproof against a little recreational slander."

Aileen laughed briefly. "This is the illusion factory, remember? And the biggest illusion is security. The higher up the pyramid you go, the more vulnerable you become."

"What about Barry Franklin? Is he vulnerable?"

"Barry? What does he have to do with this?"

I shrugged. "A natural association. Jake and you and Barry and Mexico."

"I'd like to be vulnerable the way Barry is," Aileen said dryly. "Last year he turned down a hundred million for his equity in the agency. That's more than this studio's annual net profit."

"Not bad."

"It gets better. He's a majority stockholder. I'm just a hired hand."

"No platinum parachute?"

"Oh, I've got stock options, but why would I buy stock in a company as shaky as this one?" Aileen smiled bitterly. "In this economy stock options are like bad jokes—everybody has some and nobody wants to hear about yours."

"What kind of a guy is Barry Franklin, anyway?"

"Powerful," she said succinctly.

"Funny. He never seemed the type. But then, I didn't know him very well back when Jake was alive."

"Barry could teach smart to Einstein. When he's not hatching deals, he plays tennis to hone his body and poker for his jugular instinct."

"Sounds like a well-rounded life," I said.

"He was a fanatic about poker," Aileen said.

I didn't have to prod. She was more than willing to share Franklin's human shortcomings with me.

"That's why our partnership broke up," she said. "I didn't fit into the Wednesday night game. A woman at a poker table made the boys self-conscious."

"Does Franklin carry grudges?"

"Only as long as it takes to get even."

Again, the bitterness. Abruptly Aileen focused on me instead of on the past.

"You can't be serious," she said.

"About what?"

"Jake. Barry's a bastard, but murder isn't his style. His lawyers might gut you in a figurative sense, but he doesn't have the balls for the real thing."

"Who did, then?"

Aileen stared at me uneasily.

"You really think there was more to Jake's death than an argument with his connection, don't you?" she asked.

"Do I?"

"Is that why you came here? Do you think I had something to do with it?"

"Did you?"

Aileen's eyes widened.

"You *are* serious. Seriously crazy! Good-bye, Fiddler. I won't say it's been nice seeing you, because it hasn't."

"I don't think you had anything to do with Jake's death. I need your help to find out who did."

She started to say something, then stopped. Slowly she got up and circled the desk until she was standing within arm's reach of me.

"I can't help you," Aileen said distinctly. "It's not worth getting involved. Too many sad memories. Too many bad ones. I've spent years putting them behind me."

Before I could speak, Aileen's cool fingers slid through my hair, traced my eyebrows, my cheekbones, my mouth. Her eyes were almost closed. Her fingers were shaking. I knew it wasn't my face she was touching.

"Damn you," she whispered. "Why did you have to look so much like him?"

Her hands fell to her sides as she stepped back and turned away.

"Don't come back, Fiddler."

I stood and went to the door. As I opened it, Aileen spoke again.

"Are you still with her, that little blonde? What was her name? Fiona?"

"Fiora," I corrected. "We're together again."

"Married?"

"In every way that matters to us."

"Then she was right and Jake was wrong."

I waited, but Aileen was through talking.

I closed the door behind me. And I wished the door to the past could be closed so easily.

fIFTEEN

The concierge caught me in the lobby of the Chateau Beverly and said that everything was arranged.

"What everything?"

"Your suite and the adjacent suite for Mr. Speidel."

I must have looked blank, because she launched into an explanation.

"Ms. Flynn wanted to book them until further notice. I've done some switching, and everything is set through the end of the week. If you need the rooms longer, please let me know as soon as possible."

"You'll know as soon as I know," I promised.

The concierge smiled slightly, thanked me, and went about her work of seeing that not one of her guests' whims went unfulfilled.

The Chateau would be a real change of pace for Benny. He lives in one half of a faintly disreputable West Newport duplex. He works in the other. When he travels, he favors Motel 6.

Fiora was still on the phone when I reached the suite. Benny was on the balcony watching three young women in bikinis bare their legal all to the sun. The poolside beauties were the lush brown of well-tanned beach bunnies, but their hair was dark and cropped short rather than long and bottle-blonde.

"Don't you see enough flesh on the sand in front of your place?" I asked.

"A man never gets enough beauty."

Benny wheeled his chair back into the room with quick, powerful strokes that made his shoulders ripple. From the waist up, he's in better shape than Schwarzenegger, and better looking, too. From the waist down, Benny has been on wheels ever since a single round of friendly fire cut his spinal cord in Vietnam.

The condition has done little to hamper his social life. Fiora tells me there's something enormously attractive about any man who genuinely likes women. Benny does. He makes female friends like a big, confident tomcat does. He likes to strop himself on their legs, and they like to stroke his fur and make him purr.

It's fascinating to watch. If I tried something like that, I'd be arrested.

"Those are three devout young Muslim girls getting away from the repressive control of their fathers," Benny said, "who just happen to be princes and members of the Saudi royal family. They invited me over for drinks later."

"The princes or the girls?"

"You're in a bloody frame of mind, aren't you?"

"I'm working on it."

He grunted. "Let me know when you get there. Until then, get on with telling me what the hell you've stepped in this time."

"Didn't Fiora explain?"

"She left a message on my machine this morning asking me to come here. So here I am."

"Oh."

That's the Ice Cream King of Saigon. He earned the name working undercover in Vietnam during the war. During the day, he made vanilla, chocolate, and *nunc mam* sherbet; at night he fought the kind of shadow war that calls for ruthless pragmatism and unflinching loyalty. Benny still practices that kind of loyalty. He is why I need so few other friends in the world.

Loyalty is not the word, really, for it suggests something consciously given or withheld. Benny doesn't choose. He's simply there, always there, when either Fiora or I need him.

The rest of the time, Benny rockets around his workshop and his life on his high-tech wheels, plugged into the entire world with data links and modem connections and telephone lines. His legs don't work anymore, but he gets farther, faster, than any five people I know.

I got two beers out of the little refrigerator and handed one to Benny.

"Make it last," I muttered. "Damn things cost five bucks apiece here."

"I've got a six-pack of St. Stan's down in the truck. I can bring it in right under their noses."

"Don't bother. This is Fiora's treat."

"In that case . . ."

After we both took a swallow to cool our throats, I stretched out on the long couch and told Benny about the past couple of days. By the time I was done, he had finished his beer, my beer, and one more. He belched with gusto and rocked back and forth on the titanium wheels of his chair, thinking hard. Then he belched again and shared his thoughts.

"In other words, you've killed some poor sod who probably had it coming, you've run around Southern California for two days in pursuit of the great albino kangaroo, you've lost a rucksack full of greenbacks, and you have bugger all to show for it."

I winced but didn't disagree.

"You're slipping into bad work habits, mate," Benny said. "Good job Fiora called me."

I sailed the brown envelope containing the photos and the bank statement toward Benny. He snagged the envelope out of the air, opened the clasps, and scanned the contents.

"They real?" he asked.

"Pictures don't lie," I said with a straight face.

He rolled his eyes, said something in Urdu, and tilted the photos first one way and then the other.

"In other words, you don't know whether they're real or not," Benny said after a moment.

"In other words, they appear to be authentic," I retorted.

He grunted.

"The street in the picture looks very much like what I remember of the main drag of Puerto Peñasco," I said. "The little details, like the license number on Jake's truck, are right on. I can positively identify the three guys in the close-ups."

Benny grunted again.

"But," I admitted, "this is Hollywood. They make their living here fooling people."

Without a word Benny fanned the three photos in the best light. Tugging at his long black beard, he studied the images as though he were a flat scanner. He has a scary gift for the black applications of modern technology, which makes him keenly aware of the tricks others can play.

At the other end of the suite, Fiora hung up the phone and stretched. As she walked toward us, Benny turned his attention to the Xerox.

"Bloody good month he had," Benny said.

"Yeah."

"Xeroxes are even easier to fake than photographs," he pointed out. "Have you got any friends in the bank who could go back and resurrect the original data on this account?"

"Yes," Fiora said. "The operations director. It took him a while, but he confirmed that Barry Franklin was the signatory on that account."

"What about the rest of it?" Benny asked her.

"Two days after Jake was killed, Franklin did indeed make a whopping wire deposit from an offshore account in the Netherlands Antilles."

"That doesn't prove the two events necessarily were connected," Benny said.

"Somebody wants us to think so," I said. "This was supposed to be the kind of evidence that could put a man in prison for murder one."

Fiora stretched her neck, trying to get rid of the telephone knots. While Benny went back to the photos, she rummaged for something in the refrigerator. She came up with a liter bottle of Evian. The plastic safety cap resisted her.

"Where's the bottle opener?" she asked.

I held out my hand. She gave me the bottle.

"I dropped by to see your old friend Aileen Camp," I said.

"With friends like her, no one needs foes."

Benny glanced at Fiora. I doubted he had ever heard that particular tone of voice from her before.

"But Aileen spoke so highly of you," I said blandly. "She even went so far as to say that you had gotten exactly what you deserved."

"Really. What was that?"

"Me."

The bottle opened with a snap. I handed it back.

"You must have really irritated her," Fiora said, saluting me with the bottle. "She wanted you for herself, once she figured out she wasn't going to get Jake."

"I didn't mean to piss her off. I was angling for her help in getting to Barry Franklin."

"Did you get it?" asked Benny.

"No."

"That woman wouldn't help a drowning child unless her poodle needed a playmate," Fiora said.

Benny's black eyebrows shot up. "Am I missing something?"

"Aileen was the bitch who called me after the fact and told me Fiddler had been shot down in Mexico. She didn't do anything to help Fiddler herself. That might have involved chipping her nail polish. Thank God I knew already, or Fiddler would have died by the time help got to him."

"Who told you?" Benny asked.

Fiora's expression shut down. She hates talking about the part of her mind that defies rational, logical, bookkeeping explanation.

"One of her dreams," I said. "She knew Jake was dead and I was alive before I did."

"Bloody hell."

"The hellish part is that she knew an hour before any of it happened."

"Any more beer?" Benny asked.

I got one, opened it, and handed it over. When I looked at Fiora, she was watching me with brooding eyes.

"You never told me the bit about Aileen before," I said.

Fiora shrugged.

Subject closed.

"Anything else I should know and don't?" I asked.

"Depends on what you've remembered since then," she said cryptically.

"Is it time for me to check out the handicapped access for the diving board?" Benny asked.

He hates it when we argue.

"My last clear memory is Jake meeting me at the airstrip outside of Puerto Peñasco," I said. "From that point until seven weeks later, my recollection is as fragmented and useless as the bone chips they fished out of my cerebral cortex."

"Lucky you. I remember . . . too much."

Benny cleared his throat. "So. What we have are three photos of dubious truth, a Xerox copy of probable truth, and an old 'friend' who isn't interested in digging up the past."

"Maybe she has good reason," Fiora said tightly.

"Such as?" I asked.

Fiora flashed me the kind of look she usually reserves for stuff that sticks to the soles of her shoes.

"That bitch has never had a motive that wasn't ulterior," Fiora said.

"Tell me something I don't know."

"Are you sure you know that?" she challenged.

"Hell, yes. I turned her down flat."

"Why?" Benny asked. "Was she ugly?"

"No, she was Jake's. And I had seen Fiora. After that—" I shrugged. There's no explaining that kind of attraction.

Benny tilted his head. "Weren't you a bit green for bedroom roulette?"

"I was an early bloomer."

"Even back then," Fiora said, "Fiddler looked like Jake. A better Jake. Less hard. Less jaded. Less violent."

I kept my mouth shut even though it made my jaw ache. Now wasn't the time to get in a wrangle over what Jake had or hadn't been like.

"So Aileen likes the rough trade?" Benny asked.

"Yes. No." Fiora gestured impatiently. "I don't know if I can explain Jake to a man. God knows I've never succeeded getting the truth through to Fiddler."

I tightened the jaw lock.

Benny listened to Fiora with the kind of attention he usually reserves for delicate computer problems.

"Jake had a kind of raw masculine charisma," Fiora said slowly. "He wore it the way fire wears heat."

Something cool tiptoed down my spine. I started listening as hard as Benny.

"There was nothing calculated about it," she said. "It simply was. Women wanted Jake. Jake enjoyed women. But he never *wanted* them, not the way

they wanted him. He had only one desire: adrenaline.

"And he loved only one person: Fiddler."

Benny looked at me.

I stared at Fiora and wondered why icy fingernails were dancing down my spine.

"Jake had great plans for the two of them," she
said. "Drinking and wenching and raising hell along
the border for the rest of their lives."

"Then Jake died?" Benny asked.

"No. Fiddler met me and the tug-of-war over his
soul began."

"Oh, come *on*," I said through my teeth. "It
wasn't that dramatic."

"Not for you, certainly," Fiora retorted. "You
never let yourself see what was going on. If you had,
you might have been forced to admit that inside
Jake's size thirteen cowboy boots were feet of clay."

"Oh, bullshit."

"Children," Benny said. "I hear the pool calling."

"We're almost through," I said. "The important
thing for you to know is that Aileen is the kind of
woman who likes pitting one man against another.
Luckily, Jake and I were both smarter than that."

Benny looked at Fiora.

She shrugged. "One of them was smarter, and it
wasn't Jake. But as for the rest, yes. I've always
thought that if anybody could shoot Jake in the
back, it would be Aileen."

"Aileen?" I asked. "What did she gain by Jake's
death? Sure as hell it would take three men to replace him in the sack, and that was where she liked
him best."

Fiora bit back whatever acid comment was burning her tongue and changed the subject.

"There's a strong rumor on the street that Visual Arts Studio is about to be put on the block," Fiora said evenly.

"Says who?" I asked.

"The entertainment industry analysts for three of the biggest brokerage houses in New York."

"Talk's cheap," I said.

"All three of them are taking strong positions in the stock. That's not talk. That's money."

I chewed on that for a minute before I got smart and did what Fiora had done: let go of the past for the present.

"How much money?" I asked.

"The stock price has run up seven points in the last two days, after being dormant for the last four months."

"Give it to me in English."

"Something is happening behind the scenes. By the time it's common knowledge, fortunes will be won or lost. It's called insider information."

"That's illegal," I muttered.

"So is murder," Benny offered to no one in particular. "Murder always hurts."

"Okay, say you're right," I said to Fiora. "What's that got to do with Aileen and Jake and Barry Franklin?"

"I don't know yet," she admitted.

"When will you know?" Benny asked.

"Maybe next minute. Maybe never. These things are like reading smoke signals on a foggy day. The pattern is hard as hell to pick out against the background."

"Maybe there isn't a pattern," I said.

"There's a pattern, all right. Nobody moves billions of dollars around the world for the hell of it."

"Billions?" Benny and I asked simultaneously.

"Of course."

"Of course? Jesus, Fiora," I said. "There's nothing 'of course' about billions of bucks! Are you sure?"

"The last studio sale was Universal," Fiora said patiently. "The one before that was Columbia. Both of them went to the Japanese. Both were ten-figure deals."

I whistled softly.

"Sony," she continued, "paid half a billion just to buy out the contracts of Guber and Peters, the two wonder boys they wanted to run the new show for them."

Benny scratched his chin and grinned savagely.

"How many theater tickets will those wankers have to sell to recoup a half billion dollars?" he wondered aloud.

"A lot," Fiora said succinctly.

"I hope they lose their nuts."

Benny's native land is a lot closer to being a Japanese colony than most Kiwis like to admit. As a result, Benny's antipathy for the economic soldiers of Nippon is fierce and pervasive.

"The smart money in New York thinks the Japanese are overpaying," Fiora said, "but Tokyo is financing the deals with dirt-cheap American dollars, so purchase price isn't a primary concern."

Fiora has more regard for the Japanese than Benny does. They are shrewd enough to be worthy adversaries, even for a world-class money mover like her.

"So Hollywood is taking a subtle form of revenge on Tokyo by peddling a worn-out studio to them at an inflated price," I said. "So what else is new?"

"I didn't say the Japanese were behind this deal."

"Then who is?"

"Good question. Nobody has been able to identify the potential buyers so far."

"So we're back to chasing rumors again," I said. "Personally, I get more satisfaction out of kicking in doors. High finance is too subtle for me."

Fiora looked at me. "An earthquake is too subtle for you, because you know you didn't cause it and can't direct or prevent it. Face it. You're into control. It's a male thing."

Before I could defend my sex, there was a knock on the door. I went over, looked through the spy hole, and saw a bored bellman holding a slender courier package. I dug in my pocket for a tip, opened the door to ransom the package, and closed the door.

"What is it?" Fiora asked.

"Dunno."

I flipped the package over and read the label: RUSH HAND DELIVER and the room number. No help there.

I tore the seal on the package. Inside was a rich cream-colored envelope. Inside that was an invitation and two pieces of heavy paper, printed and numbered in a very discreet way.

I read the note and looked at the ducats, then flashed them at Fiora.

"And here you doubted Aileen's desire to help her fellowman," I said.

"What?"

"Tickets," I said succinctly.

"For what?"

"Tonight's fund-raiser for Radical Earth."

Benny sounded as if he were trying to swallow his tongue.

"Bloody hell," he snarled finally. "Radical Earth

is the above-ground money funnel for the eco-
terrorists who tried to blow up the Diablo Canyon
nuclear power plant."

"Lovely," said Fiora. "Why would someone send
us tickets?"

"Because the party is being held in Barry
Franklin's house."

SIXTEEN

I was driving the Beast, fighting the rush-hour crowd that heads out through Pacific Palisades in a solid stream each day. Fiora's ears were laid back. She thought I was going about this the wrong way—earthquake style.

That's why she was wearing the trashy outfit I had specifically requested she save for seducing dust bunnies out from under our bed.

I was wearing black for the usual reason.

At the moment, Fiora was squinting into the blood-red sun, inspecting the mansions along Sunset Boulevard. The curve in her mouth had nothing to do with a smile.

"So much money, so little joy," she said. "God. I had forgotten how much I dislike this place."

"You're just envious," I assured her. "It's the curse of the outsider."

She snorted. "Envious? Not bloody likely."

I caught Benny's smile in the rearview mirror. Fiora takes much of her black language from him.

"I left this place voluntarily when I got sick of economic astrology," she said.

"Economic astrology," I repeated, as I dodged a Porsche Carrera that had delusions of grandeur. "What in hell is that?"

"Everybody is a star or makes their living servicing a star," she said. "Agent to the stars or lawyer to the stars or pool cleaner to the stars or dog groomer to the stars. I didn't want to spend my adult life as accountant to the stars, so I got out."

"You don't like actors?" Benny asked.

He was ensconced in the back like a potentate, arms resting on the seat back, drumming his fingers idly. He feels about the city the way a fireplug feels about dogs. It was a sentiment I shared.

"Some actors are okay," Fiora said. "But the people who spend their lives worshiping stars—or, worse, sucking up to them—are intestinal parasites."

"How the hell am I going to take you out in polite Hollywood society?" I muttered. "You wear your disdain like a campaign button."

"So do they. But you have an even bigger problem."

"What's that?"

She held up the two tickets.

"As your accountant," Fiora said, "I must point out that three into two does not go evenly, so—"

"No kidding."

"—how are we all getting inside? Better yet," she

continued, ignoring my attempt to interrupt, "why are we bothering?"

"I discovered I can learn a lot about people who used to know Jake just by walking in on them unexpectedly. Not subtle—"

"Earthquake time," Fiora said under her breath.

"—but we've already figured out I'm not a shy little flower, haven't we?"

Benny's hand appeared over Fiora's shoulder. He lifted the tickets from her fingers and handed them to me.

"I'll take care of the missing ticket," he said, "but you'll have to climb back here with your great and good friend, the Ice Cream King of Saigon. And coo to me."

She gave him a sidelong look.

"Trust your old Uncle Benny," he said.

"Said the Walrus to the Oyster," Fiora muttered.

"If you don't trust me, how do you feel about guilt?"

"It's overrated."

"Not in Hollywood."

The contempt in Benny's voice would have blistered stone. Fiora gave him a wary look, but she eased over the console and onto the seat beside him without any more protests.

There are two men on earth Fiora trusts. Benny is the other one.

"I feel like a chauffeur," I said.

"Good on ya, mate," Benny retorted. "Keep it in mind when I start passing orders around."

"Yessir, boss."

Like Fiora, I trust Benny.

* * *

The Thomas Brothers map had already informed me that Barry Franklin lived in Malibu. To no one's surprise, the address was one of those gate-guarded private enclaves that exist between Coast Highway and the Pacific Ocean. Ground is hard to come by in that part of the world. Steven Spielberg once paid three million bucks for a house, just to knock it over and build a tennis court.

Franklin had dealt with the inevitable shortage of off-street parking by hiring a parking service to the stars. Crew-cut young valets in red cutaway jackets were stowing overflow vehicles along the highway out in front of the gate.

There was a quarter-mile line of Mercedes Benzes and BMWs, Van den Plas Jags, Range Rovers, and Rolls-Royces. All of them had been forced to park on the street and get dusty, just like Toyotas or Hondas or Nissans.

Democracy and the trade imbalance in action.

"Odd," I said.

"What?" Benny asked.

"The Japanese have managed to buy up a lot of studios, but they haven't cracked the high-end luxury car market in Tinseltown."

"Neither have the Americans."

The high wrought-iron gates to the estate were open but blocked by barricades. Security men in dark blue uniforms were all over the highway directing traffic and discreetly screening guests. No surprise there, except for one thing. These guards weren't studio rent-a-cops. They were members of the Los Angeles Police Department.

"The man is connected," I said, impressed.

"Just money," Fiora said.

"Nope. Just money hires cops. *Clout* hires off-duty LAPD motorcycle officers."

Benny looked thoughtful.

"Those guys are the Praetorian Guard of the Pacific Rim," I said. "They usually limit their moonlighting to studio location shoots."

One of the motor cops tried to wave us off the gates to the overflow parking out along the highway.

"Ignore him and pull on up to the barricades," Benny ordered. "Play to me and act stupid, Fiora. These people hate smart women."

A whip-thin motor cop stepped in front of the truck. His face was hidden behind a black handlebar mustache and sunglasses.

"Sorry," he said, "but you'll have to park down the road if you're headed for Mr. Franklin's party."

His tone was pleasant enough. It was also inflexible. He had no doubt he would be obeyed.

I looked in the rearview mirror.

Benny leaned out the side window. "Listen, we've got a limb-challenged man here. Surely arrangements have been made for parking closer to the house."

The motor cop dropped his chin and stared coldly at Benny over the tops of his Ray-Bans.

"Limb-challenged?" the cop asked in faint disbelief.

"My legs don't work very well, you blue-arsed baboon," Benny snapped. "I'm the president of the Limb-Challenged Alliance, and I'm not going to be pushed around."

It cost a great deal, but I didn't laugh out loud.

Fiora cooed.

The cop's Adam's apple bobbed like a man trying

to swallow a bullfrog. If he had been on the streets anywhere else, he'd have administered a quick attitude adjustment to the limb-challenged loudmouth, but Malibu requires politesse from its praetorian guards.

The cop was still weighing his options when a handsome, bullet-headed black man in a blue linen blazer and gray slacks bounced out from behind the gate barricades.

"What seems to be the problem, officer?" he said.

The second guy wasn't a cop. There was too much tooth in the smile. He moved like an athlete, smooth and springy, but he exuded the calm command of a good funeral director. To be polite to us, he removed his Wayfarers, revealing eyes that were as emotionless as a hit man's.

The combination of good manners and cold rolled steel was startling. There aren't that many polished ruffians in the world. I've often thought we should qualify for protection under the Endangered Species Act.

"I guess this *gentleman* wants handicapped parking," the cop explained. "But there isn't any."

The boss glanced over Benny's shoulder and spotted the wheelchair parked behind the seat. He also noted that Benny's legs weren't up to carrying the rest of him without help.

"I'm here as a guest of Mr. Franklin," Benny said irritably. "I have been asked to represent limb-challenged people all over the country at this important event."

The boss looked at Fiora. She was breathless in her admiration of Benny.

"We are pleased," Benny continued, "to express our solidarity with all environmentally aware and politically subjugated people of this hemisphere, but we won't use the servants' entrance. We demand the same empowerment, convenience, and dignity that has been extended to other guests.''

I could see the cop's eyes rolling skyward behind his dark glasses. The smooth ruffian in the blue blazer wasn't convinced either, but he was smart enough to be cautious. Hollywood is the font of dumb causes . . . and there was no doubt that Benny's legs wouldn't bear a man's weight.

"I'm sorry if you got the idea that we weren't sensitive to your special needs," the boss said smoothly. "We'll take care of the problem right away."

"Please," Fiora said breathlessly. "He doesn't have a problem. He has a challenge. There's a big difference."

Benny looked at her with real admiration.

"Yes, of course," the boss said, smiling with a lot of teeth. "May I see your invitation, sir?"

I grabbed the envelope off the dashboard and handed it to the cop. He verified its authenticity for himself, then showed it to the boss.

"We've got a problem," the cop said. "There's only tickets for two."

Horns honked behind us. The Beast was causing an impressive backup of expensive cars.

"Oh, for Christ's sake," Benny snarled.

He tapped me on the shoulder.

"Take us home," he ordered. "I'm not going to stay here and be embarrassed by idiots who require a ticket for my personal attendant. No doubt they want a special pass for the chair, too!"

Before anyone could get a word in, Benny turned back to the boss.

"Tell me," Benny commanded, "does the press have extra tickets for the schleps who handle the camera gear?"

More horns honked. Drivers and chauffeurs were leaning out of car doors trying to see what the holdup was. Several vehicles behind us, a door slammed on a white van. A man with a Minicam and an attitude started hustling toward us.

The traffic boss sensed an unhappy news brief in the making: *"Handicapped barred from Hollywood party. Film at eleven."*

He made a command decision.

"There's no need for you to leave, sir. And there certainly was no insult intended."

I'd been afraid Benny was laying it on too thick by half, but sacred cows are just that—scared.

Ah, the high price of political correctness.

The boss took the tickets and the invitation from the cop and stepped back from the truck. He pulled a hand radio from beneath his coat, spoke into it, and waited. After the response came, he pointed down the sloping driveway.

"Take a right at the bottom of the hill and pull up to the front door," he told me. "The valet captain will find a spot for your vehicle."

Then the polished ruffian leaned in and flashed a cold, toothy smile at Benny.

"Enjoy the party, sir. If you need anything, just let the staff know. We're here to serve."

I slipped the truck in gear and stared straight ahead while we moved through the gate. As the fancy wrought iron fell by on either side, I let out a long breath.

"Don't you feel bad, abusing noble instincts like that?" I asked.

"Those weren't noble instincts," Benny said flatly. "That was bloody old condescension. I could have spit in his face and he would have kept smiling, just because I have wheels instead of legs. Stupid sods. They think we have the IQ of our chairs."

"Be grateful," I suggested. "It's easier than taking you over the wall."

"Not me, boyo. You. How could a crip like me scale a wall?"

"You're faster climbing a rope than I am, and you bloody well know it."

Benny laughed.

Franklin's house wasn't part of a beach-front residential enclave, it was the whole damned enclave by itself. The mansion gleamed in the last light of day like a futuristic Japanese monastery.

There were several small guesthouses scattered among the eucalyptus, tall palms, Japanese gardens, and well-groomed lawns. The garage looked big enough for a used-car lot. The rest of the two acres of bluff-top ground overlooking the breaking waves was taken up with a rambling wood, stone, and glass house.

The inner circle—those people allowed to park inside Franklin's own fence—was definitely high ticket. There were fifteen cars on the clean black tarmac, with a total value of somewhere around three million seven. The Beast looked positively barbaric on the same pad with a classic Bugatti, several Ferraris, and a handful of Bentleys.

Did I forget to mention the Silver Clouds? They were as common as sand fleas.

Chauffeurs gathered off to one side, swapping lies about willing women, fast horses, and generous employers.

"At least the fund-raisers are picking on folks who can afford to contribute," I said.

"But do they tithe?" Benny asked sardonically. "Bloody hell, I'd settle for one percent of the take, much less ten."

Fiora gave a crack of unfunny laughter.

"Dream on," she told him. "Not one of these people actually gives away a cent that Uncle Sam wouldn't get otherwise in taxes."

"Say it isn't so," I said.

"I never lie about money," Fiora retorted. "You know What's-her-name, the big rock singer who's providing the entertainment tonight? I'll guarantee this is entered on her tax returns as a benefit performance—a hundred thousand dollars' worth of write-off."

Benny gaped. "You mean everyone's not doing this from the goodness of their generous souls? I'm devastated."

"Dear heart," Fiora cooed in her best bimbette voice, "most of the guests came because they know it's a great photo op for *Entertainment Tonight*."

"That explains the clown with the Minicam," I said. "Now belt up, boys and girls. It's showtime."

The valet captain walked out to greet Benny and Fiora as though they were Chuck and Di. Two strapping aides flanked Benny. One of them whisked the wheelchair out through the cargo doors of the Beast. The other opened a side door and attempted to do the same for the limb-challenged guest with the short temper.

Benny snarled at everyone, grabbed the handhold above the door, and swung himself out into his chair with one powerful, controlled motion. He will accept help when it's needed, and not before.

The valet captain got the message. We rolled through the front door under our own steam and then stopped dead, wondering which part of the real-life Disneyland to visit first.

The living room was the size of several handball courts and finished like a Persian miniature. Not one artifact out of place. Glass and leather furniture that cost more than a Rolls-Royce. African and Polynesian primitive art glowered from every corner, making me feel distinctly unwelcome.

I've never understood the attraction of primitive art. Most of it looks as if it was created to frighten away evil spirits—or, worse, to entice them.

Obviously, Barry Franklin had a taste for the demon-ridden and enough money to indulge himself. The black wooden masks on the walls and the metal statuary on the tables offered a fascinating counterpoint to the loud conversation of Hollywood business sorts dressed in snaky Italian suits and designer silk neckties.

"Don't look now, but I think those are real shrunken heads on the wall behind the tall bald guy with the eye patch," I said softly.

"Those heads aren't shrunken," Fiora murmured. "All producers look like that. Their private parts are even more shriveled. If it weren't for casting couches, none of those bastards would ever get laid."

"You really like Hollywood, don't you?"

She cooed.

The business clones were close to the front door, ready to make as early an exit as possible. They all had that impatient glance-at-the-watch kind of look that said they had reservations at Jimmy's or Michael's.

For Hollywood, a party like this was SSDD. Same Shit, Different Day.

I did detect one big change in Hollywood hospitality. My last such shindig had featured a punch bowl full of cocaine and a small bale of primo Acapulco Gold on the buffet table next to the Brie and crackers. Things were more discreet here. The strongest mind-altering substance in sight was a zinfandel that went 13.8 percent alcohol by volume.

There were additional guests on the huge deck that hung out over the ocean. These folks were more relaxed, giving every appearance of settling in for the evening. No neckties, just filmy designer silks and pastel leather, black jeans and T-shirts that cost more than the average working man makes in a week. Blue-collar schtick has always been big in Hollywood.

The bodies, both male and female, would have been spectacular, were it not for a peculiarity of the trade. The camera automatically puts twenty pounds on the sleekest of frames. As a result, when viewed in the actual flesh, some of the starlets were unpleasantly thin. Except in the chest, naturally.

Or unnaturally, in most of the cases.

"I didn't know the sight of silicone made your tongue get hard," Fiora said.

I looked away from the dark-haired Eurasian wearing a spangled bustier and tattered blue jeans frayed up to the crack in her shapely ass.

"My taste for trash with flash is well documented," I said.

To prove my point I looked at Fiora more thoroughly than I had at the Eurasian waif. There was plenty to look at. Fiora's streetwalker garb fit right into the Malibu crowd.

"I'll trash your flash if you don't quit publicly drooling over exotic women," she said distinctly.

"Do you see Franklin?" Benny asked impatiently.

"No," I said.

"If he's running true to type," Fiora said, "he'll be in a room somewhere cutting a deal. He won't appear until it's time to pass the plate through the congregation."

The acid in her voice could have etched steel.

"The check he writes," she continued, "will be displayed face up and have at least four zeros to the left of the decimal point. The check may or may not get cashed, but it gives the rest of the world something to shoot for."

Benny muttered about people who masturbated in public.

"Well, I'll be damned," Fiora said softly. "The Red Nun is still hard at work."

I followed Fiora's glance to a knot of guests clustered around an intense, plain-faced woman with mouse-brown hair. Dressed in loose trousers and a lumpy tunic, she was by far the ugliest duckling on the pond. It didn't seem to matter to the people around her. They looked spellbound by her impassioned conversation.

"Who is she?" Benny asked softly.

"A Maryknoll nun," Fiora said, in a voice that carried no farther than our ears. "Her specialty used to be so-called refugee relief in El Salvador."

"You have something against refugees?" I asked.

"No. Hypocrisy is another matter."

I looked at Fiora. The acid was back in her voice. I was surprised the words didn't smoke.

"She worked in tandem with a hard-eyed colonel and a flashy little piece of ass who begged for contributions for the poor refugees while wearing designer jeans, silk blouse, and a Krugerrand set with diamonds on a chain around her neck.''

"Tacky," I said.

"It got worse. The money was all for medicine and baby formula, right?"

Benny made an overripe sound. Apparently he had heard this one before.

"I drew the nun aside," Fiora said, "and made noises about contributing ten thousand dollars. Only catch was, I wanted the money to go for weapons to fight the good fight against capitalist imperialists."

"What happened?" I asked.

"The righteous bitch said taking my money would violate her vows, but why didn't I talk to the good colonel?"

I looked at the thin-lipped nun and decided that religion hadn't changed much since the Inquisition.

"Limousine liberals." Benny made another fruity sound. "God rot their miserable souls. If I thought it would do any good, I'd be out in the bushes throwing Molotov cocktails."

I gave the room another long look but saw nothing interesting. Time to begin moving and shaking.

"If you get bored waiting for your personal earthquake to come back," I said, "work the crowd for gossip about Visual Arts Studio."

"Where are you going?" Fiora asked.

"Hunting," I said. "If you hear loud noises and police whistles, don't wait for me. Just get in the Beast and head south."

Fiora would like to have argued, but we had nothing new to say on the subject of my methods. The subject of my drawbacks had also been thoroughly vetted. Nothing new there either.

Benny rolled past me and out onto the broad, smooth deck where a cocktail circle of beefy, bearded types in plaid shirts and Birkenstocks stood cheek by jowl with earth mothers in hand-beaded leathers that cost enough to keep a Native American family in beans and bread for a year. Earth First! buttons were prominently displayed.

Radical environmentalists and Monkey-Wrenchers, the Black Panthers of the Nineties, de rigueur at all politically correct gatherings.

Fiora chose a bunch of suits and began infiltrating. Before I crossed the room, she was exchanging insider gossip about the Tokyo stock market crash and its effect on Japanese financing for Hollywood movies. I doubt if any of the men heard exactly what she was saying. They were too busy looking at her underwear.

Later I was going to burn that damned outfit.

For now, I headed down the side stair and out onto the lawn, looking for Franklin. Sixty seconds later I discovered that social mores hadn't changed all that much in Hollywood. The smokin', tokin', and snortin' was simply more discreet. Just walking downwind of a trio of young musicians made me start to feel light-headed.

I wondered how the LAPD motor cops felt about standing eyes front on the highway for an entire evening, all the while knowing they could make dozens of felony possession arrests just down the hill at the party.

A quick circuit of the grounds gave me the layout in case I had to leave in a hurry. Then I started going through the house. There was enough primitive art to stock sixteen African villages. Franklin must have gotten off on ugly, spooky masks and on statues that were anatomically as well as politically correct.

The house itself yielded a certain irony. Its remodeled interior and huge new decks were cut from the finest heartwood taken from big, old-growth coastal redwoods. No wonder Fiora's ears were laid back. It's so easy to wear a button and so hard to use plebeian lumber in your own home.

The buffet dinner was multicultural, species-diverse, and no threat to the rain forests at all. Red meat was as absent as Kelsey's nuts. The chicken was free-range and hormone-free. The side dishes included Salvadoran *pupusas*, Mexican enchiladas, and some very good black beans and rice with Cuban spices. It was all so environmentally hip and politically correct it made my butt ache.

No Barry Franklin, though. I was beginning to wonder if his own parties bored him as much as they were boring me.

It took me ten more minutes, but I finally found Franklin ensconced in a secluded meditation garden set off by stone blocks that looked like they had been ripped off from Machu Picchu. He was just finishing a call on one of three portable phones—color coded, of course—that were arrayed on what looked suspiciously like an ancient altar.

I pulled the brown envelope out of my jacket pocket and headed for him.

Franklin had changed less than Aileen. He was still handsome and dark-haired, with a healthy tennis tan and pearly teeth that Clark Gable would have died for. Franklin was still very much the man in control, too. When I stepped into his private garden, he glanced toward me with the cold, measuring eyes of a professional gambler—lots of brain, little heart, and no nerves.

All Franklin saw was a big black silhouette. I had my back to the discreet spotlights that illuminated demons caught in a moment of indescribable ecstasy or damnation.

I held the first photo in a shaft of light and waited.

"What's this?" Franklin said impatiently.

"You tell me."

Curiosity is a funny thing. Franklin was irked, but he couldn't help looking at the first photo. The street scene in Puerto Peñasco stopped him cold.

Then I flashed him the second photo, the one that showed his face and the faces of the two Mexican assassins clearly. He made a stifled sound and looked up at me, but my face was still in shadow. I waited for a long three count.

"Friends of yours?" I asked.

SEVENTEEN

Franklin's pupils dilated with raw fear. He stood up fast.

But he was a cold customer, accustomed to masking the few human reactions he had. Before he drew another breath, he was fully under control once more.

"Do I know you?" Franklin asked.

The tone was an accusation, not a question.

"We met a long time ago," I said, "just before you went down to Mexico with Aileen Camp and a guy named Jake."

Franklin frowned as though trying to remember, then shook his head blankly.

"Mexico? I was only there once. I didn't like it."

His distaste seemed genuine. He turned away, dismissing memories, Mexico, and me.

I stepped into his path.

· "You do remember Aileen?" I asked calmly.

Franklin's nod was minute.

"Jake was the guy Aileen lived with," I explained.

"Aileen lived with a lot of guys back then. Still does."

"Jake was different."

Franklin looked bored.

"Jake delivered kilo bricks to movie types in Venice," I said.

"What do you want, a chorus from 'Yellow Submarine'?"

"If your memory goes back that far, you can remember what happened a few days after your trip to Mexico." I put the picture under his nose and added, "Can't you, *babe*."

Franklin's eyes were hooded and his face showed no expression. But his hands were slowly drawing into fists. I doubted that he was even aware of it.

"Maybe this will help you recall," I said, flashing the copy of his bank record. "You made a hell of a profit that month. A little something you picked up in Mexico from Jake's old connections?"

Franklin's response was an ironic smile. Though he seemed genuinely amused, the smile didn't light up his eyes.

"Now I get it," he said. "This is a shakedown."

"You don't have enough money to buy me off."

"Yeah, yeah, yeah," he said without conviction. "Who are you? Who sent you?"

"A dead man."

I moved into the light. Franklin made some odd noises and stepped backward real quick.

"Jake!"

"Close enough," I agreed.

"But—you're dead!"

"So are the other two guys in this picture. I put both of them in the ground."

I held my thumb and forefinger out like a gun and pantomimed pulling the trigger.

"You're a dead man walking, Franklin. Think about it. I sure as hell have."

Franklin shook himself like a dog coming out of water.

I turned to walk away.

"Wait a minute!" he said urgently. "I don't know who's been jobbing you, but you've got it all wrong!"

I kept walking.

"Last week somebody tried to sell me those same pictures, and the Xerox, too!" he called.

That stopped me.

"There's no dirty money in my accounts, and I can prove it," Franklin said.

After a heartbeat, I turned around and looked at him.

"As for the pictures," he said with returning confidence, "they're phony as a starlet's smile."

I waited for him to say something new.

"They've been digitized," Franklin explained. "The photos aren't really real."

I looked at the photo of two assassins and a Hollywood type. The photo looked back at me, a seamless instant of reality taken from the past.

Or was it?

"It's called CGI," Franklin said quickly. "Computer-generated imaging. It's how the Terminator came through the linoleum. Slick, huh? But it's fake all the same."

For just an instant, I believed him.

Then I remembered what Franklin did for a living. I also remembered the one honest, unguarded reaction I had seen in his eyes when he recognized me.

Fear.

"You say you've seen the pictures before?" I asked.

"Yeah. A scumbag screenwriter named Moreton wanted a hundred grand not to show them around. I told him to jerk off."

Franklin smiled at me. It was a good poker-table smile, cold enough to frost beer on a hot night.

"How much did you pay for the pictures?" he asked idly.

"Moreton," I said, ignoring Franklin's question. "Big fat guy with a scraggly beard and stringy hair tied back in a ponytail?"

I was describing the man who had nicked the black knapsack, the guy whose voice I couldn't quite remember on the telephone.

"That's him," Franklin agreed. "I used to represent him. No more. Stupid I can live with. No talent is a deal breaker. A cockroach has more talent than Harry Moreton."

"He still around Hollywood?"

Franklin was more than happy to talk about Moreton.

"Yeah, but he hasn't sold anything in so long he's about to lose his Guild affiliation. Then he'll be out on his fat ass."

"He was in Puerto Peñasco with you."

Franklin didn't want to talk about that.

"I remember you now," he said. "The young smartass that followed Jake around like a shadow.

He called you something . . . Fiddler? Yeah, that's it. Fiddler.''

"That's it."

"Did Aileen ever get both of you in bed at the same time? Or was it some other blonde Jake had the hots for that you both were screwing at the same time?"

"Memory coming back?" I asked, smiling. "Good. I'd hate to kill a man who couldn't remember why he was going to die."

Franklin's voice followed me as I walked away through the darkness.

"Get the hell off my property! And get out of my town! I fuck little boys like you as a warm-up for important things!"

There was more in that vein, none of it original or amusing. The man should have taken a course in cursing from the Ice Cream King. Benny always has something original and nasty for such occasions.

Fiora and Benny were waiting for me at the top of the stairs. I cruised past them without a word, headed back through the demon-ridden house and out the front door. Fiora caught up quickly and paced me without a word. Benny joined us as we waited on the smooth flagstone walk for a valet to bring the truck.

No one spoke until we were in the Beast and beyond the iron gates.

"Well?" Fiora finally said to me.

"According to Franklin, the pictures are phony. They've been thoroughly fornicated by a computer."

"You don't sound convinced."

"Pictures. No pictures." I shrugged. "It doesn't matter. Franklin is good for Jake's death. I saw it in his eyes."

"Are you sure?" she asked.

"Yes."

"How sure?"

"I could execute him with a small pistol, watch his blood run out in the sand, and walk away."

She blew a slow, deep breath from her lungs. The look she gave me was unhappy and frightened. But she didn't say anything more.

Benny did, his voice matter-of-fact.

"Then we've got a problem, mate. Franklin isn't some no-name Mexican gunsel. Greasing him will be easy enough. Getting away with it won't be."

"Why do you think he's still alive?" I asked.

"I thought you might have decided to leave him alone until you figure out who's winding you up and sending you after him like a smart bomb," Benny retorted.

"Dumb bomb," Fiora muttered.

I ignored her.

"As long as the information is good," I said to Benny, "I don't care who else benefits from Franklin's death."

"What makes you so certain he's guilty?" Fiora asked.

"He's afraid of me."

"Maybe he's scared to death of what you might do to his big deal," she said coolly. "In Hollywood, money is life."

"What big deal?"

"Franklin is behind the takeover of Visual Arts Studios."

I'm glad I'll never have to play poker with Fiora. She read my surprise as though my face were a balance sheet in full sunlight. She gave me a smug feline smile.

"I guess that explains why Aileen didn't want her tickets for tonight," I finally said. "Where did you pick up that little bundle of dynamite?"

"I used to work out at a club with Lacy Timmons, one of the junior people in Franklin's agency. I ran into Lacy in the powder room. She plugged some of the gaps in the Wall Street rumors."

"What rumors?" Benny asked.

"Franklin is brokering the takeover for Santori Shimbun, one of the big Japanese media *zaibatsu*. He's got several billion bucks behind him, and he wants to pick up Visual Arts. If he can."

"A guy with several billion bucks can do pretty much what he wants," I said. "Especially in this town."

"Keep it in mind," Benny said from the back seat.

He wasn't telling me to back off. Benny understands the benefits of surgical execution too well for that. He was simply telling me I had to be titty-fingered on this one.

"There are lots of people who don't want the deal to close," Fiora said. "Principal among them is Aileen Camp. She'd be out of a job."

I remembered Aileen's complaint about being a hired hand.

"Executives play musical chairs all the time," I pointed out. "It would be easier for Aileen to get a new job than it would be to set up a guy as powerful as Barry Franklin to take a fall for an old murder."

Fiora gave me a funny look.

"Aileen is very shrewd about the male psyche," Fiora said. "Men with a sense of personal honor are no challenge for her. They are so simple, so direct, and so *predictable*. No problem to wind up and send off in any old direction at all."

"Should I be insulted?" I asked Benny.

He shrugged. If I was insulted, he would have to be insulted, too.

"Let me see those pictures again," Benny said.

I pulled out the envelope and handed it over the back seat. He switched on the overhead light.

No one spoke again until we were in the hotel room.

"Franklin wasn't lying about the pictures being buggered," Benny said calmly.

"What?" Fiora and I said together.

Benny wheeled over to the coffee table and spread out the pictures.

"Bring me a beer and a table lamp and I'll explain," he said.

"Make that two beers," I said, heading for the bedroom.

When I came out with a lamp, Fiora was putting two beers on the table. I plugged in the lamp. Yellow light flooded the photos.

"I missed it this afternoon," Benny said. "It's a damn good job, but whoever did it left a few faint tracks. Look at this."

He pointed to the third picture, the one where the package was changing hands. All three principals in the shot were so fascinated by the bag that it became the focal point of the picture. Everything else just faded into the background.

"Look hard," Benny said.

"I'm looking," I muttered.

"Don't feel bad. I missed it the first and second times myself."

I was going down for the third time when Fiora sat beside me on the couch. We stared at the picture together.

Nothing doing.

"Turn it upside down so you don't look at the money, only at the other details," he suggested.

We did and stared some more. I caught the discrepancy just before Fiora did, but I couldn't put it in words as quickly as she did.

"The curb," she said.

She pointed to what at first looked like a break in the low brick berm that ran along the street in one corner of the picture.

"I thought it was broken," she said. "But now it looks—"

"—like two pieces that were glued together just a little bit off," I said, interrupting.

"Digitized, not glued," Benny said. "It's a discontinuity in the grain pattern."

"Translation, please," Fiora said.

"If you break the entire photo down with a high-res scanner"—Benny burped gently—"and remove a bunch of the pixels and replace them with background pixels, you can get discontinuities like this."

"Meaning that something has been removed from the photo?" I asked.

"Yes."

"They can do that?" Fiora asked.

"You bet your black bustier they can," I said.

"The technology started with satellite television transmission years ago and has mushroomed since," Benny explained. "They take a black-and-white picture, reduce it to two hundred and fifty-six shades of gray, and go to work on it."

"Go to work on it," Fiora said. "How?"

"In Hollywood the process is used to splice in special effects, create monsters inside actors' brains or bellies, that sort of thing."

I stared at the photo. Once the discontinuity had been recognized, it stuck out like a peanut in a bowl of rice.

Franklin's fear had been like that, too. Obvious if you knew what to look for.

I did.

For a time I studied the picture, trying to visualize what might have filled the fuzzy, grainy discontinuity on the ground. The suspicious area lay between two dark shapes. After a minute I realized that the shapes were shadows cast by Barry Franklin and my dead pal Loco Cardenas.

The third shape on the ground must have been another shadow, that of a person who was shorter than either of the men. But the spot that would have been occupied by the source of the third shadow was a blank wall.

"Someone stood between Franklin and Cardenas," I said.

"Bingo," Benny said.

"Who?" Fiora asked.

"It's impossible to tell, without the negative," Benny said. "My preference is Bobby Soliz."

"Aileen Camp," suggested Fiora.

"You're both guessing," I said.

"Guesses are all we have," Benny said. "The only way to know for sure is to find the original negative."

"How do we do that? We don't know who has it or who sold it to us."

"Sure we do," I said.

"We do?" Benny asked.

"Franklin told me."

"And you trust him?" Fiora asked sarcastically.

"No. But I trust my own eyes. Harry Moreton, the fat bastard who picked up the backpack."

"Where is he now?" Benny asked instantly.

I looked at him. "I got the name. The address is your problem."

Benny drained his beer, wheeled over to the computer Fiora had rented, hooked up the modem, dialed a number, and began to type at about Mach 3. He cursed at Mach 4.

Tracking down a man used to be a long process of interviewing relatives, neighbors, bar flies, cabbies, and hookers. Since the advent of the computer age, tracking the human animal has turned into a game of data bases and modem accesses.

Everybody leaves electronic tracks in this society. You just have to know where to look for them.

Benny knew where.

I drank my beer and watched Benny sniff the ether for sign of Harry's fat tracks.

"Bugger all," Benny muttered after a time.

"Problems?" I asked.

"He's such a loser that TRW gave up keeping his credit rating five years ago."

Fiora blinked, impressed that any living American could sink beneath TRW's notice.

"Try DMV," I suggested.

"Rack off."

I shut up and left Benny to do what he is good at doing.

"The California Department of Motor Vehicles informs me that the silly sod's license was revoked for DUI," Benny said.

"When?" I asked.

"Multiple arrests," Benny muttered. "The bloke

drinks the way other people breathe. They jerked his ticket about . . . five years ago."

"Same time TRW dropped him," Fiora noted.

"No hits on Lexus and Nexus," Benny said. "He didn't make any headlines worth clipping."

"So much for the easy ones," I said.

I picked up my beer and settled in for a long run. The minutes went by, punctuated by Benny's clipped statements.

"Property tax rolls, no hits. . . .

"State criminal defendant index, negative. . . .

"Federal district court index, not a bloody mention."

Benny was getting testy. He tapped the keyboard with the nail on his little finger.

"I thought this guy was supposed to be some kind of big-time screenwriter," Benny said finally.

"Small-time screenwriter," I corrected. "So small he's about to disappear from show biz completely, according to Franklin."

"I wonder if there's a computerized master list of Writer's Guild members," Benny said.

He did a directory check and came up blank.

"Bloody has-been," he muttered.

"Try bankruptcy court," Fiora suggested. "I've never known a screenwriter who wasn't bankrupt, one way or another, one time or another."

Benny looked at me.

I shrugged. "What do we have to lose?"

He started tapping and grunting and transmitting over the modem, twanging the electronic grids like a spider checking his elaborate web for fresh captures.

"Did I ever tell you how to defeat the system?" Benny asked absently as he stared at the screen, waiting for a response.

"No."

"Piece of cake," he said. "Drop a letter from your name, add an extra week to your date of birth, and transpose two digits in your Social Security number."

With that, he jabbed a function key, waited for a response, and kept talking.

"So Harold J. Moreton, DOB 4/13/43, Social Security Number 476-46-1493, becomes Hal Morton, 4/20/43, Social Security Number 476-46-1439."

I sat up straight and stared.

"The computer will search until hell freezes solid," Benny said, "and never make a hit because the quarry has gone to ground in a new hole. If anybody accuses you of lying about your background, you just shrug and talk about minimum-wage data entry clerks."

I laughed out loud. "I like it!"

"Not as much as you'll like this," he promised.

Two seconds later I was staring over Benny's shoulder at the screen.

"What is it?" Fiora asked.

"Harold J. Moreton filed for personal bankruptcy two years ago," I said. "In the process, he protected his principal personal dwelling, a house on Summer Skies Drive in Studio City."

Fiora went to her pile of personal stuff, pulled out a Thomas Brothers map book, and began tracking the address as I read it to her.

eIGHTEEN

Studio City is one of those "other side of the hill" suburbs, a place where entertainers and actors camp out in half-million-dollar houses until they get rich enough to move to Beverly Hills. What with all the high turnover of rising and falling stars, most of the houses have been remodeled a dozen times. There's hardly an original piece of stucco left. The cul-de-sacs are lined with every style from ersatz Prairie School and Pasadena Craftsman's Cottage to Cape Cod and aggressively ugly modern.

Upward mobility seemed to have skipped Moreton's place. The house was a twenties Tudor with brickwork that was coming loose and wood trim that trailed streamers of peeling paint. It looked old and scabrous in the blue-white light of the streetlamp. The roses needed pruning and the grass was knee-high because the gardener had quit coming around.

Good news. That meant the private security service whose medallion stood in the overgrown rose bed had probably quit, too.

I had Fiora circle the block several times, checking approaches and trying to spot the neighborhood watchdogs before I went prowling.

Benny found a spot for his van in a cul-de-sac down the hill. From there he could watch the main streets for any black-and-white squad cars. Both he and Fiora had cellular phones, but I would be out of contact as soon as I stepped out of the Beast.

Californians love their brush-covered hillsides, and to hell with fire season. If people ever realized how attractive those hillsides are to prowlers, the brush would be scabbed off in a hot minute. But the scrub was still in place, good cover waiting to be used.

Fiora let me off at a vacant lot two blocks below Moreton's house. I slid into the chaparral and became part of the predatory night life.

The peaked Tudor roof of Moreton's house was a good landmark. Though my eyes adjusted quickly to the darkness, I made slow progress. The brush was dry. A careless step could sound like a brick dropped into a basket of crystal.

About fifteen yards from the chain-link fence I stumbled over either a large cat or a small possum. He was more surprised than I was. I must be getting better at being a predator. Not exactly a comforting thought.

I pulled on thin rubber gloves—the kind your dentist uses—and closed in on the house. The row of pencil cypress at the rear of Moreton's yard cast deep fingers of shadow across the moonlight. I used one of them to move in close. There were lights in the Tudor windows but no sign of movement inside.

The hinges on the back gate squeaked a little. I left it open. The backyard landscaping had gone feral. What once had been a fish pond now stank of slime and produced regular crops of mosquitoes for the entire neighborhood to enjoy.

I wondered how much money Moreton had pissed away in his flush years, how many fads and fancies he had exhausted in the pursuit of new ways to feel important, how many service people had serviced him right out of every penny he made. Funny, but they all had forgotten his name when the money ran out.

Ah, Hollywood. Bloodsucker capital of the cosmos.

But then, nobody held a gun to Moreton's head and forced him to stay here.

The neighborhood was quiet. Across the small brush-choked canyon, colored ghosts flickered in upstairs windows, bedroom Sonys playing X-rated videos or late-night talk shows.

There were no shadows in Moreton's window. As I eased closer to the back door, I listened for sounds from inside. At first I heard nothing. Then the rehearsed noise of a laugh track or a studio audience welled up, faded, and returned.

I wondered whether Moreton watched Arsenio Hall or Jay Leno. The laughter gave no clue.

The basement door was locked. I went up the wooden stairs and onto the deck that overlooked the yard. The floorboards next to the chaise lounge and the redwood picnic table were lined with beer bottles, some overturned, and brimming ashtrays. The air smelled of stale tobacco smoke and something even less appealing.

At first glance the place looked like someone had thrown a hell of a party. On closer inspection, it appeared to have been a party for one. There was a solitary, sullen feel to the house.

I remembered what Franklin had said about Moreton's fortunes and the revoked driver's license. The screenwriter's downhill run appeared more precipitous than most, even for as fad-ridden and volatile a place as Hollywood.

A flicker of movement caught my eye. The sliding glass door at the center of the deck was ajar. A lank curtain stirred slightly in the breeze.

Before the curtain twitched again, I had my back against the wall beside the door, listening hard. Moreton had Arsenio on the tube. A studio audience hooted and howled as the host got off a good line.

The audience in the Moreton household on Summer Skies Drive didn't laugh. Dead drunk, probably.

I peeled the billowing curtain aside and slipped into the living room. The house stank. The maid service had gone the way of the gardener. Light from the kitchen cast eerie shadows through the boar's nest of a living room: discarded newspapers on the floor, tables littered with half-eaten microwave dinners and empty bottles, dirty clothes, and used bath towels.

Moreton was still bathing. Barely. He hadn't slurred his words on the telephone, but that meant little. Heavy drinkers often can seem to be sober for a few minutes at a time—or even a few hours—before they slip back into the stupor of the end-game alcoholic.

I bent over a beer bottle and sniffed. It was half full of flat, bitter-smelling brew. A cheap supermarket brand. The bottle had been started, set aside, and forgotten. It smelled unappealing, but not as bad as whatever was curdling the air farther inside the house.

Moving silently across the dirty carpet, I went from the living room to the hallway. The sound of the television got clearer. So did the smell. It reminded me of an open sewer with Eau de Armpit thrown in for leavening.

The next room was an office. In the old days, when Moreton was making money, he had spent a lot on his workplace. The word-processing computer system had been top of the line ten years ago. Now it was a clunky technological dinosaur.

The walls of the office were lined with bookshelves that were full of leather-bound volumes of unproduced screenplays. In Hollywood, they're known as "shelf art." The remaining shelves were filled with an arcane sound system—vacuum tubes rather than transistors, turntable for vinyl records rather than compact discs.

The flashy chrome told me the system was new. Moreton must have been lonely enough to prefer the crackle, pop, and hiss of old technology. Or maybe some salesperson had sold Moreton a bill of goods about the "warmth" of Rice Crispies-style reception.

Along one wall was a beat-up leather couch, the kind where a writer flakes out and stares at the television set or the ceiling while awaiting the muse. Harold Moreton was stretched out on the couch, dressed in a T-shirt and dirty shorts.

I had been half right about Moreton being dead drunk. He was sure enough dead. What few brain cells alcohol hadn't killed were now sprayed against the leather arm of the couch.

That explained the sewer smell. Moreton's body had lain there long enough for his bowel to void. An hour, maybe two.

The screenwriter had died easily. There were no signs of struggle. A fresh row of Heineken beer bottles, four empty, one partly full, stood on the floor beneath his bloodless hand. Moreton had been topping off before going to sleep or passing out, whichever came first.

The shooter had entered the same way I had. He had covered the gun with a throw pillow to muffle the sound. Then he had placed the muzzle against Moreton's numb forehead and pulled the trigger, turning dead drunk into dead, period.

The pillow now lay on Moreton's chest. I could smell the burned gunpowder on it without touching the cloth, the same way I could see the gore, the same way I could sense the fetid underbelly of Moreton's life.

Whoever killed Moreton might have done him a favor. There was a diseased stink in the house that went beyond the contents of his loosened bowels. Terminal alcoholism is a slow, savage way to die.

Arsenio cut to a commercial while I did a quick pass around the office. On the desktop next to the word processor there was a new plastic pack of brown business envelopes. They were the same size and appearance as the ones Koo-Koo and Moreton himself had used.

The wastebasket beside the desk held ripped-out magazine pages with ragged holes cut into them. I didn't bother to find out which page matched which word of the paste-up note I had at home. I didn't need any more proof. Even a court of law would have had to concede that Moreton was the man who had sold me the photos.

Death of a Salesman. Too bad, how sad, and where the hell did you hide the negative?

A quick reconnoiter of the rest of the house told me what I already knew. Moreton had lacked imagination. The black backpack was stuffed into a pillowcase and tossed in the back of a big bedroom closet upstairs. It felt like it still contained most of the cash, minus whatever Moreton had spent on Heineken.

I threw one strap over my shoulder and headed downstairs with the backpack. This time I gave the kitchen a good look. At a guess, nothing had been cleaned in a month. But then, nothing had been used for cooking, either, unless you count the microwave as a cooking tool.

On a table in the breakfast nook was a pile of mail. Most of it was supermarket fliers and bulk-rate postcards with pictures of missing kids on one side and ads for carpet cleaners on the other. A three-week-old letter, certified, return receipt requested, had been ripped open. It contained an eviction notice. The Los Angeles County Marshal was due in on Friday.

At least Moreton wasn't going to have to worry about sleeping in his car.

I went to the office for a last look around. In the manner of a homicide detective, I stood in the doorway, trying to see past the slab of dead meat to the rest of the room.

The trash basket invited another look. I tipped it over with a toe and spread the contents with rubber-tipped fingers. At the bottom was a shipping envelope, white with a black logo in the spot reserved for the return address. I knelt down to read it. Digital Graphics Laboratory. An address on Melrose Avenue in old Hollywood.

I wondered if they had held on to the negative or given it back.

While I was down at floor level, I looked around the room again. That's how I saw the round brass cartridge case on the floor underneath the couch, where it had fallen and rolled, or where it had been carelessly kicked aside.

Even in the dim light, something about the unusual size and shape of the cartridge dug at me. I slid a couple of Heineken bottles aside and groped beneath the couch.

The minute I felt the weight of the brass, I knew I was in deep kim chee.

The cartridge case was too familiar, altogether distinctive. The cylinder had started out as a round for a high-powered .308 Winchester hunting rifle. But this shell casing was only half as long as a normal rifle shell. It had been cut down to a straight-sided cartridge with a neck opening that was exactly .451 inches in diameter and held a slug of that size.

A chopped-down .308 rifle cartridge case fit only one firearm in the world, an exotic pistol called a .451 Detonics. There are only a handful of those guns in the world and probably no more than five in Southern California.

At that moment, one of them was in the console between the front seats of the Suburban that was parked down the street, waiting for me.

I hoped.

I picked up the phone and punched in the number of the Beast's cellular. Fiora answered before the end of the first ring.

"Look in the console. Is my gun still there?"

I heard the distinct click of the console's latch.

"The holster's here, but it's empty."

"*Shit.*"

"What's wrong?"

"Tell Benny about the holster. He'll know."

"But—"

There was a mechanical beep; Fiora had installed call waiting when we bought the Beast.

"Hold on," Fiora said.

I didn't argue. I didn't want to go into the specifics of what had gone wrong on an open cellular line.

Besides, I was too busy cursing myself for leaving the gun in the truck at Franklin's party. A lot of second-story men work as parking attendants. It gives them a hell of an opportunity to match car registration with home address and the keys to go with it. Wax impression kits are small, portable, and quickly used.

Damn.

Fiora cut back to me. Her voice was clipped, urgent.

"Benny says to get out. A squad car just turned up the hill."

"Fast or slow?"

"Slow. No headlights."

Not good news. Smart cops like to sneak up on hot prowler calls with their lights off.

"Check the map," I said. "See where the canyon in back of the house intersects a major street. I'll meet you there."

I was out the back door and into the brush when I heard the minimal sound of an LAPD cruiser ghosting lightless up Summer Skies Drive.

nINETEEN

The stub of a broken branch caught me below the left eye somewhere in the canyon. I spooked a pair of raccoons that were hunting for grubs by turning over strips of newly laid sod at the edge of someone's yard. Otherwise the retreat down the little canyon behind Moreton's house was uneventful.

Fifteen minutes after I had called Fiora, I stumbled up the bank to the edge of Coldwater Canyon Boulevard. I had traveled a bit over a mile. I was sweaty, scratched, and covered with stickers. The Surburban was just coming down the hill. No cops were in attendance.

I stepped into the roadway and flagged down the Beast. Fiora looked surprised to see the backpack when I tossed it onto the rear seat and climbed into the truck. Then she looked at my face.

"What does the other guy look like?" she asked unhappily.

I touched the spot on my face where the branch had struck me. Half-dried blood smeared my fingers.

"The other guy isn't bleeding," I said. "Not anymore."

"What?"

I fished the spent brass shell casing out of my pocket and showed it to her.

"Moreton's dead," I said bluntly. "That's bad for him. What's bad for us is that somebody shot him with a Detonics Four-fifty-one."

"Signature weapon," Fiora said.

"You've been listening to Benny."

"You should have, too."

"I know. But don't tell him I said so."

Fiora's face was quiet and composed in the glow of the dashboard, but when she looked at me, worry had etched little wrinkles around her eyes.

"So somebody used a gun that can be traced directly to you to kill a man who had stung you for twenty-five thousand bucks," Fiora summarized.

I grunted.

"Not bad, as setups go," she said. "Not bad at all."

"You needn't sound so happy."

"Do I look happy?" she asked through her teeth.

"Hell."

"What now?"

"Find Benny. Then find me some clean clothes and a little peroxide. These cuts itch."

Fiora punched in Benny's number and handed the unit to me. In a departure from his customary phone habits, Benny picked up the cellular on the first ring.

"Where are you?" he asked.

"Clean," I said.

"Your back trail isn't. Uniforms and plainclothes all over the lot."

Detective units already on the scene. Odd.

And unnerving.

"That was quick," I said. "Must have been a hot tip."

"No shit."

Benny ignores the federal disapproval of profanity on the air waves.

"Are they working the canyon?" I asked.

"I didn't see any flashlights outside."

Good news. Finally. They hadn't figured out that somebody had just been in the house.

"Meet us at the market on Highland," I said.

For once, I hung up before Benny did.

Fiora drove us over the hill and back into the great pulsing gut of the city. She found an all-night drugstore and rummaged through the cheap clothing section until she found something to cover both of us.

We were sitting in the blue-vapor daylight of the parking lot, dabbing disinfectant on my cuts, when Benny's van pulled up. He shut off the engine and looked at my face.

"You look like hell," he said.

"Go kiss a platypus."

I gave Benny a fast rundown and showed him the brass. He looked at me and decided to save the "I told you so" for a time when I was in a better mood. He took the cartridge case, squinted at it in the dim light, and handed it back to me.

"You aren't out of the bush yet," Benny said. "The second they recover the slug from Moreton's corpse they'll know they're looking for a Detonics.

You've bought some time by finding the cartridge case, but bloody little else."

"Yeah."

Benny tugged at the thick black beard under his chin.

"There's something nasty going on here," he said after a time. "Too much happening too quick. Did you ever feel like somebody was jerking your chain just to hear you bark?"

"My only questions have to do with who and why," I said. "I'm guessing it's Barry Franklin."

"Any particular reason?"

"The gun was stolen at his party."

Fiora spoke before Benny could.

"But Aileen is the one who set you up with the tickets."

"Jesus," I said, flinching as Fiora laid a cotton ball along the cut near my eye. "What is that stuff, kerosene?"

"Hold still."

"It stings. A lot."

"That's how you know you're alive," she retorted.

She slopped more disinfectant onto a fresh piece of cotton and went to work again. It stung like bloody hell. I pretended not to notice.

It wasn't easy. I would have sworn she was debriding the cut with a hacksaw.

"That should do it," Fiora said finally.

"Thank God."

"You're welcome."

I looked at Fiora. There was some fresh blood on the cuff of her filmy blouse. She dabbed at it, then shrugged. I had the feeling she would never wear the outfit again anyway.

"What now?" Benny asked.

He looked rested and ready to roll. Fiora didn't. She had dark circles under her eyes, legacy of too many of the wrong kind of dreams. I thought about the big soft bed in the Chateau Beverly.

"Why don't you take Fiora back to the hotel?" I suggested. "I've got one stop to make over on Melrose."

Benny nodded.

Fiora didn't.

"I'm going wherever you go," she said.

There are many times when I'll discuss, argue, or shout about things with Fiora, but not when she uses a certain deadly quiet tone. When she sounds like that, I might as well save my energy for something I have a chance of doing, like turning back the tides with my tongue.

"Let me rephrase that," I said to Benny. "Why don't you go on back to the hotel and get some rest? Fiora says she isn't at all tired."

"I've got a better idea," he said. "You two go and do whatever it was you wanted to do while I go out and get something to eat before I go back to the hotel. Something light. Maybe a Tommy's chiliburger and a pile of chili fries."

"Nobody around here takes orders worth a damn," I observed.

"Only because we keep getting such dumb orders," Fiora said calmly.

"She's right, mate," Benny said. "You sure you don't need me?"

"I'm sure. There's enough of a crowd as it is."

He started up the van and headed away, driving toward Beverly and Ramparts.

* * *

The film lab on Melrose was in a seedy building next to a hot-sheet motel and just east of the old Paramount lot. The neighborhood might have been bright and bustling in the thirties; now it was old and as tough as the arriving immigrants.

Signs were in Spanish, Armenian, and Thai in alternating blocks. The gang graffiti overlapped, which meant trouble. Security was brutal and cheap. Junkyard dogs snarled at the end of long chains. Concrete walls were studded with broken bottles or hung with razor wire. Mean streets, and nobody made any bones about it.

Fiora cruised the block a few times before she made one pass through the alley. The lab was on the second floor above a *farmacia* and a travel agency. The alarm box on the outside wall of the old building was new and freshly painted. That meant the damn thing probably worked, but there was no way to tell whether it called LAPD or simply yelped like a bored dog.

Fiora was tired of playing the streetwalker game, so she waited in the truck while I checked into the No-Tell Motel. I specified a room on the side of the motel that overlooked the back of the film lab.

The clerk was a sullen black woman with gold caps on both incisors and the body of an Amazon.

"Thirty minutes?" she asked.

"All night."

She looked me over skeptically and shook her head.

"Ain't no white boy can keep it up that long without black help," she said.

"Then we'll bring you in to get me restarted."

She gave a hoot of laughter and smiled like a junkyard dog. One gold cap was decorated with a cutaway of a five-pointed star. The other had a crescent moon. On her they looked good.

She glanced out at Fiora in the truck and shook her head again.

"I gotta tell you, boy. Sometimes them blond street girls just don't wanna go the distance. They turns one trick, takes the money, and stuffs it up they noses. Then they be gone."

"If that happens, I'll definitely order from room service."

The star and crescent flashed again.

Since it was after midnight, she agreed to let the Sin Bin Suite until 10 A.M. for only seventy-eight bucks plus room tax.

"But that don't include no movies," she warned. "They's extra."

"We don't need audiovisual aids. We understand the principles involved."

The Sin Bin Suite was an old, standard-issue, smelly hot-sheet room. It had dusty velveteen curtains, a contraption called a "love swing" suspended from the ceiling, and a king-size waterbed. A full, leaking Jacuzzi had been shoehorned into the spot where the shower stall once stood. The Jacuzzi needed a shot of chlorine. The steam rising from its murky surface made the room smell like Moreton's fish pond.

Fiora came back from her inspection tour with her lip curled in frank disgust.

"I love you like a field of flowers," she said, "but I'm not going to be your parboiled lust slave tonight."

I looked like Kwame when he realizes he isn't going to get a romp on the beach.

"Do people really immerse their whole bodies in that thing?" Fiora asked, pointing to the sullen Jacuzzi.

"Up to their lips," I agreed cheerfully, "which is one of the reasons why we shouldn't. If you've seen enough, turn off the lights."

The lights went off instantly.

While I raised the blind on the room's back window, the one that looked right out on Melrose, Fiora tested the waterbed with her hand. The mattress gurgled as though it hadn't been properly filled. Then it undulated in a suggestive and intriguing way.

Fiora peeled back the coverlet and the polyester blanket. The sheets, though stained, were clean. She gave me a look that I interpreted as a leer.

"It would be a shame to waste seventy-eight bucks plus room tax, wouldn't it?" she asked.

"Work first, then play."

She stuck out her tongue.

"Hold the good thought," I said. "I'll be right back."

I opened the back window and stepped out on a rickety stairway that led down to an alley. Once on the ground, I circled around the block and came at the *farmacia* from the other direction.

Melrose was quite, almost surly. I eased into the sheltered stairway and climbed up to the second floor, where the lab was. The front door was glass. Between its faded letters I could see the reception area.

Nothing unexpected. Filing cabinets, a telephone on the secretary's desk, and an alarm control panel with blinking red lights on the wall behind the desk. The glass door was wired with no-nonsense contact pads. There was a transmitter cone for a sonic intrusion detection system in one corner.

A good system, probably designed to protect expensive photographic equipment in the back room. I listened through the glass but heard nothing. I grabbed the door handle and yanked, hard.

Nothing happened.

I shook the door again and again until finally the status lights shifted on the alarm's control panel. The bell in the alarm box on the back wall cut in and rang like a dirty mother, loud enough to wake the crackheads down the block.

Satisfied, I trotted down the stairs and crossed back to the Sin Bin Suite.

Fiora was sitting cross-legged on the bed. She had changed out of her streetwalker togs. Now she wore a pair of thin cotton drawstring pants and a T-shirt that would have been too big for me. The Kliban cartoon on the front of the shirt showed two cats sitting on top of a board fence. The tom had his arm around the kitty's shoulders. The cutline beneath said, IF I HAD TWO DEAD RATS I'D GIVE YOU ONE.

True love is grand to see.

I picked up the telephone, got an outside line, and called Benny at the Chateau Beverly. He wasn't in his room yet. I left a number at the desk where he could reach us.

All the while, the photo lab's alarm bell came through the walls like an alarm clock in the next room gone berserk.

When I put down the phone, Fiora was still staring at the television. For her, that was unusual. She likes television even less than she likes Merle Haggard concerts. I walked over, wanting to know what had intrigued her.

The picture was fractured, as though the set was badly out of adjustment. The sound was clear. Fiora had turned it way up to compensate for the raging alarm. Two inept actors were reading lines from a cocktail bar seduction scene. Nothing riveting there.

Yet Fiora didn't even look my way when I crossed in front of her to reach my side of the bed.

"I assume you're responsible for that racket across the street," she said.

"Yep."

I flopped down beside Fiora. The waterbed's reciprocal wave action nearly tossed her off. When everything settled down again, I stared at the television.

No wonder Fiora couldn't make heads or tails of the picture. It was scrambled and cross-cut. Stuffing coins into the box on top of the television would put things right instantly.

"No quarters?" I asked.

"They wanted two bucks a minute. Nothing but the real thing is that good."

The seduction must have been complete, because the dialogue fell apart into distinctly sexual grunts—male—and keening, lisping cries—female.

"Oh, yes. Ohh, yesss! Ohhh."

"She might have a career in real movies," Fiora said.

"She might come, too, but I wouldn't put serious money on it."

Fiora ignored my sarcasm.

"Think about it," she said. "Anyone who can sound that wispy and vapid and still have enough brains to cross the street could go the distance in Hollywood.''

"Yesss! Yesss! Yesssss!"

"Sounds like she's going the distance now."

Fiora ignored that, too.

Fake ecstasy keened right along with the real alarm. Sooner or later, one would climax and one would quit. I wasn't taking bets on which would happen first.

"What the hell are you watching, or trying to watch?" I asked finally.

Fiora consulted the dog-eared pasteboard schedule she had removed from the top of the television.

"I think this is *Faster, Pussycat, Wham, Bam,*" she said slowly. "But it could be *Nude on the Moon.*"

I stared at the screen. "It could be one of Picasso's women playing a flute, too."

"I don't think that's a flute."

"You sure? It's awful long for a—"

"Trust me," Fiora interrupted.

I stared some more.

"This I gotta see," I said. "I've got four quarters. Do you have four?"

"Squint."

"Huh?"

"Squint and pretend the screen is a jigsaw puzzle that's about half assembled."

"But—"

"If you unscramble the picture it won't be nearly as interesting."

I looked at Fiora.

"You're sure?" I asked.

"Whose imagination do you think is better, yours or the people who make skin flicks?"

I squinted.

Slowly the scrambled picture began to make sense. What I had mistaken for a flautist on a mangy bearskin rug turned out to be a naked woman engaged in a clear-cut violation of one of the California Penal Code's most unconstitutional sections.

Every so often the camera would switch to the face of an unusually ugly customer. He was grinning or snarling. Hard to tell, under the circumstances. I do know I've seen a more appealing rictus on a corpse.

It wasn't the sort of movie most folks over the age of thirteen want to see clearly, but, half distorted as it was, the whole thing had an oddly sexy quality. Almost subliminal. That's probably why people make love with their eyes closed.

Especially if their partner looks like a moth-eaten rug.

I reached out and touched Fiora's back with my hand. The set of her muscles told me she was tense and tired at the same time. I knew all the signs. She had spent too many days and nights like that when she was running her own company.

"Lie down and get some sleep," I said. "I'll need you as a lookout later."

"I can't sleep with that damned bell ringing."

"It will stop."

"Did you see that?" Fiora asked incredulously.

"What?"

She pointed to the screen.

The blond musician seemed to have swallowed her instrument. Or his. She was making muffled sounds that were probably supposed to signify pleasure but sounded more like someone choking.

"Wonder if any of the cameramen knew the Heimlich maneuver," I said.

Fiora snickered and stretched out next to me. Her head was propped on my shoulder so she could still see the screen. Her hand came to rest across my waist just below my belt buckle in that proprietary way she has.

I like it.

"You trying to stir up a little interest?" I asked, resting my hand over hers.

She laughed softly. "A *little* interest? Not likely."

Fiora's hand slid from beneath mine and went to work tugging my shirt free, first of my belt and then of my body. When matters were arranged to her satisfaction, she slid her hand over my naked belly. Her palm was warm and smooth. Her short nails dragged lightly across my skin. Gravity got heavier and the room got warmer.

On television, the woman proved her acting ability. She began yipping and yapping as though she always reached climax while administering fellatio.

"Typical male fantasy," Fiora said.

Her breath was warm against my bare skin. She traced a random pattern just beneath my waistband with the tips of her index and middle fingers.

It was distracting.

I liked it a lot.

"Do men really like women to be so loud?" Fiora asked.

"No. Men like women who are ready, willing, and available. Noise—including talking—is optional."

Fiora tipped her head and looked at me as though to see if she had heard me right.

"Most men just want to get their ashes hauled," I said. "We are not nice people. We are cruel and exploitative. We lack finesse and sensitivity. We are also hopelessly violent. Just ask any politically aware woman.''

Fiora tried to take a pinch of my skin between her thumb and forefinger, but I thwarted her by tightening my belly muscles.

"How about you?" she said against my breastbone. "Do you like—um, vocally demonstrative women?"

I traced Fiora's right eyebrow with my finger.

"If you're noisy, I like noisy women," I said. "If you aren't noisy, that's fine, too. What I like is you."

I moved my hand down Fiora's back and fished up the long tail of her shirt until I could reach the skin underneath. It was even softer and smoother than the touch of her fingertips. As I made light tracings on the skin between her hip bone and the lower point of her rib cage, the sounds from the television simply receded, no longer real.

Fiora turned her face to me and kissed me, softly at first and then harder. When I kissed back, Fiora made a muffled noise deep in her throat. The sound was involuntary, uncalculated. It made me want to take her clothes off.

I rolled over, taking Fiora with me, enjoying the feel of her body beneath me. She smiled and moved in a way that told me she liked it as much as I did. Slowly I pushed up her shirt. Then I ran my tongue beneath the black peekaboo bra until she twisted slowly beneath me, her body hot with the kind of response that can't be faked.

Two vehicles pulled up in front of the *farmacia* building across the street. Doors slammed noisily.

"Damn!" Fiora groaned.

I seconded it.

tWENTY

There were two vehicles in the alley. One was a black-and-white LAPD beat car. The other was a solid white vehicle with a light bar on top and the trademark shield of an alarm company on the door. Both cars had pulled up beside the *farmacia* and lab building about forty feet from the back window of our motel room.

I gapped the curtain on the window a half inch. Fiora and I watched to see how good they were.

The two units had taken more than ten minutes to respond to the alarm. No burglar worthy of the name would still be inside. But the two real cops went through the motions anyway, checking the front and back doors of the lab and making sure all the windows were intact. The job took them about two minutes.

The guy from the alarm company was in uniform, too, but he looked way too thin to have passed the LAPD physical. He wore a rumpled brown uniform and carried a four-inch .38 on his service belt. The gun was probably more a comfort to the customers than a threat to the crooks. The kid was an alarm technician, not a paid warrior.

When the real cops had finished their work, the thin kid got a folding stepladder out of his trunk. He unfolded the ladder against the wall and scrambled up until he could pull the face plate off the alarm box. There was a circuit breaker below the bell assembly. The kid punched it. Suddenly the night was quiet.

The technician checked the assembly and the wiring while the cops waited, looking as bored as they no doubt were.

"Everything looks good," the kid called down.

The first cop said something I couldn't hear.

"I checked the log," the alarm tech said quickly. "No record of false activation in the last six months."

"Well, this one was sure as hell false," the second cop said.

He wore two stripes and the hollow-eyed, tired look of a cop holding down two jobs to pay the mortgage and still have enough left over to go fishing once a year.

"Don't blame me," the alarm tech said plaintively. "Talk to the alarm supervisor in the morning."

"I'll do more than that," the younger cop retorted. "I'll get the watch commander to post a 'do-not-respond' notice for all shifts."

"Yeah," said the tired cop. "Your company's

equipment gives us more trouble than any two private outfits put together. We're getting sick of it."

The alarm tech shrugged, fitted the hinged cover back on the alarm box, and climbed down the ladder.

"Don't gripe to me," the tech said. "Gripe to the customer. He's the guy with the outdated equipment. What do you expect from crap that's older than I am?"

"Boy, that damn bell better stay quiet the rest of my shift," the old cop said.

He and his partner climbed back in the squad car and drove off. A moment later, the alarm tech followed.

I let the curtain fall into place.

"This is going to be too easy," I said.

Fiora looked skeptical. "What are you going to do?"

"In a few minutes, I'm going to check out the neighborhood for cops. Then I'm going to kick in the back door of the photo lab."

"Lovely," Fiora muttered.

"Then I'm going to park my own private ladder in the alley."

"But—"

I kept talking. "Then I'm going to climb up and reset the breaker, just like that alarm tech did."

"Won't they be back?"

"Doubt it. If they are, I'll do it all over again and then again until the cops get fed up and don't respond."

"You've done this before," Fiora said.

"A time or three, yes."

"It really works?"

"So far so good."

Fiora sighed a deep sigh. The two cats on her T-shirt shifted around intriguingly.

"Benny's right," she said.

"He usually is. What is he right about this time?"

"In your own way, you're just as dangerous to the system as he is."

"Can you think of a way *within* the system to get a straight answer out of Barry Franklin or Aileen Camp?" I asked.

"No."

Fiora put her arms around my waist and held on for a moment, plainly uneasy. I stroked her hair and said the only thing I could.

"I won't actually be inside that lab more than three minutes. Even if somebody decides to respond, I'll be long gone by the time he gets here."

"What am I supposed to do?" Fiora asked against my chest. "I'm not very good at waiting around to see if things are going to go south."

"You're the lookout. If you see anything wrong, call the photo lab. I'll hear the phone and know there's trouble."

She muttered something I chose not to hear.

"Once I've reset the alarm, I'm going to park the truck on the street out in front of the *farmacia*," I said. "When you see me come out the back door, come a-running and we'll leave. Got it?"

"Yes, for all the good it will do."

Fiora wasn't happy. At all.

"Can you think of another way to get the job done?" I asked as patiently as I could.

"What's the phone number?" Fiora asked.

We found a tattered Yellow Pages and looked up the lab's number. Then I got ready to leave.

Fiora watched me silently until my hand closed over the doorknob.

"We're supposed to be equal partners," she said. "How come I always have to be the lookout?"

"The usual reason."

"What's that?"

"Brute strength."

"But—"

"If it came to it," I continued reasonably, "I could tie you to the bed and go prowling. You couldn't do the same to me. Brute strength has its uses."

"Three minutes," she said in a tight voice.

"What?"

"Three minutes inside. No more."

"Three minutes," I agreed.

I shut the door behind me and stepped out into the night.

The two LAPD cops had looked like good candidates for parking the car in an out-of-the-way place and grabbing some sleep. I drove quickly around the neighborhood to make sure the alarm wouldn't wake up anyone that mattered.

Two truck drivers were drinking coffee and smoking cigarettes in a Dunkin' Donuts shop. Five blocks east, at the base of a Hollywood Freeway offramp, a dusky *indio* teenager wearing a dirty T-shirt, shorts, and a pair of cheap sandals hawked bags of oranges and one-dollar roses to the darkness. He forced a half-frightened, half-drunken grin when I drove up to the traffic light.

I bought one bag of fruit and all the roses for a twenty. Fiora isn't by nature a patient person, but I can usually win her back with flowers. Besides, the kid was too young and too drunk to be selling stuff on mean streets late at night.

No cops were anywhere in the neighborhood. I parked right behind the photo lab, got a pair of Channel-Lock pliers from the truck's tool kit, and walked to the back door of the lab. Despite the tech's crack about the age of the equipment, the alarm pads still were sensitive. The alarm went off the first time I shook the door.

With the bell ringing in my ear, I slapped the pliers on the doorknob and twisted hard. Channel-Locks are so efficient at breaking and entering they used to be classified as burglar tools. They still should be. The knob resisted, then gave a sweet little metallic *pop*. The door swung open.

As I went back down the stairs to the truck, I saw the curtain in the Sin Bin move. Fiora waved. I waved back.

Then I climbed up on top of her new truck to reach the alarm box and punched out the relay. As I swung down from the Beast's roof, I knew I was going to need those roses for sure, because I left some scratches on her new paint with my big feet.

I drove the truck to the street out front, parked half a block away, and went back to the rear of the building again.

The light from the reception area was bright enough to show me the digitizing scanners and pixel readers that were the heart of the photo lab's operation. Benny would have loved the equipment, but they could just as well have been sausage grinders to me.

The files in the front office weren't locked. I started on the middle drawer. There was nothing between Miner and Mosberg. Not a file, not a gap where a file had been, nothing.

Damn.

Knowing how hard it is to get reliable, literate clerks, I worked the alphabet on either side of Miner and Mosberg. Still nothing. I'd have to do it the hard way.

I went to the top drawer and started to check file by file. Most of the lab's business was commercial. Corporate names, studio special-effects departments, magazine publishers who wanted cover art cleaned up, photo retouchers trying to avoid using the air brush.

None of the file names in the first drawer were familiar. Each file had billing material and the working negatives the processor had used.

I knew I was on the right track, but I was beginning to feel a bit naked. It had been three minutes since the alarm had gone off. I had been inside the building for two of those three minutes.

Three minutes inside. No more.

I hadn't liked the look in Fiora's eyes. Dream-haunted.

I worked faster. The middle drawer was a bust all over again. I tried variations of Moreton's name. Still nothing.

Three minutes inside.

No more.

I slammed the drawer irritably. I was doing exactly what I had promised Fiora I wouldn't do.

The third drawer began with Parish Entertainment. I flipped files so quickly I almost quit reading. I raced past the second one under the *V*s. Then I doubled back to make sure I had read the name lightly penciled onto the corner of the negative envelope.

Harold Moreton. Will Call.

I grabbed the file and read the carbon copy of the invoice: *Bill to Visual Arts Studio, Attn. Mr. Bishop, Security.*

Bingo.

The negative envelope felt thick enough to hold several prints and a strip of celluloid.

I was about to open it when the phone rang. An instant later the sound of tires braking hard on dusty asphalt came from the rear of the lab.

I grabbed the receiver from the secretary's desk and lifted it but didn't say a word.

"Get out!"

Fiora's voice was frightened. Before I could reply the room at her end exploded with sound—shattering wood and snarling men.

Someone had just kicked in the motel room door.

"Don't move!" someone yelled. "Drop the phone!"

"Do it," I ordered. "Don't give them any excuse to shoot."

The phone hit the floor.

For an instant I thought I would throw up. But that wouldn't change anything, so I swallowed hard and tried to squeeze the receiver into a new shape.

Jake, you bastard son of a wandering man. What in hell do we do now?

"Face the wall," the voice ordered. "Don't move. You're under arrest."

The man was closer to the phone now. I could hear the sounds of others in the room with him. I expected to hear footsteps thundering up the stairway to the back door of the photo lab.

No sounds came except through the phone.

"Who you talking to, bitch?" the hard voice demanded. "Where's your man?"

"I'm not talking to anybody, and I don't own a man."

Fiora's voice sounded distant, small, unnaturally clear.

Someone picked up the receiver and spoke into it. "This is the Los Angeles Police. Give yourself up, Fiddler. Make it easy on all of us. Especially your woman."

The voice sounded faintly familiar, but no name came into my mind. Nothing but blood and adrenaline howling.

I hung up the phone very gently, shoved the negative envelope into my hip pocket, and went to the back door of the lab. There were two cars in the alley between the motel and the back of the lab. One was a uniform car and the other a maroon Ford LTD with tax-exempt plates and a pigtail antenna. A detective unit.

The uniformed officers were in felony raid positions behind their unit, one with a riot gun at the ready and the other with drawn pistol. Both plainclothes officers were plastered against the stucco wall beneath the window of the Sin Bin, waiting with drawn guns for someone to appear in the back window of the motel room. Me, no doubt.

Nobody seemed interested in the photo lab, which meant that no one knew where I was.

The cops stood in waxwork tableau for another thirty seconds. Then the raid team finished searching the room and decided they had missed me. The radio in the black-and-white grumbled something I couldn't hear.

The cops in the alley could. They visibly relaxed. The senior patrol officer snapped the riot gun back into its keeper on the dashboard. The detectives put away their guns. Cigarettes flared into life. The fun was over.

My forehead felt numb and hot at the same time.

You happy, Jake? You've finally managed to bring my "tight-assed little blonde" down to your level. *Our* level.

Jake's cold chuckle sounded as though he were in the room with me.

Don't lay that trip on me, Fiddler. You have a problem, it's with yourself, not with me. I didn't invite Fiora along. You did.

Sometimes, Jake, just sometimes, I wish I had never known you.

I tried not to think about Fiora being pawed by cops looking for guns and maybe copping a little feel along the way. She has always been very particular about who touched her. Like a cat.

An irrational feeling consumed me, emptiness and rage at once. Fiora was gone forever to some place I could not reach.

Then I felt her in the room with me. Nothing more, just the feeling of calmness at her center. Fiora, who was so intense, so passionate, was capable of immense self-control.

Slowly, the feeling of permanent loss began to ease. I drew several deep breaths and felt the numbness dissolve in my mind and body. I stepped back from the window of the lab.

And I waited.

After about five minutes, the cops came down the back steps from the second floor of the motel. Fiora was in handcuffs, being escorted by a female patrol officer. The lady cop was massive, dressed in a dark blue uniform and bulked up by the Kevlar vest beneath her shirt. She made Fiora seem small and fragile in her cheap T-shirt and slacks.

Not once did Fiora look toward the lab. Her head was high and her back was straight. She ignored the cold appraisal of the street cops who watched while she was loaded into the back seat of the black-and-white unit.

I knew then how Fiora must have felt when she saw me led away from the beach at Venice in handcuffs. But unlike Fiora, I had known what awaited me.

Now she would know, too.

She would receive the full rites of initiation into a world I'd never wanted her to know about. Pat-downs and body-cavity searches, booking and fingerprinting, seeing the world from the wrong side of the bars. All of it another step down the far side of the divide that separates good people from the rest of us.

It was all right for me. I had chosen the other side of the divide. But Fiora had not. Her only mistake had been in choosing me.

A final cop came down the stairs from the Sin Bin and started issuing orders to everyone around. I knew at least one of his names.

Dugger.

He still had the streetwise look and smug arrogance of an undercover narc. But the way everybody jumped when he barked told me he was in charge of something bigger than a vice raid.

Jesus, Jake. What have you gotten us into this time?

tWENTY-ONE

Dugger's appearance told me more than I wanted to know. For openers, it told me there wasn't a damn thing I could do to help Fiora. Legally. It also made me wonder why LAPD was chasing me and a twenty-year-old dope case with the same bloodhound.

I stepped back from the window, fished out the envelope with Moreton's name on it, and broke the glued flap with my index finger. The three prints inside were old news. I already had a set of them. But the thin glassine negative envelope was brand new.

I held the strip of three thirty-five-millimeter color negatives up to the light that was filtering in from the reception area. The images were too small and ghostlike to read.

There was a light table in one corner of the lab. I couldn't risk turning it on but hoped to find a magnifying loupe nearby. I did. The ten-power magnifying glass ate light like a black hole.

The only illumination in the place was the lone hundred-watt bulb in the reception area. I went there and tried again. The loupe was awkward. I held the strip of negatives in one hand and tried to find the proper focal length.

The negative images were bizarre. Light was dark and dark was light, and the colors were from nightmares. The human figures in the three consecutive frames looked like monsters from a special-effects sequence. Once I got used to the reversal, it wasn't hard to recognize the two Mexican assassins and Barry Franklin.

Aileen Camp was recognizable, too. She had been the mystery figure standing between Franklin and the shooters.

She was wearing a skimpy little polka-dot halter that had been the source of more than a few leers in Puerto Peñasco. Looking at the undoctored pictures told me that Koo-Koo had been staring at her breasts in two of the pictures. In the third one, he had been staring at a sack full of money.

Portrait of a conspiracy. Scene one, the down payment. Take one. Roll cameras and *Action!*

There were a lot more details I would like to have known, but the thrust of the plot was pretty damned clear. Jake and I were sucked into the middle of the action later. One of us had died on cue. Now Fiora and I were part of the surprise ending.

I wondered who was doing what and with which and to whom this time around. Did Aileen do

Franklin this time or did he do her? Or did a narcotics task force twist one to screw the other?

Not that it really mattered. Dead was dead and revenge was revenge.

Still, Aileen must have been fairly desperate to take the chance that the original negatives would be discovered. But then, she must have been confident that I would behave as expected when she wound me up and pointed me at Barry Franklin.

As Fiora said, old-fashioned men are predictable.

Aileen's bet had nearly paid off. Koo-Koo was dead. Barry Franklin would have been, if the setup at his party had been different. But it hadn't been. Franklin was still alive.

For the first time I realized that if Jake had been in my boots, Franklin wouldn't have survived. Jake had done what he wanted when he wanted and let the devil take the hindmost.

But Jake had never found a woman like Fiora.

There was a telephone on the wall of the lab. I picked it up, got a dial tone, and started punching in numbers. My first call was to Ray Bently. It took thirty seconds. Then I dialed Matt Suarez. He picked up on the second ring. His answer sounded like a groan.

"Did you ever find out anything more about those cops who went to see Bobby Soliz the other day?"

"Your timing sucks," Suarez growled.

"I'll make it up to you."

"It's not the sort of thing you could make up."

"Tell her I'm sorry."

His response was a grunt.

"Does the name Dugger mean anything?" I

asked. "Big guy with a ginger beard, wears loud Hawaiian shirts."

Suarez hesitated. He would trust me to guard his back in Spring Canyon at midnight, but I was still a civilian and he was still a cop.

"Let me put it to you this way," I said. "You want your walkaway money back?"

"Shit Marie, as Daddy used to say. If you know about LAPD's caper, it can't be all that hush-hush."

I waited.

"Dugger's the principal street agent in a supposedly secret task force that's trying to twist Bobby's nuts," Suarez said bluntly.

"I'm staring out a window at Dugger right now. He just took Fiora away in handcuffs, and if he knew I was here, he'd probably call out SWAT and burn the place down and me with it."

"*¡Putame!* What the hell have you gotten into?"

"Good question. The major players are Dugger and a bunch of very smelly show-biz folks, all of whom were involved with Jake."

"Good old Uncle Jake," Suarez said ironically. "It's nice to know he can still cause trouble after all these years."

I wasn't interested in rehashing the bad old days.

"Who do I need to see at La Mesa to talk to Bobby again?" I asked.

"I'll take you."

"Negative. I've just become a real detriment to anybody's career. LAPD probably has a bulletin out on me right now for murder."

"That dude on the beach?"

"No. A fresher body."

Suarez grunted. "You've been a busy boy."

"My gun killed a man, but this time I wasn't on the other end of it."

He read my voice with the accuracy of a cop who has been lied to often enough to recognize the truth.

"You're amazing," Suarez said. "You waste a guy on purpose and skate, only to get framed for a killing that wasn't yours."

"It's a great life if you don't weaken. Now who do I have to buy to see Bobby?"

"When do you need to get in?"

"As soon as I can get to Mexico," I said.

"Knock on the gate, *compadre*. Somebody will be waiting for you."

"Don't burn yourself. I'm pretty hot at the moment."

"So am I," he muttered. "Just do me a favor."

"Name it."

"If something else goes wrong in the next ten minutes, don't call me."

It would have been easier to hop a plane out of Burbank or LAX, except that at 3 A.M. nobody's flying but the folks on the freeways. Once I cleared the Los Angeles Civic Center, Interstate 5 was hammer down—just me, the bakery trucks, and the gasoline tankers.

With the cruise control set to keep up with the general flow of traffic—seventy-one miles per hour —I began trying Benny every five minutes. He wasn't answering in his van, and no one claimed to have seen him at the hotel. His home number rang and rang and rang and rang until the answering machine finally kicked in.

I left a message, but I doubted it would be picked

up. I was developing this brilliant ability to get friends and lovers into trouble.

Ray Bently called back when I was passing Via de la Valle in Del Mar, sometime after four in the morning.

"Parker Center lockup has Fiora," he said. "They're trying to make a booking charge of homicide."

"Bullshit! She was nowhere near the—"

"I know," Ray cut in. "They know it, too. But a homicide charge isn't on the bail schedule. That means she sits there until I can get a judge to set bail formally."

"Did you talk to Fiora?" I asked.

"I'm headed downtown now, but the cops are playing games. Hollywood station made me chase my tail for thirty minutes before they'd even admit there had been cops at the motel."

"Dugger is a badge-heavy prick. I hope he falls down some stairs real soon."

"Some people might call that a threat," Ray said.

"Some people would be wrong."

It was a promise.

"Is there any way I can talk to her without sticking my neck in a noose?" I asked. "She's not used to jails."

"Let me talk to her first. Then maybe we can get her access to a phone, whether they've booked her or not."

"If I don't answer the cellular right away, keep trying. I'll be away from the car for a little while."

"Where?"

I hung up the phone without answering, kicked the cruise control up to eighty, and dialed a Mozart disc into the CD player. The Beast roared along on its knobby tires like a top-sailed schooner in a world of supertankers and container ships.

I wondered where Jake was. He hadn't whispered in my ear since I had yelled at him for getting Fiora in trouble.

The Border Patrol 4 × 4s were crawling the walls of Spring Canyon like big cockroaches as I parked the truck on the U.S. side of the line. I got out and walked toward the Mexican port of entry.

The Mexican border guards were busy watching a couple of North Island marines toss an entire night's tequila shooters, *chicharones,* and half-digested tacos on the cracked pavement beside the gate. One of the guards glanced at me and shook his head sadly, silently commenting on the foolishness of young gringos who come to Mexico to be wild.

I thought about the half-scared and quite drunk Mexican kid who had sold me the roses on the Melrose off-ramp. He was crazy, too, in a way he'd never think of being at home. It must be something about crossing borders that brings out the craziness in people.

Then I thought of Bobby Soliz. I wondered how he really felt about Mexico, now that he had had a chance to live it for a couple of decades.

I woke up one of the cabbies in the hack stand on the Mexican side. He looked groggy until I told him where I wanted to go. Then his eyes got big. An extra twenty soothed him, but he drove so slowly I finally asked what was wrong.

He answered in clear, formal Spanish. Silently I translated: No good comes from a fare to the prison or to the graveyard.

No argument there. No help for it, either. What I needed was on the other side of prison walls.

The sky over Otay Mesa was starting to brighten as we headed into the *colonias*. There were lights on in some of the little houses, immigrant guides coming home from their nightly run north or working men with *micas* or *permisos* getting ready to head north to pick tomatoes or haul garbage.

A milkman rattled along the rutted street in a panel truck that was at least as old as the border fence. His glass bottles made a cheerful, almost forgotten sound in their metal crates, music from my Western childhood, where milk was delivered in bottles long after cities discovered paper cartons. The sound was cheerful and melancholy at once, like the *colonia* itself.

The cabbie pulled up in front of the penitentiary and waited while I looked around. Sometimes you see an alien land most clearly at dawn, the common threads of darkness and light, death and life. It was a good time to have a talk with Bobby.

Even La Mesa looked promising at daybreak.

I gave the cabbie a ten, with the certainty of another twenty if he would wait to take me back to the port of entry. He didn't like the idea, but he stared at the money a long time. It was more, in pesos, than he could make in a day.

I knew how he felt. Money is power. In Tijuana, ten dollars made you a *patrón*. In Hollywood, ten thousand dollars made you a *peón*.

The cabbie finally took the ten and nodded a little sadly. He told me he would wait one hour, no more. Then he would go home to his wife. He needed to see his children for a time before they went to school.

"I understand," I said. "I won't make you late."

The gate guards had no trouble taking the tens I gave them. They snapped off sharp little salutes across the actions of their assault rifles and held out their palms for the grease as though they were taking tickets at Disneyland.

Inside the heavy steel gate stood a professorial little Mexican in a rumpled suit and round steel-rimmed glasses. Matt Suarez's buddy, no doubt, the ambitious junior administrator. The man gave me a perfunctory smile. This was business, not pleasure, to him.

That surprised me. Most men who are on the take aren't fussy about who they take it from.

"You wish to see the prisoner Soliz, yes?" he asked.

I nodded.

"Are you carrying any weapons? I cannot permit any weapons to go inside the prison."

"No weapons," I said.

It was a lie but that didn't bother me very much. I knew there were a lot of weapons inside the prison already.

"I will have to check, *señor*. I am sorry."

I was sorry, too. I didn't expect him to find the little blade that was disguised as the shank of my belt buckle—Aaron Sharp's gift—but the man's thoroughness suggested he might be trying to protect Bobby.

Maybe he had decided Bobby offered a quicker route up the administrative ladder than Matt Suarez did. Not good news.

I lifted my arms and let the bureaucrat run his hands over me. As searches go, it was strictly pro forma. Maybe he hadn't sold out to a higher bidder after all.

The bureaucrat led me through the interior gate and across the main yard, which was now littered with sleeping men. At the second gate, he stopped.

"You wish an escort?" he asked.

"No. Does Bobby sleep alone?"

"Ah," he said, "well. . . ."

"Let me rephrase the question," I said curtly. "Are there bodyguards with him?"

The man removed his glasses and rubbed the lenses with the end of his tie. The cloth looked frayed, as though he had worn the tie and repeated the gesture for a long time.

"At the moment, no," he said finally. "There is a young woman who comes to see him quite often and . . ."

The bureaucrat looked uncomfortable.

"I understand," I said.

His eyes flashed with anger. He took off his little round Lenin glasses and studied me with the bitter defensiveness that only a patriotic Mexican can muster.

"Do not judge all of my country by its prisons," he said. "They are full of men who have become wealthy and powerful by selling drugs to your country."

"I know the cost of the narcotics traffic. Sometimes I think I've spent most of my life picking up the pieces."

He looked thoughtful for a moment, then nodded.

"Mateo says you are to be trusted," the bureaucrat said briskly. "I have issued instructions that any disruptions in this part of the prison are to be disregarded until dawn."

"What is your name, *señor*?" I asked.

"Carlos Pacheco Quezada," he said.

I offered him my hand.

"*Mil gracias,*" I said. "If you ever need a favor in the United States, please get in touch with me through Matt."

Pacheco hesitated, then nodded, accepting my offer.

Forget politics, forget diplomacy, forget high-sounding principles and coalitions and rule books. The whole world operates on one fundamental, personal obligation. Whatever else is said about the Mexican culture, it is a place that still honors obligations such as the one I had just incurred.

Pacheco took my hand and shook it with the softness that is characteristic of the Latin.

"Mateo is *mi primo*, my cousin," he said.

It explained a whole lot. Pacheco wasn't on the take. He was simply taking care of family.

And so was I.

I turned and walked quietly across the inner yard to Bobby's cottage.

tWENTY-TWO

Shanks—homemade knives—are the weapon of choice in most prisons. Eating utensils, shop tools, scrap metal, even hard plastic have all been used to make shanks. The weapons have to be carefully designed to be undetectable during searches, including skin searches. Real cons have developed a practice called keistering to hide contraband . . . but that's always a dicey method of dealing with knives. Getting the thing out in a hurry is a real bitch, too.

Aaron Sharp had given me the kind of weapon that doesn't need to be keistered to survive a search. The knife is a shark's-tooth dagger with a triangular blade three inches long. The blade is attached to an ordinary-looking belt buckle, which serves as a haft. The blade can be inserted into a special sheath in the end of a standard leather belt.

I fished the tooth out as I walked across the La Mesa prison yard. The little dagger had limited intimidation value in a prison full of men who sneered at machine guns, but it was more visually impressive than fingernails.

The front door of Bobby's little cottage had been left open overnight for ventilation. I stood on the concrete stoop for a minute and listened. Somebody was snoring inside. A real ripsaw snorer. Sounded like Bobby was finally paying the price of prizefighter's chronically broken nose. The space between snores was filled with the drone of a fan.

I could have come in riding a tap-dancing elephant and old Bobby wouldn't have heard me. He had gotten careless in his old age. Or he thought he had paid enough in protection to ensure safety.

Stupid of him. That much protection money doesn't exist.

I pushed the door open the rest of the way and went into the cottage. The air inside was stale, close, and musky: stale beer, recent sex, and old sweat.

As my eyes adjusted to the deepest shadows, I saw a tiny sitting room, a kitchen with a kerosene burner, and a sink stacked with dirty dishes. Another open door led to a cluttered little bedroom. Two figures lay tangled in a sheet on a narrow bed.

By La Mesa's standards, these special quarters were palatial. By the standards even of East Los Angeles, the place was marginal.

I went to the bedroom door. Bobby was on his back, his thick arms thrown up over his head. A woman lay beside him with one arm draped across his tanned, hairless chest. She had a tangle of long dark hair and the mature breasts of a woman, yet in the thin light from the window her face looked like that of a thirteen-year-old. Both of them were nude.

The fan in the corner of the room droned endlessly. Even so, I was careful not to kick anything as I circled the bed to stand looking down at Bobby.

His face was lined and the skin around his eyes was heavily scarred. Yet there was a curious, almost hopeful look to him, as if he thought he was getting away with something. Every crook knows that he's going to get away with it, that he'll never really pay.

As I looked around the nasty little cottage, I wondered how Bobby managed to keep his illusion intact. On the other hand, Bobby's illusion was a more potent weapon against reality than the blade I had in my hand.

I bent down and unplugged the fan. Slowly its noise faded away, leaving the room silent.

Neither of the sleepers stirred for a while. Then the girl shifted and rolled onto her back. Her breasts lolled like loose sacks of grain. Slowly her eyelids opened.

My presence began to register on her face. Surprise came first, then the beginnings of fear. Within two seconds she lost the air of thirteen-year-old innocence. She looked like what she was, a hard, frightened whore.

I held my index finger to my lips and showed her the knife. She caught on instantly and lay still without making any attempt to awaken Bobby. Prostitutes are the ultimate realists.

I spoke softly, without urgency. "Wake up, Bobby."

Bobby's sightless eyes rolled open. He turned his face in my general direction.

Slowly he sat up and asked calmly, "Who is it?"

"Someone from the bad old days."

Bobby gathered himself as though to leap off the bed. I was behind him with my arm barred across his throat before he knew what had happened. When he struggled, I shut down his windpipe. By the time I let up, he was ready to listen.

"Steady, Bobby," I said. "If I wanted you dead, you'd be dead."

He had figured that out. The corded muscles of his body slowly relaxed but not completely. He was still ready to spring at the least hint of an opening.

No good. I didn't want to spend the rest of the night wrestling with a blind man.

Deliberately I drew the point of the knife across Bobby's throat. The whore gasped at the thin trail of blood. Then she realized the wound was not deep.

"Just remember how thin your skin is," I said softly.

Bobby wasn't afraid of a cut or the small burning pain that came with it. He had known worse wounds, much worse pain. The difference was that now he couldn't see anything. He couldn't see death as it stalked him, nor could he see life as it leaked out of him.

He was the kind of man who would fight anything he could see. But now he couldn't see.

The fight slowly left him. He lay slackly against me. I moved aside, letting him fall back onto the bed. When color came back into his face, I started talking.

"Explain to your lady friend that you and I need to talk privately."

I knew enough Spanish to tell her myself, but there was no need to give that away. I listened while Bobby relayed my statement and then fell silent.

"I think it would be a real good idea," I said, "if she put her clothes on and got her ass out of here without speaking to a single person. You understand?"

Bobby understood. He started giving the woman marching orders that included not raising an alarm.

The prostitute's face told me she already comprehended that part of the deal quite well. She got out of bed, grabbed a dirty dress from the floor, and stood up. She was heavy and squat, like an Aztec fertility goddess. Her face could have stopped trains.

Bobby was still giving orders when she vanished through the door and into the dawn. Silently.

"Somebody's cheating you," I said, "renting you ugly whores because you're blind."

Bobby told me to do something obscene and intricate with my mother.

I told him my mother was dead.

"What do you want?" he asked petulantly.

"I want to know why you killed Jake Malverne."

"Jake Malverne?"

Bobby thought a moment, silently trying to recall the names of the men he had killed. It must have been quite a list. He didn't say anything for two minutes.

"Jake?" Bobby asked finally. "Big dude with pale eyes, shoulders like an ox, and hands fast enough to catch flies?"

Bobby knew exactly who Jake was, but I played the game anyway.

"Yeah," I said. "That's Jake."

"Jesus, that was a century ago. He would have made a great fighter, for a gringo."

"Yeah."

Bobby shrugged. "I didn't kill him."

"You didn't pull the trigger, but the men who worked for you did."

"Who told you that?"

"Nobody, Bobby. I was there. They tried to kill me, too."

For a moment he looked terrified again. He expected me to pull the knife across his throat, but this time with muscle behind it. His beefy arms pinched in against his sides and he raised his hands as though to ward off an attack.

"They weren't doing it for me, man! I swear it on my mother's grave!"

"Yeah, yeah, yeah."

"It's true! Both of them took off after Jake died. I heard one of them died a few months later."

"No kidding."

"In fact," Bobby said, crossing himself uneasily, "I heard Jake's ghost killed him."

I laughed.

"Then I heard the other one was killed just the other day up in LA somewheres," Bobby said quickly.

"Jake's ghost strikes again."

Muscles rippled as Bobby shrugged.

"Maybe, maybe not," he said. "Koo-Koo was a bad dude. He killed thirty-two men that I know of. A lot of them had family. Lots of people were looking to cut Koo-Koo's throat."

"They can stop looking."

Bobby tilted his head as though listening intently.

"Wait a minute," he said abruptly. "I know who you are now! You were here the other day, with that *pendejo* Suarez."

"Yeah."

"What do you care about who killed Jake?"

"He was my uncle."

Finally Bobby made the connection.

"You were the kid who played the violin. You were damn near as big as Jake. But quicker. Best hands I've seen on a gringo."

I looked at my scarred hands. I wasn't as quick as I once had been, but I was a hell of a lot meaner.

And I was tired of talking about the dead past.

"Who hired Jake's killers?"

Bobby's face went blank, like a stone mask. "I tell no one."

"Bullshit. You've been telling any gringo who asked. Talk to me or I'll send you to talk to Jake."

Bobby drew a deep breath, stuck out his chin, and corded the muscles of his thick neck.

"What gringos you talking about?" he asked cautiously.

"Those cops from LA."

Bobby flinched.

"The guy named Dugger," I said. It was a guess, but not a wild one. I knew LA cops were nosing around and Dugger was the likely prospect.

I waited for Bobby to deny it. He didn't. He changed the subject.

"You accusing me of being a snitch?"

"Yeah."

Now he bristled.

"Personally, I don't give a damn who you talk to," I said. "But your good buddies out there in the prison yard might not feel that way."

An ugly look settled over Bobby's face.

"I run this joint," he said. "No one here will take the word of a gringo that Bobby Soliz is a snitch. They'll spit in your face."

"Maybe," I said. "Maybe not. But Dugger is different."

"Huh?"

"How would Dugger feel if I told him you were dealing dope to federal agents with one hand while you're stroking him with the other?"

Bobby's Adam's apple did a quick lap up and down his throat.

"Who's the fed?" he demanded.

I said nothing.

"Who is it? Suarez?"

I didn't say anything.

"I knew it," Bobby said bitterly. "I knew that smooth homeboy bastard was wrong the first time he showed up in here."

"You're wrong about Suarez," I said calmly. "But it doesn't matter. I know who the fed is. You don't."

Bobby swore.

I kept talking. "One word from me, and your sweetheart deal with the Los Angeles cops blows up in your face like a cheap pocket pistol."

Bobby tried to interrupt. I didn't let him.

"LAPD can't afford to protect a snitch who's going to fall on a federal beef. So walk tall and talk straight to me. *¿Comprendes?*"

With a silent snarl, Bobby looked away, an animal caught in a trap.

"If those two burros who offed Jake hadn't gotten in the wind," Bobby said distinctly, "I would have killed them myself. Jake was *mi compadre.*"

That fit with my own memories of Jake and his opposite numbers on the border. Wolves run with wolves.

I swept a pile of clothing off a little chair beside the bed and sat down.

"Who ordered Jake's death?" I asked.

"I don't know!" Bobby said savagely.

"Guess."

"It had to be one of his partners, maybe both. I don't know. I wasn't part of that deal."

"Why would they want to kill him?"

"Chrissake," Bobby hissed. "Why do dope dealers ever get killed? For the money!"

"But Jake wasn't dealing dope. He was making a movie."

Bobby gave me a sad look through blind eyes.

"What the hell have you been smoking, man?" he asked softly, scornfully. "Jake was down here to put together a load."

"Jake had given up running dope."

"Is that what he told you? Huh. I guess he really did want to make sure you stayed out of the business."

I didn't like it.

Sorry, kid. I thought it was best that way.

Your best way damn near got me killed, Jake.

"I should have known," I said aloud. "Jake always did love the weed trade."

"Weed?" Bobby gave a crack of laughter. "He and that blond bitch were down here negotiating for twenty kilos of coke."

I reacted before I could think better of it.

"You're lying," I said. "Jake never ran anything stronger than Acapulco Gold."

Yet even as I spoke, the past shifted again, painful shards of memory returning, changing everything. It was almost like being shot all over again. A really unhappy feeling settled in the pit of my stomach.

My gut told me Bobby wasn't lying.

Jake was.

tWENTY-THREE

"**N**o shit, man," Bobby said. "I'm telling you the truth."

Then he grinned like a kid, remembering.

I had that age-old impulse to flatten the bearer of bad news. But I didn't. I had spent too long remembering the wrong things to start complaining now when the right things were finally dredged up from the past.

"Back before the Colombians moved in, twenty keys of coke was a big load," he said.

"Yeah. Big load."

My voice said "Big deal."

"It was probably the best stuff ever to hit Hollywood," Bobby said earnestly. "Rock crystals as big as your thumb. You could shave one all day long and never get through it. Rub a little on your cock and you could bang all night long, man. It was fine."

I grunted.

My response wasn't good enough for Bobby. He wanted me to be as impressed by the good old days as he was.

"That blonde went crazy for it," he said slyly.

Bobby laughed again, differently, the sound of a man remembering something special and sexual.

"Bitch must have gone through a whole ounce in the three days she was here with Jake," Bobby said. "Every time he zipped up his jeans, she unzipped them again. She liked it best with both of us at once."

I didn't care if Aileen liked it with a burro and a dancing bear. I was still feeling the aftershocks of discovering that Jake had gone against his personal principles and smuggled something that *he* considered a drug.

LSD? Leave it alone, Fiddler. No matter what you hear, leave it alone. Same for heroin.

Coke? Man, it's worse than anything but Angel Dust. Burns out your soul. Bad shit.

But our sweet Mary Jane? No bad karma there. Weed is like beer you can smoke. Gentle and clean and just wild enough to keep you interested.

It was good advice to a kid who had a taste for life on the wild side.

I had followed that advice, because I respected Jake's words more than I respected moral codes delivered by people who didn't practice what they preached.

But, if Bobby was to be believed, Jake hadn't respected his own offbeat rules, his own moral code.

Jake?

The only sound I could hear was the faint crowing of a rooster somewhere out beyond the prison walls.

I felt a little sick and a lot foolish, like Kwame must feel when he finally bites that thing he's been chasing and discovers it's his own tail.

"Jake didn't know anything about buying or selling cocaine," I said finally. "He was a weed man."

"That's why he left most of the deal to the woman. Buying and testing and negotiating. His end of it was to get the stuff over the border."

"Why?" I asked.

Bobby knew what I meant. He sighed and rubbed his hand over his eyes.

"The weed trade was getting rougher," he said. "The independents like Jake were being shut out. I tried to get him to organize and go big, but he wouldn't listen. Said if it was a business, it wouldn't be fun anymore."

That fit with my memories of Jake. It was the outlaw life that appealed to him, not the money.

"How much coke did Jake smuggle?" I asked, not sure I wanted to know the answer.

Bobby shook his head. "It was his first load of snow. Jake was going to dump it in a can of white gas and make it disappear. Said it was so safe it would hardly be any fun."

I chewed on that one for a time.

"Did he ever tell you why he changed his mind about coke?" I asked.

Bobby shrugged, his heavy deltoids bunching. Then he sighed again.

"Maybe Jake just grew up," Bobby said. "He saw how things were going."

"Things?"

"The border. The weed. Machine guns and big gangs."

"Civilization."

"Yeah," Bobby said. "A week before he died, Jake told me he knew how the Indians must have felt when the railroad went through."

That, too, sounded like Jake.

"Then he told me how he was going to buy a big ranch in Mexico where the twentieth century would never come," Bobby said.

"And then he ran a load of coke to pay for it," I said.

Bobby's smile was feral. "Like I said, kid. He grew up. Twenty keys of coke or twenty tons of weed. Same net profit for a lighter load."

"Quick and dirty."

"Those Hollywood dudes would pay anything for coke. They snuffed it, shot it in their veins, rubbed it on their dicks, and shoved it up their women's pussies."

The rooster crowed again. It seemed louder now, closer. Reality coming up with the dawn.

I didn't want to hear any more.

And I had to hear it all.

"Know what, kid?" Bobby asked into the silence. "If it weren't for Hollywood's cocaine habit, the Colombians would still be smuggling emeralds and killing each other with machetes."

"The Colombians I know deal to black crackheads in run-down neighborhoods, not to Hollywood."

"Not back then. Coke was like diamonds. Big, big bucks."

"Big bucks," I said. "Hooray."

Bobby looked pained by my attitude about the good old days.

"Colombians wholesaled coke to weed smugglers like me," he explained. "Then they saw how it was —money and starlets that would blow you for a pinch of snow, famous actors lined up to kiss your ass—and they moved in."

The cock crowed for the third time, a rising, urgent cry. Outside the prison, dawn flared softly over the horizon, sending clean light through the sky.

Bobby never noticed. He was caught in a past where he could see as well as feel all the Hollywood ass that cocaine brought him.

"Then those Medellín bastards gave me this," Bobby said, pointing.

I looked at the star-shaped scar on the side of his head.

"They wanted me out of the way," he said.

"They got it."

"Yeah. By the time I could work again, there was nothing left for Mexicans but small stuff. Sometimes . . ." Bobby's voice faded.

"Sometimes?"

"Sometimes I think Jake was the lucky one," Bobby said simply.

I closed my eyes and lived for a few breaths in the world of the blind.

It wasn't an improvement.

"You mentioned Jake's partners," I said, opening my eyes. "Who were they?"

"Well, mostly it was the bitch he was sleeping with. And then there was a fat guy who hung around with her, hoping to get some of what she was giving to Jake."

Aileen and Moreton. Quite a pair.

"What about Barry Franklin?" I asked.

"Who?"

"Big handsome guy with dark, wavy hair and a Valley tan. He was down here just before Jake was killed."

"Oh, that one," Bobby said. "I stayed away. I didn't trust him."

"Why?"

"He could have been a cop."

"But you trusted the woman."

"No cop sucks the way she did. She really dug it."

Good old Aileen. The ultimate whore, always making the mark feel like the biggest cock of the walk. She didn't like sex. She used her body the way a plumber uses a wrench, to get a stronger hold on a pipe. As a way of getting power over a man, it worked a lot of the time.

But then, as Fiora has pointed out more than once, any man who is ruled by his crotch deserves whatever he gets. Apparently Bobby had deserved a life where cocks crowed up another dark night instead of a dawn.

"Is this what you told the LA cops?" I asked.

It went against Bobby's grain to admit he was an informant. He ran his fingertips delicately over the red line I had drawn across his throat. Though the blood had congealed, the cut must have stung.

"Yeah," Bobby said. "That's what I told them."

"What about Barry Franklin?"

"What about him? We never did business. Hell, I never even knew his name until today. The bitch was my connection."

Franklin could just as well have been a million miles away, so far as the LA cops were concerned. Free and clear—and, what the hell, blood washes off money.

And if what goes around comes around years

later, good old Franklin could gently guide the Los Angeles cops to an expatriate dope dealer named Bobby Soliz and use him to destroy Aileen.

Even way back then, Aileen must not have trusted Barry Franklin completely. She had used Harold Moreton to film the payoff so Franklin couldn't cry innocent.

But the pictures were a double-edged sword. Aileen couldn't use them publicly without implicating herself. So she did the next best thing. She and her henchman, Bishop, doctored them, used Moreton to lay them on me, and waited for the homicide headlines.

But I wasn't Jake. I had learned that everything has its price, including freedom. If I wanted to stay free, I had to start thinking and stop reacting.

Older and wiser.

Older, anyway. And wise enough to hang on to a good woman rather than let a man-eating snake crawl into my bed.

I wondered how much of it Fiora knew, had already known for years. I wondered if she had just let me blunder along, guiding me here and there as woman so often do with the men they love. Indirection, the woman's way. Every bit as successful as frontal attack, so long as the polite fantasy of male primacy is observed. And ever so much kinder.

I had repaid Fiora's tact by dragging her over to the wrong side of the divide.

It's a good thing you're dead, Jake. I don't like either one of us very much right now.

"Get dressed, Bobby."

He didn't like my tone of voice.

Neither did I. It belonged to the kind of man I didn't want to be.

"What are you going to do?" he asked shakily.

"Wear you like armor to the front gate."

The cabbie was waiting beyond the gate. He was so eager to go that he started the engine while I was still across the street. He dropped me a block from the port of entry and vanished into the seething streets.

I joined the flow of green carders and *permiso* holders headed north.

The Beast was waiting on the other side with the patience of a machine. I called Suarez on the cellular while I was still in the border parking lot.

"We need to talk," I said. "I'll buy you and your lady friend breakfast, if you trust her."

"She already went home."

"Where shall I meet you?"

"Take the Eight-oh-five and get off at Midway. Café on the corner of Midway and Taninger. Tell Jorge you're my friend."

I made better time getting to the restaurant than the law allowed. When Suarez pulled into the parking lot in his jacked-up Ramcharger, the cook started cracking eggs and dropping hotcakes. Suarez sauntered in, lean and springy as a young stud horse. He kissed the waitress, called the grill man *primo*, and pulled up a chair across the table from me.

"You look like hell," he said.

"So I've been told," I said.

Suarez looked at me. I didn't keep him waiting.

"My woman's in jail for something I did," I said, "the cops are looking for me on a murder charge, one of my best friends has disappeared, and another one is going to be pissed off when he finds out that I've burned his undercover operation.''

"You've had quite a night.''

"That's just for openers.''

Suarez drank coffee and looked serious while I told him how I had loosened Bobby's tongue by threatening to burn him to LAPD. Suarez whistled tunelessly through his teeth. I had blown his operation and both of us knew it.

"Did he talk to the cops?'' Suarez asked.

"Yes.''

"What did LAPD use as a twist?''

"A clean record,'' I said.

"That would do it. Bobby would sell his daughter to go home again.''

Suarez moved his coffee cup so the waitress could put a huge platter in front of him. *Huevos rancheros* swam in salsa at one end, hotcakes swam in butter and syrup at the other. A dike of frijoles with cheese separated the cultures.

I got the platter's twin, the Great Mexican-American Heartstopper Breakfast.

Without a word, Suarez stabbed the *huevos* with his fork, letting the yellow yolks run through the clean red salsa and mix with the beans that were the color of Santa Fe adobe.

I started at the other end. After a few bites, my stomach suddenly remembered that it hadn't been fed since the trendy anti-beef buffet at Barry Franklin's party. I ate the hotcakes, then breached the dike of frijoles, and kept going, finishing the platter before I looked up.

Suarez took his time, thinking through what I had done to his case but making no comment either way. When his platter was empty, the waitress removed the dishes, refilled our coffee cups, and disappeared. Suarez fished out a Lucky Strike, lit it, and made me wish for the first time in a long time that I still smoked.

"I'm not pissed about losing the buy money," Suarez finally said. "LAPD fucked up my case anyway."

I waited, knowing Suarez had more to say.

"What are you going to do?" he asked.

"Blow Barry Franklin and Aileen Camp right out of the water."

Suarez took a drag on the cigarette and blew smoke toward the ceiling.

"Same way you did Koo-Koo?" he asked.

"I might if I could, but I can't."

"You're in pretty deep shit."

"Up to my ass."

He drew on the Lucky and held the smoke in his lungs for a moment. Then he blew it out.

"You're in up to your lips," he said flatly, "and someone has you lined up to drown."

"You're getting paranoid, Matt," I said.

"You know what they say. Even paranoids—"

"—have real enemies," I cut in. "Yeah. I know. But we're talking about a fire fight between Hollywood heavyweights. I'm just a piece of spent ammo that missed its target."

Suarez shook his head. "No. You're still a loose cannon."

I opened my mouth to tell him he was crazy. But when I looked at him, Aaron Sharp's shrewd streetwise eyes looked back at me.

"I'm listening," I said.

"Do you have any idea how hard it is to get a

major narcotics investigation going in Hollywood?" Suarez asked.

"They bust dopers all the time on the Walk of the Stars."

"Penny ante," he said impatiently. "I'm talking about a case that goes all the way to the structure of the business itself."

"Okay, tell me. How hard is it to get a case like that going?"

Suarez's smile was hard, like his father's. They were both human bird dogs, the kind of hunting machine that would follow a trail wherever it led. In the end, the trail had killed Sharp. Suarez had the same kind of drive but he was smarter, if only for the experience of watching his father.

"The biggest industry in Hollywood is entertainment," Suarez said. "The second biggest is entertaining the entertainers."

I took a swallow of coffee and listened to Suarez.

"There are fifty kinds of whores in that town, a hundred kinds of dope dealers, and more kinds of vice than you want to know."

"Nothing new there," I muttered.

Suarez smiled thinly. "Lots of pictures are financed by dirty money that's been laundered through offshore banks."

"Nothing new, Matt."

His smile became wider and colder. "When was the last time LAPD threw star-quality dopers or their dealers in jail for possession, much less for trafficking?"

"Never."

"When was the last time DEA had a significant undercover operation that targeted the entertainment business?" Suarez demanded.

"Never."

"And there never will be. Hollywood is a company town. The press and the politicians work their asses off to protect the stars, because without them Hollywood is just one more overpriced whorehouse."

"So?" I asked.

"Three times I've had informants lined up, quality informants who'd make Bobby Soliz look like a washed-up old *campesino*. Each case was turned down."

The coffee cup paused halfway to my lips.

"That's new," I said.

"Not to me," Suarez said savagely. "The regional director himself shit-canned the third one. When I complained, he said, 'Grow up, Suarez. Get a life.'"

Carefully I replaced the coffee cup on the saucer, thinking hard and fast. Nothing I came up with was comforting.

"If this guy Dugger is running around putting heat on Aileen Camp," Suarez said, "Dugger isn't just an undercover cowboy looking for a headline bust. He has some very heavy backing. You understand what I'm saying?"

I understood.

I was in shit up to my lips and someone was trying to drown me.

tWENTY-FOUR

On the way back, I kept trying the same numbers over and over. Benny at the hotel. The house phone in Crystal Cove. Ray. Benny on the car phone.

And then I started all over again, mix and match.

Just north of Oceanside on the flat coastal plateau, I finally connected with a live number. Benny picked up on the first ring of his hotel room phone.

"Where the hell have you been?" I demanded.

"And a good morning to you, too."

Benny sounded tired and flat.

"Out carousing?" I asked.

"Depends on your idea of a good time. I've been playing games with some pals of yours. They send their regards."

Uh-oh.

"LAPD?" I asked.

"They were waiting for me at the hotel, mate," Benny said irritably. "Snapped me up like a swagman on a goanna."

"I take it they cut you loose, though."

"I'm being watched. A wanker in a maintenance uniform has been fishing the same cigarette butt out of the pool for the last ten minutes."

"You meet a dick named Dugger?" I asked.

"Not directly, but I heard the name."

"What did they want?"

"Your balls," Benny said succinctly.

"Any special reason?"

"Moreton."

Shit.

I backed off on the accelerator just before I rammed the butt of a northbound semi.

"So quick?" I asked.

"So quick."

"What about you? Any charges?"

"All they had against me was that you paid for my room at the Chateau Beverly," Benny said.

"In other words, they were staked out there even before you got back."

"Too bloody right."

That explained how the cops had gotten to the No-Tell Motel so quickly. I had left a callback number there for Benny. I might just as well have left a map.

But I still didn't know how the cops had gotten to the hotel in Beverly Hills in the first place. Or, for that matter, to Moreton's house.

"Where are you two now?" Benny asked.

"One of us is down south, headed back from seeing an old friend in Mexico. The other is . . . in jail."

The cellular connection hummed hollowly for a long time. I wasn't looking forward to whatever Benny said next. He is as protective of Fiora as I am, and for the same reason. He loves her.

"You made a royal bollocks of that," he said coldly.

"I've got Ray working on springing her."

"When?"

It was a demand, not a question.

"It could be slow going," I said. "This clown Dugger is trying to make a homicide charge stand against her."

"So what are you doing for her besides running about like a blue-arsed fly?"

"Back off, *mate*."

It was the second time I had used that particular tone. I didn't like it any better this time.

There was silence, then the sound of Benny's harshly expelled breath.

"What's your plan?" he asked carefully.

"I need to have a real heart-to-heart talk with Jake's former lady."

"Why?"

"She was the missing face in the picture," I said.

"Bloody hell. Fiora was right."

"See what you can do about getting a home address for the bitch. The trick I used getting into her office won't work twice."

"Affirmative. Did you use your correct vehicle registration number when you checked in at the hotel?"

"Damn!"

"You'd better ditch the truck, mate. Every cop in the Southland is looking for it."

"ASAP."

I hung up and cut my speed back to a sedate fifty-three. Up until Benny mentioned the Suburban's registration I had been feeling bulletproof, but I wasn't. I had counted on the fact that the Beast is registered to the foundation Fiora set up after she sold Pacific Rim. But I had forgotten the registration slip at the Chateau Beverly. One little speeding ticket, one little computer check of my license and truck registration, and I'd have been in jail.

I told you, kid. You ain't been using your head. You've been using Fiora's. A man who lives on the wild side can't have a steady woman. Too distracting.

Dry up, Jake. When I want your advice, I'll ask for it.

The rest of the world had awakened and was pouring onto the freeway, taking away the lure of the open road. I switched on a traffic station and discovered that the morning commuters were snout to ass from San Juan Capistrano to the LA Civic Center. No particular reason. Just business as usual.

I got off at Crown Valley Parkway and took surface roads to minimize my exposure to cops. The ticket machine at John Wayne Airport long-term lot handed me a check that said the time was 8:59 A.M. I clapped the cellular on the battery pack, locked the Beast against suburban prowlers, and walked a hundred yards to the airline terminal.

From there, Avis was just a phone call away. We cut a deal. I gave them money and they gave me the ugliest scow on the road. The feds use thousands of Caprice Classics; I had always wondered why. Now I was going to find out.

The commuter crush thinned out by nine-thirty. I was northbound on the San Diego Freeway at Beach Boulevard when the cellular went off on the seat beside me. I thought about not answering, fearing a trap or, worse, bad news. But curiosity overcame caution.

"This is Mr. Bently's office," a cheerful voice announced. "Please hold on a moment."

When Fiora came on the line, I almost ended up in the center divider.

"Hello, love," she said.

"You're free, then?" I asked urgently.

"Not exactly. I'm in something called Sybil Brand Institute. If I ever meet the lady, I'll give her the name of a better decorator. This place is butt ugly."

I listened, trying to hear the emotions that she was working to conceal—fear, anger at being caged, relief that I was still free. I heard none of them. She was well in control of herself.

It didn't surprise me, but it made me damned glad. No one knows how they'll react to prison until they're put in one. Fiora needs freedom more than anyone I know, including me.

And neither of us does very well with the kind of authority that comes from a billy club.

"The girl said you were calling from Ray's office," I said.

"I assumed the phones here were monitored except for the line set aside for attorneys and clients. That's the one I'm using. Ray's office forwarded the call to you."

"You would make a frighteningly good crook," I said.

"Comes from hanging around with suspected felons."

"Suspected murderers, to be precise."

"Then I don't need to warn you. You already know."

"I do?"

"The cops are convinced there's a link between Koo-Koo's death and Moreton's."

Breakfast did a back flip in my stomach. I wasn't as far ahead of Dugger as I needed to be.

"When did they decide the two were linked?" I asked.

"Before they arrested me."

"You're sure?"

"The first question they asked was about Koo-Koo. The second was Moreton."

Not good news.

"Anything else unexpected?" I asked.

"I don't know. I've never done this before. They worked on me in relays. Three hours, eight detectives, including the commander of special investigations."

"Christ. Are you all right?"

"No worse than some business negotiations I've been through. The guy with the weakest bladder loses. They lost."

"That's a hell of a lot of heat. Are you sure about the commander?"

"He introduced himself as plain old Gene Hansen, but I saw his name and title on a door down the hall."

The woman should have been a spy. Most people would have been scared witless, and there she was, gathering information and impressions like a sponge.

Scared, but not witless.

"Bad news, love," I said simply. "LAPD is in a full-court press on this. Task force, commander, pit bulls, and all. I'm sorry."

"I'm an informed, consenting adult. I lived with you long enough to know this could happen."

"Are you all right?" I asked.

"The cops are polite enough. Some of them are even polished. Except for Dugger. He's a turd."

"What did he say to you?"

"He has a special-weapons team waiting to kill you. He won't use them if I lead him to you. And then he'll let me go. And—"

I held the cellular so hard my hand ached, waiting for Fiora to get her voice under control again.

"If you die, it's my fault—"

"God *damn* him!"

"—because I could have saved you."

"Fiora, that's not true and you know it!"

"Do I?" she whispered. "I—"

In the background, a voice called, "Time's up."

"—love you."

The line went dead before I could answer.

There are a lot of places to hide in the Los Angeles basin, but I went for the anonymity of the city itself. With all the manpower Dugger had available, he was probably tracking credit card transactions, so I paid cash for my room at the Bonaventure, hauled out the alternative ID, and lied.

My only luggage was the cellular phone. The bellman insisted on carrying it. After he left, I lay on my back on the king-sized bed for ten minutes, staring at the cottage cheese curds of soundproofing on the ceiling, trying to figure out how the cops had caught on to so much so fast.

No explanation came.

I called Luz Pico, who runs our household when

we're not home. She had sent one of her best maids by to feed Kwame and tell him he was beautiful. Then I called the Crystal Cove answering machine.

There was only one message. "This is Aileen, call me at the office."

There were also five hang-ups. Aileen, or some other player, trying to get me.

I dialed up the studio switchboard and asked for Aileen's office. What I got was a man's voice.

"Security, Bishop."

"I asked for Aileen Camp."

"She's not here at the moment. I'm handling all her calls. Can I help you?"

"Yeah, you can let me talk to Aileen. She's been trying to get hold of me."

"Fiddler, right?"

Chilly little fingers went down my spine. Having a distinctive baritone voice can be a real pain. The wrong people are forever recognizing it.

"I'm afraid Aileen's not around right now," Bishop said.

"Where can I reach her?"

It wasn't a request or a question. It was a demand.

"I'll have to have her get back to you," Bishop said. "Give me a number."

His voice had a nasty little edge. He was tired of the secretarial waltz around the subject of whose boss calls whose boss first.

"Blow it out your ass, Bishop. I've been leaned on by bigger fleas."

"Listen, you—"

I talked right over him.

"You ran some errands for Aileen," I said. "LAPD would like to know about them."

"What the hell does that mean?"

"Remember the errand you ran to that lab over on Melrose?"

He waited a second too long before asking, "What lab?"

"It's me or a task force, Bishop. Where's your boss?"

Bishop thought it over for about four breaths before he answered.

"She's not in real good shape at the moment," he said.

"Drunk or stoned?"

"She's been under a lot of pressure."

"She'll be under a lot more if she doesn't talk to me. Now."

Bishop made a command decision to disturb his boss.

"Give me a number where she can call you," he said. "She'll call. You have my word."

I gave Bishop the number of the cellular. Modern technology is wonderful; cellulars can be monitored but they can't be traced. Cops can find out who pays the bills, but not where the phone is at the moment.

Five minutes later, the cellular rang. I picked up.

"Yes."

"Hello, Fiddler. How are you?"

"Better than you."

"What does that mean?" she asked.

"You tell me. Why did you stay up all night calling me and then turn your phone over to a rent-a-cop with an attitude?"

There was a silence followed by the faintly crystalline sound of ice cubes bobbing against glass. Apparently she liked her breakfast juice high-test and fully fortified.

"Did you make any progress on that matter we discussed yesterday?" Aileen asked.

Her tone was businesslike, but there was a gentle slur over the middle syllable of "yesterday."

I played as dumb as she thought I was.

"Yesterday?" I asked vaguely.

"Yes," she snapped. "The photographs."

I hadn't mentioned any pictures. I wondered how long it would take for her to remember that.

"I talked to Barry Franklin," I said.

"Well?"

"He claims you were in the pictures, then doctored out."

There was an odd sound, as though Aileen had swallowed the ice cube instead of the antifreeze.

"That lying b-bastard."

I let her hang for several extra beats before I sympathized.

"Yeah, he's a real putz," I agreed. "Everyone knows how much you loved Jake."

She swallowed again, more easily.

"You told me yesterday," I said. "Harold Moreton told me the same thing. Bobby Soliz told me, too. You were always very careful of Jake's feelings, even when you had Bobby's dick in your mouth."

"I n-never—"

"Yeah, yeah, yeah," I interrupted. "Old history. Dead and almost buried. Unless you want to be dead and buried with it, you'll shut up and listen."

I waited for a protest. Nothing came but silence. Even half drunk, Aileen wasn't stupid.

"We're being set up to take the fall for Moreton's murder," I said.

"Harold Moreton? He's *dead*?"

No slurring there. She was truly surprised.

Enough adrenaline had flooded her system to hold the alcohol at bay. It was only temporary, but so is life.

"When? How?" she demanded.

"I found him yesterday. He had been shot with my gun."

"Did you—"

"No," I interrupted curtly. "I'm not as predictable and honorable and stupid as good old Jake."

"What are you talking about?"

"Simple. If the cops get me, I'm going to give them you, Moreton, and the lab over on Melrose. Then I'm going to give them Franklin. You two better pray the cops don't catch me."

There was a long pause while Aileen breathed shallowly, fumbled with a cigarette, and finally got it going. The sound of her exhaling was followed by the muscular gurgling of liquid being poured from a fresh fifth. She took a swig, hissed breath out through her teeth, and laughed.

"Well, well, well," Aileen said. "You look like Jake, but you don't think like him. He'd never have ratted on a girl. Or is it just that I'm older now, so you see past the tits?"

"I saw past the tits in Puerto Peñasco."

"Only because of Fiora," Aileen said. "The little bitch. Jake came to a point every time her name was mentioned."

I was really getting tired of talking about the old days.

"Did you know that your hero tried to get in Fiora's pants?" Aileen asked. "Said it was the only way to cure you of lovesickness. He—"

"Jake's dead, and you have a history of lying like the whore you are."

Liquid sloshed, ice clinked, Aileen swallowed. When she spoke again, the adrenaline was gone.

"You fin'ly remembered, d'in ya?" she asked.

"Did I?"

"The coke. Jake thought it was weed."

"Bobby Soliz told me it was a coke deal from the word go."

Aileen chuckled into the glass, getting closer with each mouthful to the oblivion she sought.

"It was," she mumbled. "But only for Bobby. Jake still wanted weed. Bobby said there was more money in coke. I thought Bobby made more sense, so I told him I'd find a way to get Jake to agree."

No one needed to tell me she had failed. Jake was dead and Aileen was in Hollywood.

Maybe Bobby was right. Maybe Jake had the best of it.

"Jake was pissed off when he found out," Aileen said. "Wouldn't even touch me no matter what I did."

"So you paid to have him killed."

There was a silence and a broken sigh.

"Yes. . . ."

I've killed men. I know about the cold that begins in the pit of your stomach and slowly eats away your body.

But I didn't know about the kind of cold that comes from buying a good man's death.

"Was it worth it?" I asked.

Silence, a swig, a sigh.

"Sometimes," Aileen said.

"When?"

"At first. The load bought us a star and a screenwriter. The picture got us a little gold statue."

"And now?"

"Now?" She laughed brokenly. "Now I'd trade it all for a night in bed with an honest man."

"It will never happen."

"Because I'm not young anymore?"

"No. Because you had the last honest man killed."

tWENTY-FIVE

There was a long silence broken by a sound from Aileen. It could have been a laugh or a sob. Frankly, I didn't much care.

On the other hand, I couldn't see Aileen keeping her mud in a ball long enough to creep up on Moreton and blow his drunken head off.

"What's Barry Franklin's part in all this?" I asked. "Was he the shooter? Or did you both hire it done this time, too?"

Silence.

"Wake up, Aileen."

"I can't help you."

"Wrong answer. LAPD has me on the hook for one murder. What's a few more?"

"Is that a threat?" she whispered.

"Yes."

"You wouldn't—hurt me."

"Remember how mad Jake was when he found out about the coke?"

Aileen gave a shattered laugh. "Yes. I remember."

"I've been that mad since my woman was hauled off in handcuffs to jail."

"Fiora? She's in jail?"

"Jake is dead. Fiora is in the slam. You're responsible both times. Tell me again why I wouldn't hurt you. I'd like to know."

"Oh, God."

I could hear her breathing unevenly and trying to think.

"W-what do you want?" she asked.

What I wanted wasn't possible, so I settled for what was.

"You and Fiora are going to trade places," I said.

"Huh?"

"The cops have Bobby Soliz."

"They've had him for years," she said.

"These cops are American."

"So?"

"So you're going to put a cork in that bottle long enough to make a statement to the cops," I said impatiently.

"But—"

I kept talking. "Barry Franklin will be a big part of your statement. So will the old cocaine sale that was laundered through his account from overseas."

"I can't," she whispered. "I'd be ruined."

"You're already ruined."

"No. It will all—work out."

"Keep dragging your feet and I'll mention Jake to the cops. How would you like to be deported to Mexico on a murder charge?"

There was a strangling, keening sound at the other end of the line, as though Aileen was crying and denying that her life had changed and gagging on the truth at the same time.

Abruptly the phone went dead.

I didn't bother dialing again. I had done as much to Aileen as I could over the phone. I was going to have to get my hands on her and deliver her to the cops myself.

I called Benny. He answered on the second ring.

"You have any luck with Aileen's address?" I asked.

"No," he snarled. "That's why I didn't call."

"She's close to cracking, but I'm going to have to lean on her in person to get the job done."

"You better call somebody else to find her."

"You're the best I know."

"Then you're in trouble, mate. I haven't been able to find a trace of Aileen in the public record. When fans started snuffing stars, Hollywood got real good about concealing addresses."

I stared at the glass door to the balcony. The city was still hot, but the Santa Ana winds were dying. Smog was building at the base of the San Gabriels.

An LAPD helicopter went whacking by at eye level, hunting something on the streets below like a mechanical raptor. The city reminded me more of *Blade Runner* every day.

"Is somebody still babysitting you?" I asked.

"I think so, but I can lose them if I have to."

"Stay put. I'll call you back."

I rang off, then dialed Ray's office. When he came on the speakerphone, he sounded as testy as Benny had.

"Don't start in on me," I warned Ray. "I'm not

ready to turn myself in yet. Not until I'm damned sure I'll survive the arrest.''

"As an officer of the court, I must advise you to give yourself up. As your lawyer I can tell you it would be safer. Dugger really wants you.''

"He'll get me when he least expects it.''

Ray didn't like the sound of that, but he didn't say anything.

"Is Fiora all right?'' I asked.

Ray made a sound that was hard to decipher on the speakerphone. It sounded like a snort.

"That's quite a tiger you have, son. She just called here to ask for a copy of the LA County jail regulations. It seems she and the chief turnkey disagree about certain basic female amenities.''

"Such as?''

"Showers.''

I let out a long breath. If Fiora was fighting over showers, she wasn't being hurt in any other way.

"Any progress on getting her out?'' I asked.

"No bail,'' Ray said bluntly. "I've been trying all morning.''

"Dugger?''

"Yeah. He and LAPD are pulling too many strings. I can't find a judge who'll take them on.''

"Does your investigative file contain a copy of the original police report, the one when I shot Koo-Koo?'' I asked.

"Of course.''

There was no "of course'' about it. Few lawyers are as thorough and tenacious as Ray.

"Good,'' I said. "Give me Koo-Koo's home address.''

Papers rustled, Ray muttered, and then he read me an address in East Los Angeles.

"What are you going to do?" Ray asked.

"You don't want to know."

I hung up, called Benny, and told him to start losing his tail. Then I headed for East LA.

The Los Angeles barrio was concentrated around the Plaza, west of the river, north of what is now downtown. Once it was called Sonora Town. Today the barrio sprawls from the mid-Wilshire area all the way to Pomona and is called many names, none of them designed to sell real estate.

The sprawling neighborhoods are tight and insular. Most of them are little more than villages that have been transplanted as a whole from Mexico or farther south. In Koo-Koo's neighborhood the bumper stickers on the rusty urban assault vehicles read YO ♥ HERMOSILLO and MULEGE ES MAS MACHO!

The little street was potholed and lined with battered cars. Fighting cocks crowed aggressively from cages in the converted garage behind the drab white and green bungalow whose address I had memorized. Two lop-eared curb setters sniffed the wheel of the Caprice as I parked and got out.

A stout woman in a faded cotton dress answered my knock. She stood behind the latched screen door and watched me with dark, ancient eyes. Her Spanish was heavily flavored with some regional *indio* dialect. She wiped her hands on a white apron and eyed me with a wariness that went deeper than different cultures.

My belly felt hollow when I looked over her shoulder. Four children on the floor in front of the television. Three of them were boys.

One looked like Koo-Koo.

"Is this where Refugio Armijo lived?" I asked in Spanish.

"You *policia*?" she responded in marginal English.

I tilted my head to one side and shrugged fractionally. The gesture is Mexico's greatest contribution to western culture, ranking right up there with four-letter Anglo-Saxon obscenities and the New York bagel.

"*Sí,*" the woman said. "Here Koo-Koo live."

She glanced over her broad shoulder at the children. Her face showed no emotion.

I hoped mine didn't either.

"Where did Koo-Koo work?" I asked in Spanish.

"He no work," she said bluntly. Then, in scornful Spanish, she added, "He too important to work. Only burros work."

I looked past her into the house. It was clean, well kept, and had decent furniture. The fragrance of meat, chiles, and *masa* told of ample food.

"How did Koo-Koo provide so much for his family?"

She looked disgusted.

"This? This is not his family. We are his brother's family. Koo-Koo lived here, drank, and bought whores."

Koo-Koo hadn't changed much from Puerto Peñasco.

"How did he get his money?"

"He said he did gardening for some Anglo woman."

"What do you think?" I asked.

She shrugged massively. "I think his hands were soft."

"Where did the woman live?"

"Out there with the rich gringos."

"Beverly Hills? West Side? Hollywood?" I asked.

Her heavy bosom lifted and fell in another shrug. The places where the rich gringos lived were all the same to her.

"How long had he worked for this woman?"

"A long time," she said. "Ever since he came north."

Bingo.

Maybe Aileen was being shaken down by Koo-Koo. Or maybe she was still running on exotic fuels he supplied for a price. Either way, Koo-Koo was in touch with her, still running errands for her.

I doubted, though, that he called her at the studio.

"Did Koo-Koo leave you a telephone number where you could call him when he was working for this woman?" I asked.

She shook her head.

"Did he ever call her from here?" I asked.

"All the time. Ten, fifteen dollars a month for the phone. And my poor husband paid the bill himself rather than ask Koo-Koo for the money. My husband, who drives a trash truck and washes dishes to support us."

"Do you have this month's bill?"

Abruptly the woman looked uneasy. "Why? My husband, he do nothing wrong."

"I know. It's a new program."

She blinked.

I kept talking. Fast.

"The city's Crime Victim Assistance Program will pay Koo-Koo's telephone bills due to his unfortunate demise," I said.

The words didn't make much sense to her, but the bills in my money clip spoke a universal language. She nodded once, turned on her heel, and disappeared into the back of the house.

One of the kids, the one who looked like Koo-Koo, got up and came over to the door. He studied me with cool brown eyes.

"You going to catch the man who snuffed my uncle?"

The boy's English was unaccented, idiomatic, legacy of television and compulsory education. He was also wearing gang colors, legacy of clashing cultures.

"We know who killed him," I said. "It was self-defense. Koo-Koo shot first."

The kid wasn't interested. "The asshole should go to jail anyway."

"He just might."

A wide grin flashed.

"My uncle was okay, no matter what Ma says. He took us to Disneyland once. And he always bought us ice cream when the wagon came down the street."

El Patrón. Koo-Koo had always had a lot of that in him, along with the meanness.

From somewhere in the distance came the tinny, scratchy sound of music over an ice-cream vendor's loudspeaker.

"My uncle was killed, too," I said. "It's tough. But things aren't always as simple as they seem. When you grow up, you'll look at things another way."

Or maybe he wouldn't.

Maybe when he grew up, the kid would come looking for me.

The boy's mama reappeared with a gray envelope. She unhooked the screen and passed the paper out to me through the crack.

"Gracias," I said.

I pulled out the telephone bill and checked the toll list. Two expensive calls back home to Mexico and four toll calls, one a week, to the newest area code in California, 310: West LA, Beverly Hills, and the Beach. All four calls to the same number.

I handed the envelope back through the crack in the door, along with a fifty-dollar bill. Mama's dark eyes got big.

"I have no change for you," she said simply.

"Ni modo."

As soon as I got back in the Caprice, I called Benny.

"You get rid of the lice?" I asked.

"I shed every last one of the little buggers in the parking structure at Beverly Center."

"Good. I have a number my gut tells me belongs to Aileen's home phone."

"Give it to me."

I did.

tWENTY-SIX

Benny's van was parked in the shade of a tulip tree at the far corner of the Holiday Inn parking lot, just off Sunset. He must have been tired. He had cranked his seat back while he waited for me. Now he was sleeping hard, eyes squinted and beard lifting in the breeze from the open window.

As soon as I pulled alongside and shut off the engine, I could hear his snoring. Then he straightened up, stretched, and was wide awake. Catnaps are his specialty.

"Food," Benny said.

I handed him two burritos and a tamale in a paper box.

"No *menudo*?" he asked.

"Tripe soup is reserved for weekends."

"What day is it, anyway?"

"I don't know."

"Then how do you know it isn't the weekend?" he asked.

"No *menudo*."

I pulled myself into the passenger seat of the van and cranked back the seat.

"Address?" I asked.

He nodded, gestured with a dripping burrito at a clipboard that was fastened to the dashboard, and fell to eating with unnerving speed, four bites and two swallows per burrito. He knocked back the last of the molten salsa straight from the plastic cup, licked his lips, and was ready for action.

By that time I had realized Aileen's home was in Bel Air.

"I went by a few minutes ago," Benny said. "It's set back from the street. Lots of green stuff. About five million bucks of LA real estate."

"Is anybody home?"

"No way to tell," he said. "Porch light on and garage doors down. Couldn't see if her Jaguar Van den Plas was there. Want to know her license tag?"

"Not yet. Anything else useful?"

"Technically this is LAPD territory, but the dog work is being done by Bel Air security. Efficient buggers, too. They already put me on their clipboard."

I grunted. "No worries, mate. I'm just dropping by to talk over old times."

"You armed?"

"No."

Benny reached for the glove box. I stopped him.

"If I kill her," I said, "it will be with my bare hands."

"Wear rubber then. They can get prints off of corpses now."

Like a lot of neighborhoods built by too much money, Bel Air is surreal. The developers tried to mix a Southern California chaparral habitat with a landscape architect's impression of the forest primeval. The resulting fire was historic. Half the houses in the place burned down.

But Bel Air residents had more money than sense. They just rebuilt, brought in forty-foot potted palms and eucalyptus to replicate the original overgrown effect, and sat back to wait for the next one.

Aileen's house was a single-story rambler with a low, slanting roof and dark trim. At least four thousand square feet under the kind of English roofs and dormers that were popular when Shirley Temple was a kid. The lawn was manicured and the shrubs were as perfect as a Japanese gardener or a Hollywood set dresser could make them.

I opened the door of the van and stepped out.

"Cruise around," I said to Benny. "It will make the rent-a-cops feel better."

"If I see anything, I'll call Aileen's number."

"One ring only."

"Roge," Benny said. "If it goes from sugar to shit, slide out the back way and climb up the hill to the next cul-de-sac."

I closed the van's door and started up the hand-split flagstone walk that led to the front door. The door chimes played the first five notes of the theme from Aileen's Oscar-winning film, the one that had been bought and paid for with Jake's blood.

The chimes set off a small dog somewhere toward the back of the house. He yapped neurotically for fifteen seconds, then stopped. I rang again and the dog barked again. Same for the third time. I began to wonder if the dog wasn't wired into the chimes.

Aileen had been too drunk to drive. By now she was probably out cold, beyond the reach of yaps and chimes. The knob on the front door felt big, cool, and smooth as it turned beneath my grip. Unlocked.

I pushed the door open and stepped inside. The dog started to yap again. No other noise, no matter how hard I listened. The air seemed heavy, lifeless.

Aileen's taste in interior decor was less savage than Barry Franklin's. Her living room was filled with handsome Santa Fe furniture done in fine woven fabrics and even finer leather. The walls were covered with paintings, not one of them a print. Each was lighted better than it would have been in a museum.

An O'Keeffe held center stage, cottonwood trees on a riverbank somewhere around Abiqui. A mediocre painting by a top-notch painter. The cottonwoods were surrounded by better paintings done by much lesser names. Leave it to Hollywood to showcase inferior work by an established name and ignore superior work by an unknown.

My boot heels knocked solidly on the polished tile, but the rest of the house was silent. The hallway that led toward the back of the house was lined with more art, expensive but unexceptional. The dining room was large and formal, the sort of place to throw important little dinners for a dozen intimate enemies. The kitchen had a first-rate range, a huge refrigerator, and everything else the caterers would need.

A sound came between footsteps. I stopped and listened. The dog was whining like a lost puppy. Maybe Aileen had been too drunk to take care of it.

I moved down the hallway toward the desolate

sound. The French doors at the end of the hall were
open, inviting me to enjoy the patio and its surrounding acres of well-mowed sod. The slight breeze
pulled a few leaves from a giant sycamore and sent
them drifting down the surface of the curved swim-
ming pool.

Just beyond the pool, in the doorway to the bath-
house bar, Aileen Camp lay on her back. A shattered
glass threw shards of light on the concrete pool deck
beside her. A little white poodle lay next to his mistress, gently trying to lick the blood from her shattered skull.

I pitied the hapless poodle, player in a game he
would never understand, only lose. His god was
dead.

The poodle looked at me and wagged his tail ten-
tatively, asking me to help. If I had been carrying a
gun, I might have shot him, for that was the kindest
thing to do.

I went through the French doors and crossed the
patio toward the dog. He cowered and began bark-
ing hysterically, terrified, ready to bite any helping
hand but the one that could help him no longer.

There were no surprises when I got close. The size
of the entrance wound in Aileen's forehead and the
exit wound in the back of her skull told me that she
had been shot with a heavy-caliber gun.

The piece of brass gleaming in the bottom of the
pool where it had been flung by the ejector told me
that the murder weapon was a semiautomatic pistol.
My gut told me the brass was a .308 Winchester cut
down to fit the breech of a .451 Detonics.

I swallowed hard, but the feeling of a noose
around my neck didn't go away.

The phone in the pool-house bar rang.

Once.

I went out over the back fence, up the hill, and through the brush, and I never looked back.

tWENTY-SEVEN

When I burst through an oleander hedge onto the uphill cul-de-sac, Benny was waiting for me. The cargo door of the van was wide open. Before I got the door shut behind me, the van was rolling.

"You're bad luck, boyo. Get down and stay down."

I hunkered down beside the refrigerator. Woodsy foliage streaked by the side windows.

"What's up?" I asked.

"Cops. A regular holstein caravan, with a few unmarked cars thrown in."

"Where?"

"Queuing up outside the Bel Air gate. When one of the private security cars showed up to pilot them, I got on the blower."

One ring.

"Thanks," I said.

He grunted.

"Can you see them now?" I asked.

"They're just turning into your lady friend's street."

"Bloody hell, as a good friend of mine would say."

"What happened?" Benny growled. "Did you give her time to punch an alarm button?"

"No."

I dug a cold beer out of the refrigerator, cracked it, and settled back against the bulkhead to think and think hard.

"Some of those alarm systems are more subtle than you are," Benny said.

"Nothing subtle about the big hole in Aileen's skull."

Benny whistled softly and shook his head.

"Did you have time to do a ballistics check on this one?" he asked after a moment.

"No need. There was another piece of three-oh-eight brass in the bottom of the pool."

"Some wanker really wants you in the ground."

"No shit."

I took a slug of the beer. St. Stan's. The beer that made Modesto famous. It was rich and flavorful, like taking a pull on a bottle of vanilla extract. My mouth began to taste less like tarnished brass.

"Want me to drive to Franklin's place?" Benny asked.

"Why?"

"He's the man with the motive, boyo."

Benny was impatient. He gets that way with me when he thinks I'm being too slow to drop the hammer on a known assassin.

"Franklin's not the kind of man who gets blood on his hands," I said. "That's been bothering me ever since Moreton got killed."

"Franklin did what everybody in Hollywood does when they want to eat but don't want to cook. He sent out for it."

I drank some more beer. And thought some more.

"If you won't do the little sod," Benny said flatly, "I will."

"That may help me, but it won't do anything for Fiora."

Benny's big hands flexed on the wheel. I was right and he knew it. He just didn't like it.

Neither did I.

"You have a better idea?" Benny asked.

"I need the kind of proof that will convince Dugger to let us all off the hook."

I took another swallow of beer.

"Wish to hell Aileen hadn't been killed," I said.

"Christ. You get any softer and I'll use you as boot polish."

"Now I'll have to break someone who isn't a lush."

Benny glanced at me in the rearview mirror. "Who?"

"What we really need now is a cop."

"You've lost your bleeding mind."

"No, I'm just starting to use it."

"Leave the brainwork to Fiora. It makes me nervous when you start thinking."

Benny rolled the spotlight at Sunset and merged with the commuters and day students leaving UCLA by the back way. When he was certain we weren't being followed, I got into the front seat and started punching up numbers on the cellular.

Suarez was at his desk in the San Diego Federal Building.

"Yo," he said in a bored voice.

"I've got an idea for a high-profile case that your regional director won't be able to shit-can," I said.

"Who do I have to kill?" he asked, no longer bored.

"I hope it doesn't come to that. I'll need two operators."

"You're talking to one. Who else?"

"Soliz. In LA. Can you do it?"

There was a pause while Suarez thought.

"How long do I have?" he asked.

I looked at my watch and did a few calculations.

"I need you in West LA by evening," I said.

"Santa Monica Airport?"

"Done."

Suarez laughed like his daddy, low and hard.

"If I'm not there by seven," he said, "you can figure Bobby opted to be buried in Mexico."

I called Ray's office next. He was already at Sybil Brand, so I paged him with the cellular as a callback. He responded so fast I suspected he was carrying a cellular himself. The line wasn't secure, but I didn't need to worry greatly about cops eavesdropping. I was probably going to end up with the cops fairly soon anyway.

One way or another.

"Are you with Fiora?" I asked.

"Yes."

"Let me talk to her. Then do whatever she asks."

"Fiddler—" he began.

"I swear it won't involve you in anything that could allow the state to jerk your ticket."

"Why am I not comforted?" he muttered.

But he gave the phone to Fiora.

"Are you all right?" we asked simultaneously.

"I'm fine," I said quickly. "Now listen carefully and don't talk back for once. Call Dugger and tell him I'm ready to give myself up."

"Are you sure you want to do that?" she asked evenly.

"I'm sure I *don't* want to do that, but it's the only way I can think of to nail the bastard who's killing people with my Detonics."

"People? Plural?"

"Plural," I said flatly.

"Am I going to like this idea?" she said after a moment.

"It has a certain symmetry—"

"So does a barbell."

"—even if I did think it up all by myself," I said.

"Where do you want Dugger?"

"Remember the fund-raiser?"

"Yes."

"That general neighborhood."

"Line of sight or does Dugger have to be close enough to eavesdrop?"

The woman is quick. Frighteningly so.

"Gladstone's will do," I said.

It was a beach-front restaurant at the south edge of Malibu.

"All right," she said.

"Tell Dugger I'll meet him at the take-out window. My treat."

"You'll end up with a big tab. Coyotes like him travel in packs."

"I'll put it on plastic. Bring Ray and his cellular. When I call, come running. I might not get a chance to raise more than one holler."

"Fiddler . . ."

We both listened to the sound of the carrier wave, knowing there was nothing more to say except the words we knew as well as we knew our own hands.

Be careful. I love you.

Fiora broke the connection first. I punched out the phone and dropped it on the dash. Suddenly I felt as though I had been three days without sleep. I yawned wide enough to crack my jaw.

"Crank back the seat," Benny said. "Three hours?"

"Not a minute more. Or less."

I was asleep before I took the next breath.

When I woke up, Benny was shaking me and holding a cup of tar-colored coffee under my nose like smelling salts. Caffeine and a burned mouth woke me up enough to get on the cellular to DEA. When I gave my name and asked for Suarez, the sector radio operator gave me a message: ETA 1815.

Benny had us on the flight line at Santa Monica Airport with two minutes to spare. Suarez climbed out on the wing of a Cessna twin that had just landed.

A moment later Bobby Soliz came out of the cabin. He was dressed in scruffy Levi's and a T-shirt. In prison, he had controlled his surroundings, but he wasn't in prison any longer. He looked old and shabby and lost.

I met Suarez and Bobby at the gate in the chain-link fence behind the flight line.

"Have you told him anything?" I asked Suarez.

Bobby recognized my voice. "Fiddler."

"Yeah. Welcome to the good old U.S. of A."

I took Bobby's arm and steered him toward the front door of the van. He looked a little less uneasy when he was sitting down.

Suarez and I got in the back. He took off his hat and laid it on the seat beside him. Then he adjusted the pistol that was wedged into the waistband holster inside his Levi's.

"What do you have in mind?" Suarez asked.

He was as cool as an iced Corona, like we were going fishing.

"Anyone ever tell you that you take after your daddy?" I asked.

Suarez smiled slightly and waited.

"Do you still carry Mexican credentials?" I asked.

He studied me a long time, deciding whether to answer.

"Why?" Suarez asked.

"Franklin hates Mexico."

"And Mexicans?"

"Yeah. Them, too."

"Mos' gringos don' like us," Suarez said, thickening his accent until he sounded like the worst kind of Tijuana puke. *"Ni modo*. We no like them neither."

"Exactamente," I said. "You do that very well."

"Dad told me it would come in handy. He was right."

Benny looked from one to the other of us with black narrowed eyes. For the first time I noticed that he was sitting on the Browning Hi-Power that he favors for sniping. When I looked at Suarez, I saw he had noticed it, too.

"Is it finally hunting time?" Benny asked.

"Show-and-tell," I said firmly.

"Shoe polish," he retorted.

Benny bulled the van out into Coast Highway traffic. We cruised past Gladstone's, headed north. Three plain-jane sedans were scattered among the Saabs and Mercedes Benzes and Corvettes in the restaurant parking lot.

There were four figures seated in the sedan closest to Gladstone's take-out window. I caught a flash of Fiora's honey-colored hair in the setting sun.

I tried not to think about what could go wrong. For now, Benny was right. Thinking would just get in the way.

At least my kind of thinking would. I was feeling bloody-minded.

I pointed out the cars and told Suarez what I had set up.

"Looks like Dugger brought most of the task force with him," Suarez said.

"Yeah."

"They'll be pissed when they find out that DEA is in the middle of their case."

"Yeah."

Suarez smiled.

I offered him the cellular.

"You want to call somebody in your office downtown," I asked, "maybe have them ring up LAPD, just to cover yourself?"

"Did LAPD call me when they went to La Mesa?" Suarez asked sardonically.

Benny laughed like the assassin he once had been.

Suarez turned and looked at him, then back at me.

"I don't know who he is, but I'm glad he's on our side," Suarez said.

I asked Benny to keep track of the mileage and time as we headed toward the Malibu colony. Then I poked Bobby.

"What did LAPD promise you in return for cooperation?" I asked.

"A clean rapsheet up here. No hassles. I could come home as soon as I found a way to get out of La Mesa."

"Well, *hombre*, you're out. If you want to stay that way, you'll take orders from me."

Bobby gestured toward Suarez. "He ain't gonna take me back?"

Suarez adjusted the gun butt where it was digging into his side. "You want to go back?"

"No!"

"Do like Fiddler says and you stay here. Screw up and you're face down in Mexico."

Bobby nodded. It was the kind of deal he understood.

We clocked the run to Barry Franklin's front gate. Three minutes and twenty seconds at sixty miles an hour.

"Too long," I said. "Franklin's too clever. But there's no help for it."

I read Benny the number on Ray's cellular, our only link with Fiora.

"I'll try to give you the high sign," I said, "but if I get distracted, use your own judgment. This is hell's own little fandango."

Benny nodded.

"Okay. If I can have your attention, gents," I said, "this is a cross-cultural collaboration on a murder investigation."

I talked fast, giving them the bare outlines of my

plan because there was no time for anything fancy. Everyone listened intently.

Without warning Benny turned across three lanes of southbound traffic and stopped with the nose of the van resting against the big wrought-iron gate that stood between Barry Franklin and reality.

All gates have locks.

But this time I had brought the key.

tWENTY-EIGHT

Franklin depended too much on his gate. It was impressive as hell, big and black and tied together with a length of chain. But there was no backup, no retired cop in a little gatehouse, not even an alarm box.

Benny turned to Suarez.

"You're a federal agent, right?" Benny asked.

Suarez nodded.

"You're here on official business? A murder investigation?"

Suarez nodded again.

Benny reached over and pulled down into four-wheel drive, low range.

The battered bull bar in front of the van's bumper inched forward, taking up slack in the chain that secured the gate. The chain growled, then squealed, and finally snapped with the sound of a pistol shot. The gates flew open. We rolled down the long tree-lined driveway unchallenged.

"Barbarians through the gate," Benny said with satisfaction.

"Did you know that there was a full program of events at the Coliseum the day the hordes breached the walls of Rome?" I asked.

"You've been reading again, boyo. I warned you about that. Turns your spine to shoe polish."

Shaking his head, trying not to laugh aloud, Suarez checked the load in his pistol with the easy motions of a man who has done it thousands of times.

When we came to the circle drive in front of the house, there was a big black Mercedes parked within three steps of the oversized front door. The car's trim was all in gold.

"Looks like the emperor is at home," I said.

Benny drove past the Mercedes and stopped. I stepped out of the van's cargo door, pulled the passenger door open, and helped Bobby out. He wobbled before he caught his balance.

"What are you doing?" he asked.

"We're going to talk with the man you thought might have been snitching off Jake's last load," I said.

"Oh. That asshole."

"Yeah. That one."

Suarez was already at the front door, waiting. He had shifted the pistol in his belt so the butt was fully visible. When Bobby and I took our places, Suarez punched the brass button on the wall.

Somewhere inside, chimes rang quietly. No Oscar-winning theme, here. But then, Franklin hadn't ever won an Oscar. It must have ground on him that Aileen had.

If Franklin had servants, they had gone home early. He opened the front door himself. His eyes focused first on me, then on Suarez, and finally on Bobby. I stepped forward, wedging my foot in the door in case Franklin tried to slam it.

I needn't have worried. Franklin was frozen in the moment he had recognized Bobby Soliz.

"Hey, Barry," I said pleasantly. "Glad I caught you."

Franklin didn't move. He didn't even breathe.

"I want you to meet some friends of mine," I said. "The guy in the black hat is Comandante Mateo Suarez of the Proceduria de Justicia Federal in Tijuana."

Three of us knew it was a lie. The fourth was too numb to care. Franklin could barely force himself to glance at Suarez.

"He's what the Mexicans call a *federale*, a Mexican federal agent," I explained. "Sort of like the FBI, only he wears a hat."

Suarez grinned like a wolf.

I touched Bobby on the shoulder. "And this is—"

Franklin made a sound low in his throat.

"Ah, you remember Bobby. And here I was afraid you'd forgotten all about Puerto Peñasco."

Franklin's mouth worked once but nothing came out. He tried again, looking at Bobby but speaking to me.

"What the . . . ?"

Franklin's voice dried up.

Suarez stepped forward.

"*Señor*, I am investigating the murder of an American in our country," Suarez began.

Franklin looked more unhappy than ever.

"The murder took place many years ago," Suarez said in clean, earnest English, "but unlike the custom in your country, we Mexicans take the death of another man, even a gringo, very seriously."

"Amen," I said.

"We will reopen a murder investigation any time we obtain new evidence," Suarez continued.

Another odd sound came from Franklin, but Suarez was still lying with the assurance of an undercover narc.

"These two men," Suarez said, "have brought me new evidence in the killing of a man known as Jake Malverne."

Suarez's English was precise and beautifully accented. He wore a faint, sad smile that looked just like a portrait of Emiliano Zapata.

Then he turned to Bobby and spoke in machine-gun Spanish that I had to strain to follow.

Like most crooks, cons, and undercover cops, Bobby was a born actor. He lifted his face and stared directly at Barry Franklin's ashen face . . . or at the source of the odd sounds Franklin had been making.

Bobby nodded solemnly and spoke in English. "Yes. This is the one. There is no doubt."

"*Señor* Franklin," Suarez said briskly, "you are under arrest for the crime of murder. You will come with us."

Franklin finally discovered his voice.

"Wait! You can't arrest me! You have no power here!"

Suarez touched the butt of his gun. "Your DEA has been kidnapping Mexican citizens for years. This time we return the favor."

Suarez took a firm grip on Franklin's arm. Franklin bleated like a goat and tried to draw back but Suarez was well trained. He barred Franklin's wrist and propelled him forward.

"Come, *pendejo*," Suarez said. "In my country there are many questions waiting for your answers."

Franklin's face was a study in rising terror. Not once since Jake died had Franklin considered this possibility. Mexico was the other side of the moon. What happened down there didn't really count. Franklin was like the drunken marines I had seen that morning, retching and reeling back across the line at dawn, leaving sin behind as though it were a belly full of tequila shooters and half-digested tacos.

"No!" Franklin said hoarsely.

I stepped to his other side and clamped down on his arm.

"Quit whining," I said. "You did the crime, now you'll do the time."

"You can't prove that without Aileen, and she's—"

Franklin stopped speaking as though he had run into a wall.

"Aileen's dead," I agreed. "How did you know?"

"It—it was all over the radio. They're looking for you for her killing and Harold Moreton's."

Franklin's brain had finally thawed out.

I looked at my watch. I knew three plus minutes had been too long.

"That is in America," Suarez said, shrugging. "We do things differently in Mexico. Come."

Suarez frog-marched Franklin toward the van. The agent struggled, but it did him no good. He hadn't worked out enough.

"You can't do this!" Franklin said.

"Wrong again," I said. "You'll like Mexico, Barry.

None of this probable-cause and beyond-reasonable-doubt bullshit. No fifth amendment, either.''

''*Sí*,'' Suarez said. ''You are expected to assist in your own prosecution. It is our way.''

''No!''

I glanced at my watch and kept talking. The van was only a step away.

''It's the Napoleonic Code, babe. Comandante Suarez is judge, jury, and prosecutor,'' I said. ''But there's no rush on the trial. *Mañana* is still the style.''

''You can have Bobby's cell in La Mesa until the trial,'' Suarez offered. ''He's not going back.''

We started to lever Franklin into the van. He grabbed the steel doorpost and braced himself so that he couldn't be forced into the van.

''Wait, wait, you can't do this! It's wrong!''

''So is murder,'' Suarez said dryly.

I began peeling Franklin's short, manicured fingers off the post. As soon as I let go of one to work on another, the first fastened on. It was like trying to shove an octopus through a keyhole.

''Let go or I'll break your wrist,'' I said.

''For Christ's sake, stop!'' Franklin pleaded. ''I didn't do anything!''

''Bullshit,'' I said. ''Aileen told me everything. The two of you hired Koo-Koo and Cardenas to kill Jake.''

''You can't prove it!''

''Wrong.''

My conviction was so great Franklin stared at me.

''I've got the picture,'' I said. ''The real one.''

''Huh?''

''The picture of you and Aileen paying the two hit men. I've got Bobby's testimony and I've got your bank records showing the sudden rush of cash that came after you sold the load of coke."

Franklin's sudden laughter was almost hysterical.

"That money wasn't from the coke!"

"So you say."

"It's true! The money came from a New York brokerage house that invested in the movie. I can prove it!"

Bingo.

"Yeah? How?"

"I can show you the entire paper trail," Franklin said eagerly. "Aileen just used the bank statement to make me look bad. She wanted you to kill me."

Close, but not close enough.

I slackened the pressure on Franklin's fingers but kept pushing him in other ways.

"I've heard this story before," I said indifferently. "I like my version better. It ties up more of the loose ends."

"What? What, for Chrissake?"

"If that was clean money, where did the cash from that coke deal end up?"

Franklin laughed shrilly again, still frightened but beginning to believe he could talk his way out of this mess.

"There was no cocaine money," he said. "We never sold it. Aileen used it all."

"Won't fly, pal. Aileen used a lot of coke in her younger days, but twenty kilos? She would have had to get a nose transplant."

"No, I don't mean she snorted it all herself. She *used* it."

"For what? Mopping up grease in the driveway?"

"She threw big parties with it," Franklin said. "She gave ounces to actors and directors and writers. She entertained the money men. She used to cut it up on a mirror and pass it around in the banquet room at Ma Maison, just to show she had balls."

The story made more sense than the one Aileen had told me.

"I'm listening," I said.

Franklin drew a deep breath and kept talking.

"How the hell do you think she got that picture made?" he asked. "The star was snorting every minute he wasn't in front of the camera. So was the crew. They went through a kilo and a half on location in Montana."

I was still listening. Franklin knew it.

"She had her film," he said. "She had her Oscar, too, and after that it was all easy. The coke ran out, but she didn't need it anymore."

Suarez looked at me.

I shrugged.

Franklin drew another deep breath and kept talking.

"Aileen was the ultimate producer," he said. "She knew what everyone wanted, what their weakness was, and pandered to it. They believed what she said because she was telling them what they wanted to hear."

Somewhere in the back of my mind, I heard Jake grunt, like someone had just punched him in the solar plexus. Franklin was telling the truth.

Good, but not good enough. Too little, too late.

And I was running out of time.

"Nice story," I said.

I stopped playing at removing Franklin's fingers from the post. I bent his little finger across his palm in a come-along hold that is both harmless and so painful you see stars. I know, because it had been used on me more than once.

"It's true!" Franklin cried.

"So is Jake's death," I said. "You're good for it. You're going to get it."

"Wait!"

"Why?"

"The cops have your lover. They're after you. But I can get you—"

From the corner of my eye I caught a flicker of movement.

"—off the hook. I know who killed Moreton and—"

The heavy barrel of the Detonics emerged from the dark shadows inside the front door of the house.

"—Aileen with your gun, and I know—"

It was too late, but I tried to throw Franklin aside as the world exploded and gore sprayed.

"Bishop, you son of a bitch!" I screamed.

Too late. The sound of the shot made everything else silent.

tWENTY-NINE

As I flung Franklin aside, another shot rang out.

Suarez leaped sideways toward the Mercedes, clawing the pistol from his belt at the same time.

Benny yelled a warning somewhere along the way and then opened up from the relative cover of the van with his Browning.

A third shot rang out from the Detonics but Benny's first two slugs blew chunks out of the door casement, distracting Bishop and throwing off his aim.

I was on my way into the interior of the van when I remembered Bobby Soliz. The little boxer stood square to the fire, knowing his danger but not knowing where safety lay. I grabbed the back of his pants and yanked him inside with me.

"Stay down," I said.

Bobby hugged the rug.

The Mercedes screened Suarez from everything but Teflon-coated bullets. He was down behind the doorpost and had his gun arm laid across the hood. He tripped off three shots in quick succession, chewing up the other half of the big double door.

Benny and Suarez had Bishop bracketed. As coolly as a man in a penny arcade, Suarez walked his next shot toward the center of the killing zone. Benny pinched in from the other side.

The muzzle of the Detonics appeared, but only for an instant. Bishop had once been a cop. He could foresee the end of this ballistic ballet. The staccato beat of hard leather over tile came back like an echo of gunfire.

"He's running," I called.

Suarez eeled to the front of the car and exposed his shoulder briefly, trying to draw fire. When no shots rang out, he started forward, covering the blank shadows with the muzzle of his gun.

"Matt! Stay put!" I yelled. "He's an ex-cop. He knows every move you're going to make."

"Yo."

Suarez held station just outside the front door, waiting for backup.

"Call in the reserves," I said to Benny.

"I'm on the blower now."

He held up the cellular so I could see.

"Tell them there's a federal agent here so nobody gets shot," I said. "Get an ambulance for Franklin, and for Christ's sake give me that extra gun."

Benny grinned through his beard like a buccaneer as he handed me a flat five-shot revolver with a hidden hammer.

"Feeling naked, mate?" he asked.

I bailed out of the van and up to the front door.

"I'm point," I said in a low voice. "I've been over this ground before."

Suarez nodded curtly.

I went from dusk to dark shadows in one rolling motion.

There was a light at the far end of the main hallway, probably from Franklin's office. I scrambled forward, covering the far doorway with the little pistol.

A flash of memory came, reminding me what a mess the Detonics had made of Aileen's skull and Moreton's as well. It hadn't done much for Franklin's chest, either.

Another flash of memory came—the primitive art Barry Franklin had collected, death masks and wooden idols and rattles carved with demons. Scraps of hell collected on the way through life.

I wondered how Franklin liked the hell his life had become.

The doorway of the office stared vacantly at me. A credenza in the hallway gave me as much cover as I was going to get.

"Move," I said over my shoulder.

Suarez came through the door. He raced with surprising silence over the tile hallway. Just as he came past me, we both spotted the muzzle of the Detonics sliding around the door casement. I fired twice before Suarez cut loose with his 9mm. Our reports were lost in the howitzer boom of the .451.

The splinters exploding from the doorframe made Bishop flinch. His bullet blew a hole in the wall behind me. He didn't try for a second shot.

The Detonics vanished. Bishop's retreating footfalls thundered on the wooden deck.

"Cover me," I said.

Before Suarez could argue, I leaped over him on the way to the doorway of the office. When I got there, Suarez was right behind me, taking up a covering position.

The room was empty. I crossed to the open French doors and listened. A shoe scraped on wood. I snatched a look through the door.

Bishop had guessed wrong.

He should have gone left. Left was the way to the stairs. Right took him to the end of the deck, toward the best view on the whole California coast.

View, but no stairway. Only a long step into the twilight.

Bishop had already recognized his mistake. He didn't waste any time wringing his hands. He vaulted onto the railing and teetered there, preparing himself for the forty-foot drop to stones or to the sea, whichever hit first.

His peripheral vision must have picked out the movement of my head in the doorway. He snapped off a shot in my direction. Bad mistake. The Detonics had a recoil like a field cannon. The shock unbalanced him.

I tried two quick shots with the short-barreled revolver. They both went wide.

Bishop's arms flailed as he fought for balance. If I had wanted to risk it, I might have saved him. Or I might have pushed him.

Suddenly the rail was empty.

A few seconds later the impact of his body striking rock came back up through the damp evening air.

When I reached the end of the deck and looked over, Bishop lay on one of those phony concrete rocks that California landscapers use because the real ones don't come in convenient sizes. Bishop's head was resting on his shoulder, his neck at a perfect right angle to the rest of his body.

A hangman could have done no better.

How about it, Jake? Are we quits now?

There was no answer.

I suppose that's as good as it gets.

Suarez and I put away our guns, he dug out his DEA badge, and we went back to the front of the house to wait for the cavalry to arrive.

It didn't take long. The unmarked detective units came helling down the sloping driveway, tires squealing and antennas whipping and red lights on the dashboard flashing to clear traffic out of the way. The lead car hadn't stopped rolling when Dugger popped out of the passenger door and leveled a .357 Magnum at us.

After the Detonics, I wasn't impressed.

"Drop the guns!" Dugger yelled.

The driver bailed out on the other side, his gun drawn. Two plainclothes types piled out of the second unit and assumed positions as strategic reserves.

Suarez and I dropped our guns on the shiny black hood of Franklin's Mercedes and stepped back.

"I'm a federal agent," Suarez called out. "Everything's under control, so don't do anything dumb."

"I don't care if you're Christ himself," Dugger said. "You're in LAPD territory."

He motioned us back a few more steps before he advanced and collected the guns. Then he stepped back and took in the whole scene.

Barry Franklin lay in a pool of blood on the driveway.

Benny sat at the wheel of his van. He snapped off

a mocking salute with the cellular phone he was still holding.

Bobby Soliz smiled blindly from the back of the van.

Suarez and I stood in the pool of light from the doorway, waiting for Dugger to realize his fun was over. After about three breaths, he got the message. He flipped the safety on, holstered his gun, and signaled for the rest of the cops to do the same.

When all the weapons were stowed, the back door of Dugger's car opened. Fiora got out, dressed in an orange Sybil Brand Institute coverall. She moved awkwardly because her hands were cuffed in front of her and attached to a steel chain around her waist.

I was hit by a cold, violent rage. Mentally I added another black mark by Dugger's name.

"Hold it," Dugger yelled at Fiora. "Stop!"

Fiora ignored him.

So did I.

I met her just a few steps from Dugger. When she tried to throw her arms around me, she couldn't move her hands far enough apart in their chains.

I picked her up in my arms. Her hands felt cool against my face. Her warm, familiar scent was mixed with the sour smell of an institution.

"It won't happen again," I promised.

Fiora just smiled and shook her head and buried her face against my neck. There were only a few tears against my skin, but each one was another mark against Dugger's already impressive score.

"Fiora?" I said softly.

"It's all right," she whispered. "You're alive and it's all right."

Then Fiora stopped talking and started kissing me. She made a thorough job of it.

It irritated the hell out of Dugger, who was trying to get my attention.

"You're under arrest for two murders," he said for the third time.

I turned toward him, still holding Fiora.

"Take off her chains," I said.

"You don't give the orders here. You're under arrest for—"

"Dream on," I said, cutting across Dugger. "Your informant and sole evidence for that murder case is lying down the hill with a broken neck. You're shit out of luck."

"What makes you think I have an informant?"

"Ned Bishop," I said.

"What about him? What do you—"

"Last chance. Take off Fiora's chains."

"Fuck you."

"Thank you. A clean conscience is a wonderful thing."

I turned toward the cops who were closing in. It wasn't hard to pick out the boss. He had command presence at thirty yards.

"Do you know a man named Ned Bishop?" I asked.

"Yeah. Used to be Dugger's partner."

I looked at Dugger. "Are you as crooked as Bishop or just butt stupid?"

There was an abrupt silence. Before Dugger could say anything, his boss did.

"What's this about Bishop and Dugger?"

"Take off Fiora's chains and I'll talk to you," I said. "Otherwise I'll talk to the press."

The boss spotted Suarez's DEA badge. "You really DEA?"

"Yeah."

"You know what happened?" he asked Suarez.

"Yeah."

"Well?"

Suarez shrugged. "Do yourself a favor. Keep it out of the papers."

The boss looked at Dugger. "Turn her loose."

Dugger's jaw worked for a while, like he was trying to crack walnuts with his back molars.

"How embarrassing for you, Detective Dugger," Fiora said.

Smiling like a cat, she held out her handcuffs.

Dugger turned his head, spat, and fished in his pocket. He took his own sweet time finding the key ring and opening the locks that held Fiora's chains in place.

Then he turned on me.

"She's free, but you aren't," he snarled. "It's going to be a long night."

He didn't know the half of it.

ePILOGUE

"Ouch!" I said. "What is that, steel wool?"

"Hold still," Fiora said.

She swabbed at the cut over my eye. Benny sat nearby, sucking on a beer and watching us. An unholy light gleamed in his black eyes, as though he was enjoying a private joke.

I shot him a look that told him to keep his suspicions to himself. I didn't need another argument with Fiora. It had been a hell of a day already, and the sun wasn't even up yet.

"Clumsy of you to fall that way," Benny said neutrally.

"The stairs at the police station were wet."

"You ought to sue them," Benny said. "LAPD has deep pockets."

"They can keep them."

Fiora frowned at the cut on my face. "I still think you should have some stitches."

"Good idea," Benny said. "We could get Bobby's old fight doctor. He's had a lot of practice with cuts over eyes."

I gave Benny another look.

He smiled and took another swig of St. Stans.

"What happened while we waited for you?" Benny asked. "How did you get that prick with ears to turn you loose?"

"Which prick with ears?" I asked.

"Dugger."

"Oh. Him."

Benny made a sound like he was swallowing his beard, but he managed not to laugh out loud.

"Yes," Fiora said. "What did happen while the rest of us cooled our heels in the lobby?"

"Remember the bug the cops found in Aileen's phone?" I asked.

"Bloody idiots," Benny said. "They wouldn't recognize a Micro S-Seven if it bit them."

"They didn't want to recognize it," Fiora said. "It meant their dear ex-cop buddy was a murdering crook."

She dunked another swab in disinfectant and went to work on my hands.

I hissed under my breath and tried to think of something more pleasant. Like how my hands got scraped up in the first place. Now *that* was pleasant.

I must have smiled, because Fiora gave me a wary look.

"They didn't want to buy my theory even after they found the receiver for the bug in Ned Bishop's office," I said.

"I told 'em so," Benny said.

"Sure you did, but Dugger's a trained skeptic. He even insisted on checking the bug for your fingerprints."

"If I had done the job, I wouldn't have left a print."

"Bishop did," I said.

"Amateur," Benny said with disdain.

Fiora swabbed, I hissed, and Benny looked like a cat trying not to burp canary feathers.

"So Bishop listened in while you leaned on Aileen," Fiora said, "and knew the whole thing would come unraveled on him unless he put a cork in her."

"Yeah. So he went around snipping off loose ends."

"With your gun," Benny said.

"I guess Dugger gave up on you after he found the receiver in Bishop's office?" Fiora asked.

"No such luck," I said. "He needed a motive for Bishop."

"I already told Hansen the motive," Fiora said.

Hansen was the task force honcho who had command presence at ninety feet.

"You should have told Dugger," I said.

"Why bother? The man has cement for brains."

"I'll drink to that," Benny said, lifting the bottle of beer.

"Dugger wouldn't have understood," Fiora continued. "He only understands direct power."

Benny and I exchanged a glance.

"Hollywood works on indirection," Fiora continued. "Franklin was brokering the Visual Arts deal, and Aileen was trying to kill it. Bishop took one look at the odds and decided who would win. The next step was easy. He bugged her phone and sold her game plan to Franklin.''

''Money,'' I said. ''The root of all evil, and so forth.''

''Power,'' Fiora corrected. ''If Franklin pulled off the Visual Arts deal, he would have become the single most powerful person in the new, internationally owned Hollywood. Bishop would have been his right hand, hatchet man to the stars, the new Rasputin. Indirect power, the kind the Japanese understand.''

She looked at my hands and made unhappy noises.

''But what I don't understand,'' she said, ''is how you got the cuts on the tops of your knuckles. If I fall, I scuff up my palms, not my knuckles.''

''Those mulish retrograde types use their knuckles on everything,'' Benny said. ''The rest of us use baseball bats.''

I gave him a look.

''Other than that,'' Benny said distinctly, ''it was a good job, mate.''

He saluted me with the beer bottle.

''Good thing Dugger was there to help you,'' Fiora said, touching my hands lightly.

Benny damn near dropped the beer bottle.

I stared at Fiora.

''Ray told me all about it,'' she said. ''How you slipped, and Dugger tried to catch you, and you both went headlong down the stairs together.''

I made some noises.

So did Benny.

''Poor Dugger,'' she said serenely. ''He was on the

bottom all the way down. It was a very long flight of stairs."

Fiora smiled, brushed her lips slowly over mine, and whispered, "A *bloody* good job, mate."

THICKER THAN WATER
by Bruce Zimmerman

From the Edgar Allan Poe Award-nominee comes a new thriller featuring San Francisco therapist turned sleuth, Quinn Parker, in another suspenseful adventure. This time, Parker's old pal, stand-up comic Hank Wilkie, invites him to Jamaica for a sunny all-expense-paid stay at the half-million dollar estate Hank has just inherited. It's just too good to be true.

THE WOLF PATH
by Judith Van Gieson

Low-rent, downtown Albuquerque lawyer Neil Hamel has a taste for tequila and a penchant for clients who get her into deadly trouble. *Entertainment Weekly* calls Hamel's fourth outing "Van Gieson's best book yet — crisp, taut and utterly compelling."